JOHN PARRISH

FREE FALL

A Mathew McKenna Thriller

Thanks to Paul Schumacher, my Beta Reader.

Cover designed by Robin Ludwig Design Inc.
Formatting by Polgarus Studio

Also By John Parrish

Free Fall

Cold Awakening

Artifact

Eighteen Years Ago

CHAPTER 1

Mediterranean Ocean
USS *Reagan*, Aircraft Carrier

"Lieutenant Commander Rayman, get your team on deck," said Captain Alex Preston, startling Samantha Johnson out of her thoughts.

"Yes, sir." Rayman stood up from the padded black seat in the ready room, reached down, and grabbed his gear. He said to his team, "Grab your gear and let's go. Follow me."

Samantha Johnson, future First Lady of the United States, leaned forward and picked up her gear. She stood to discover Commander Rayman standing directly in front of her. A soft half smile encroached upon the left side of his face. He was known for that crooked smile.

"Welcome to the Rapid Response SEAL Team," said Rayman. "This is your first mission since graduating, correct?"

"Yes, sir."

"Congratulations on becoming a Navy SEAL." He placed his free hand on her shoulder. "Once a SEAL, always a SEAL."

"Yes, sir."

"It's OK to be a little nervous. You're not going to let anyone down. I won't let you. The training is hard so the missions are easier. Just do as you were trained, and you will be fine."

"Yes, sir. Thank you, sir."

Lieutenant Commander Rayman walked through the metal doorframe and out of the second ready room aboard the aircraft carrier the USS *Reagan*. The hallways were narrow and the stairways were steep; new recruits quickly learned to climb up or down them carefully.

Rayman's five team members followed him closely, moving through the hallways like a centipede. Samantha was the last one in the line. Suddenly her face was hit by a cool, salty blast of Mediterranean Ocean air. She gazed up into the dark sky as the wind blew her hair back; there was a quarter moon on this cloudless night. She was outside now.

To her left were eight aircraft of different sizes and shapes parked neatly in rows. The wheels had blocks under them, and the aircraft were chained to the deck. Most things were chained to the deck when not in use. A small list could send anything sliding around. The deck of an aircraft carrier was one of the most dangerous places to work in the world, and that's *without* things sliding around.

Commander Rayman walked over to a designated spot on the carrier's flight deck and dropped his bag. "Suit up," he said.

Elaine was six feet tall, with broad shoulders, and short dark brown hair. She dropped her duffel bag, unzipped it, and withdrew her combat flight suit and a hard bulletproof vest with a hard-shell chest plate and a small but highly efficient jet pack on the back. She reached in and grabbed her combat flight helmet, which resembled an expensive motorcycle helmet, and put it on. It was ultralightweight, like every piece of equipment they used. It had to be. If it wasn't lightweight, it wasn't theirs.

Lieutenant Commander Rayman stood in front of his team. Everyone was suited up. Samantha flipped a switch just inside the helmet and it came alive, showing all relevant information about the jet pack. The heads-up display also showed a map of where they were and where their target destination was. It also displayed the preprogrammed flight path leading to the target.

Rayman turned to the officer in a green jersey standing close to him and gave him a thumbs-up. The officer scanned the deck, then returned the thumbs-up signal. "Cleared for preflight test."

"Preflight," ordered Lieutenant Commander Rayman. "Double-check your fuel."

Samantha read her heads-up display. *Fuel—100%. percent.* "Check," she said.

In a few seconds, the other four members also sounded off: "Check."

Samantha moved her flight-control glove, and it sent a signal that initiated a preflight systems check. Item by item, the jet pack tested itself. Thrust venting, stabilizers, and computer systems were all checked and confirmed. When the jet pack was done, it said to Samantha, "Preflight systems check is complete. All systems confirmed and ready for flight."

"Anyone have any problems?" Rayman asked when every

member of the team had done the same.

One by one, they confirmed that the systems checks were OK.

The mission included two crab units, Betty Crab and Sally Crab. These crabs were AI combat units. Each had a flat, disklike body twelve inches in diameter. With six legs, they looked, well, like crabs. Calling them anything else would have been unnatural. But these crabs were deadly.

The shape made them very hard targets to kill, and they were made from a synthetic stronger and lighter than steel. Each had one automatic gun. These crabs were smaller than the usual combat crabs, designed to be ultralightweight and small; otherwise, they couldn't fly with the team. But they were deadly accurate, highly mobile, and very durable. Frankly, they were almost impossible to kill. Each crab rode piggyback with one designated person. The crabs were designed to fit right on the shoulder of the jet pack.

Samantha and Elaine each took a kneeling position, and Samantha felt Betty Crab hop onto her back and climb into position at her shoulders.

"Betty Crab in position and secured," said Betty Crab through the comm.

To Samantha's right, Sally Crab was climbing into position on Elaine.

The green shirted officer gave Rayman a thumbs-up. They were clear to launch.

Rayman faced the officer and snapped a salute back.

"Let's go," said Lieutenant Commander Rayman.

Samantha moved her flight glove, and the jet pack's thrust increased and lifted her up into the air. She followed her team as they moved over the deck of the carrier at a height of only six feet.

Flying lead position, Commander Rayman said, "Remember, radio silence till you hear me at the target."

Without warning, Samantha was suddenly over the dark, undulating waters of the Mediterranean Ocean, the carrier moving quickly into the distance. She felt a surge of exhilaration. No one had ever built a thrill ride this awesome.

She wondered what Steve would think of her now. *No, scratch that.* That jerk didn't deserve her anyway. He'd dumped her the week she graduated for a dumb, big-breasted, redheaded flirt. *Jerk.*

The captain of the USS *Reagan*, Alex Preston, picked up the comm in his right hand. "Red Fox, this is Dark Sky. Good luck."

"Dark Sky, thanks. Over," said Commander Rayman.

CHAPTER 2

They flew at an extremely low level, just above the waves of the ocean. If not for the night-imaging system, the mission would have been all but impossible. The team would be in flight for forty-seven minutes.

Athletic in build, a tomboy by nature, Samantha had attended college on an athletic scholarship for baseball. Samantha never did anything second best. Trying out for the Navy SEALs was a natural career path for her. Succeeding was also natural. Seventy percent of the people who try out for the Navy SEALs end up dropping out.

She smiled to herself, thinking about what her college friends were doing right now. Here she was, flying a jet pack on a rescue mission as a Navy SEAL, her target a coastal city inside Libya. It was amazing and normal all at the same time. Intelligence believed the daughter of a Jordanian minister, Eva Jaikal, was being held captive along with a United States Army colonel. Eva was only twelve years old. My God, she had to be terrified. If she was, in fact, still alive.

As they approached the coast, the team banked right and flew parallel to the coastline for several miles. Then they banked to the left and flew over a beach, heading inland.

They continued to hug the terrain, flying below tree level whenever possible. As they reached the outskirts of the city, they suddenly went vertical, flying straight up. The strategy was to fly low approaching the coast and then high over the city to avoid visual detection.

The heads-up mapping display inside their helmets began to flash. The jet packs spoke to them in a soft, clear woman's voice: "Ninety seconds to target."

CHAPTER 3

Samantha could feel the adrenaline as it entered her bloodstream. Her whole body was anticipating the task ahead. She reviewed her duties and went through what she would do under different scenarios. The US Navy had trained her well. She was ready. The training for all military combat personnel was intense and hyperaccurate. That was especially true for the elite combat units: the Navy SEALs, the Army Rangers, and the Green Berets. She was the newbie on the team; she'd been active with this team for only six days. She didn't know it at the time, but in a few months, combat would become routine.

"Thirty seconds to target," said the jet pack.

Flying high enough to be out of any visual contact with anyone in the city, they flew as quietly as a whisper. The city was asleep, but a few people were walking the streets below. It was two in the morning, local time.

"Fifteen seconds," said the jet pack.

Lieutenant Commander Rayman came on the comm. His voice was even, calm, containing no hint of emotion. "No heroes. Everyone do your job. Trust the SEAL next to you. Weapons on. Go live. Let's do this and go home."

Samantha pulled her weapon from her waist and clicked the On switch. Everyone else did the same thing as they descended.

The target was an upper-class house, located in a suburb near the beach on the outskirts of town. A brick wall surrounded the property with a gated driveway entrance.

They hit the compound in two teams of three SEALs each. One team took the front, the other the back. Each team had been assigned a crab.

Sue, Bill, Samantha, and Betty Crab landed at the back door of the house. Rayman, Jack, Elaine, and Sally Crab landed at the front.

Upon landing, they killed the engines. Just as Samantha touched down, Betty Crab let go of her and fell to the ground, landing like a cat on its six padded feet.

Betty Crab quickly scanned the backyard for threats. All clear, she moved into the yard twelve feet away to a strategic dip next to a tree. Betty Crab hunkered down into the grass and said over the comm, "Betty Crab in position."

Each member of the team wore a comm set comprised of two bone conduction earpieces and a small, nearly invisible mini bone mic designed to pick up and transmit whispers. The bone conduction design allowed their ears to be unobstructed for clear normal hearing. Bone conduction technology transmits sound using the cheekbones and jawbones to transmit the sounds instead of using the eardrum. Every member of the team was connected. If any member said anything, every other member would hear it, including the crabs.

Kneeling to one side of the door, Sue glanced around the

backyard. It was empty. Samantha and Bill were in position behind her, leaning against the wall of the house. Sue was tasked as team leader B.

Rayman, Jack, Elaine, and Sally Crab took up positions in the front of the compound and at the front door.

Sally Crab raced into the middle of the yard and lowered herself into the grass. "Sally Crab in position."

Rayman took hold of the door handle. "On my signal."

Jack and Elaine each gave Rayman a short nod.

"Sue, let me know when you're in position," said Rayman.

Samantha gave Sue a thumbs-up, as did Bill behind her.

"In position. All is quiet and clear," said Sue.

Rayman pressed the door handle. It was not locked. "Go!"

* * *

On the deck of the USS *Reagan*, two Viper attack helicopters started their engines. They had gone through their preflight checklists and were now ready. The captain gave the signal, and the deck officer cleared the Vipers to lift off. The pilots throttled up at the same time, and they gently lifted vertically into the air. Cleared to two hundred feet, the two additional aircraft joined the other aircraft flying combat air patrol.

Their mission, their real mission, was to wait. Two Vipers were already off the coast, waiting to move in for support, hopefully including the extraction of the hostages.

The original mission had called for only one Viper for the extraction; Captain Alex Preston had decided to send two. The two additional Vipers he'd just launched were plan C.

The captain had a bad feeling about this mission. Honestly, he didn't like it. The intel they'd received had been pretty convenient—maybe just too convenient. Anyway, the Vipers were ready.

* * *

Rayman opened the front door slowly and entered the living room as softly as he could. Sally Crab watched as Rayman, Jack, and Elaine disappeared into the front of the house. As Elaine entered, she closed the front door behind her. Rayman and Jack had withdrawn their knives. There were two dark shapes of men lying on the living room floor. A third man was lying on the couch under a blanket. All three were sleeping. Each man had a weapon next to him.

Rayman motioned Elaine toward one of the men on the floor, and Elaine pulled her knife. Rayman walked around everyone in a giant arc that ended at the head of the couch. Bill and Elaine each knelt next to a man.

They struck all at once, driving their knives deep into the spines of their targets, killing them instantly and, more importantly, quietly. At least this much of the intel was correct: the house was being used by terrorists.

"Living room clear. Three targets down. Careful, team B, there are bad guys here," whispered Rayman. The mic of the comm picked up his barely audible voice and transmitted it to the earpieces of the members of the team.

* * *

Sue slowly opened the back door. As it cracked open, she saw the dark shape of a man leaning in the doorframe between the back room and the kitchen. She stopped opening the door. "Target to the right, in the doorway," she said to Samantha as she pointed to his location.

Sue opened the door farther, her weapon ready. Samantha slipped inside the kitchen, moving sideways through the door, her knife in hand. Bill followed her.

The terrorist heard something behind him and pivoted toward the sound, still leaning against the door. His weapon was held casually across his chest. He seemed to have no thought of danger, much less the notion that a US Navy SEAL team had just entered the house.

Samantha was on him in two quick steps. She sent her knife deep into the side of his neck, severing his spine and ending his life. Sue and Bill rushed to Samantha and took hold of the terrorist before he fell. They laid him down gently on the tile kitchen floor. Together Sue and Samantha leaned him against the wall, making it look as though he had fallen asleep sitting up. Bill stood by, ready to defend them if needed.

Sue, Samantha, and Bill stood still, listening and watching for any movement or sound. After a moment passed and there were no other sounds, Sue said to Lieutenant Commander Rayman, "Kitchen clear—moving toward the basement. One target down."

"Roger, we'll check the upstairs," he said as he motioned for Jack and Elaine to follow him. He went up the stairs in the lead with Jack and Elaine right behind.

Sue, Samantha, and Bill gathered at the top of the

basement stairs, and Sue opened the door and began to descend the steps. When her foot touched the fourth step down, something slammed into her chest. It was as if someone had punched her. Then they heard the sound of gunfire. Sue's trained reflexes pushed her down onto the steps of the stairs, making her a smaller target. "I've been hit," she said as she scanned the basement below.

Samantha passed Sue, who was squatting on the stairs, and reached the basement floor. She saw a flash of movement as a figure with a gun dove behind an old chair. Samantha sent a quick stream of bullets into the back of the chair, and a figure fell away from it, spilling onto the floor. The stuffing in the chair offered little protection from a semiautomatic.

Even with night vision, they had to be careful. They were supposed to rescue hostages, not get them killed in a gun battle. Sue got up from her crouching position and rushed down the rest of the stairs, and the three of them panned out into the basement.

Bill spoke first. "Two hostages, north wall." He positioned himself to defend them if needed.

Sue fired three times toward the south corner; a target fell dead. Samantha fired twice, killing another man attempting to hide. Carefully Sam and Sue walked the length of the basement. They checked every nook and cranny, anywhere they thought a person could hide.

Bill had already cut the hostages loose when Sue and Samantha arrived at his side. The hostages sat on the floor.

"Colonel Taylor?" said Sue as she gave them a cursory examination.

"Yes?" said the man sitting in front of her.

"Navy SEALs. You're safe now." She placed a hand on his shoulder.

"Get us the hell out of here." He smiled through a face filled with bruises.

"Working on it." They had clearly been beaten, but they had no broken bones. Though they were weak, they could move under their own power.

"We have secured Colonel Taylor," said Sue.

"Roger that," said Rayman.

Next to the wall where the hostages had been tied was a small table with an assortment of tools that had clearly been used to torture. A larger table was next to it with hand and leg shackles. The table was just long enough for a person to lie on.

Samantha let her eyes wander down the length of the table. There were ugly brown and reddish stains on it, more brown stains on the floor beneath it. She glanced at the small table next to it and let her mind scan the tools sitting there. Lying on the floor next to a drainage sink was something familiar, something round with threads running from it. It was an eyeball, and the eyeball was looking back at her.

Samantha bent over and threw up. Bill grabbed her arm and pulled her away.

"Basement is secured and cleared. Four targets down, and we have two hostages," said Sue.

All was quiet in the basement.

Upstairs was a different story.

CHAPTER 4

In the upstairs hallway connecting the bedrooms, Rayman, Jack, and Elaine branched out, each taking a bedroom. Rayman burst into the first bedroom; it was empty. He opened the closet door with his weapon ready. Also empty.

When Elaine entered the master bedroom at the end of the hallway, she heard a scream and saw two naked men scramble to the wall next to the bed. In the bed was a girl cowering beneath dirty white sheets.

One of the naked men grabbed his rifle lying against the wall. Elaine fired at both men, and the wall was splattered with ugly red and clear fluid. Both were dead as they slid against the wall and fell to the floor. Two large red smears marked their slide. In Elaine's night vision, she could see their eyes were frozen open. One of the men lying on the floor, angled against the wall, still clenched his gun in his right hand.

Elaine heard a burst of fire from the next room. That was Bill's room.

"Target down. Room clear," said Bill.

"We have company," said Sally Crab. Sally Crab's voice was lower than Betty Crab's voice. All AI units had independent voices that made them easy to distinguish from each other.

"Sally, hold ground," said Rayman. "Take any action needed."

"Copy," said Sally Crab.

Betty Crab spoke: "We have company in the back."

Again Rayman said, "Betty, hold ground, take any action needed."

"Copy," said Betty Crab.

Having cleared his room, Commander Rayman reentered the hallway. "Elaine, I'm on my way to you."

Elaine approached the bed. "US Navy SEALs," she said, holding her hand out toward the girl on the bed as Rayman arrived. He checked the master bathroom and the closet. All was clear.

The girl was crying, clenching her bedsheet to her chin, her eyes wide in fear. The girl climbed out of the bed and ran over to Elaine, nude. She had clearly been beaten and raped. Her left cheek was swollen to the point that her left eye was closed, and what appeared to be cigarette burns covered both arms and inner thighs. From the girl's face and height, Elaine figured she could not have been fourteen. She fit the description of the minister's daughter.

From her night vision system, the image was analyzed for identification. "Ninety-seven percent probability the subject is Eva Jaikal," said her helmet. She was the daughter of the Jordanian minister.

"Eva, you're safe now," said Elaine.

Elaine yanked a bulletproof shawl from a pouch on her side. It was for the hostages. Designed to wrap around the person, it had Velcro to keep it in place so it could offer protection from gunfire on the move. It was not as good as the protection worn by the combat troops, but it provided reasonable protection from stray bullets.

Elaine bent down to secure the shawl around the girl. "Two targets down. We have the minister's daughter," said Elaine.

"I see that," said Rayman, standing beside Elaine. He placed a hand on her shoulder.

She smiled at him, then moved back to her charge. Eva trembled, but she seemed to sense that she was now safe.

Sally Crab fired in single shots to preserve her ammunition. The troops coming over the wall were slowing dramatically. The dead and wounded bodies lay at the base of the wall, a testament to Sally's deadly accuracy. The troops changed their strategy. They continued to press directly toward the crab, just to keep it busy, while they sent most of their troops to the side of the house and out of the crab's vision.

Betty Crab ran from tree to tree in the backyard, attempting to suppress the onslaught. She ran to one side and fired at the targets, then to the other, then did it all over again. Too many targets. They charged toward the house wherever Betty wasn't.

"We are in danger of being overrun," announced Sally Crab. She continued to fire rapidly at the lead targets, but there were so many of them. Sensing that they had changed tactics, Sally ran farther out into the front yard to get a better look. As she ran, she pivoted back and forth, firing in a wide arc. Targets were everywhere.

"Targets have reached the house. They are at the west wall," she said.

Betty Crab said, "Overrun is imminent in the backyard."

Rayman directed Jack to the front yard to support Sally Crab and Samantha to the back to support Betty Crab.

"Sally Crab, Jack is on his way."

"Roger that," said Sally Crab as she dashed to and fro.

"Betty Crab, Samantha is on her way."

"Roger that."

While Sally Crab and Jack defended the front and Betty Crab and Sam attempted to stem the tide in the back, Rayman clicked a switch on his comm. "Viper One, this is Lieutenant Commander Rayman. Request emergency assistance. We are being overrun. Copy."

"This is Viper One. Looks like you landed in the middle of an anthill. Help is on its way."

The strike by the Vipers came without warning. They hovered at cloud level and released a torrent of lead into the backyard, then another in the front. The weapons officer sent waves of lead, covering a wide swath of the yards on either side of the house. Then it stopped and the Vipers vanished.

"Status, Sam and Jack," said Rayman as he, Sue, Bill, and Elaine gathered up the three charges and secured them all quickly in their protective blankets. It was clear that only the little girl, Eva, could run. The others would need to be assisted if they were going to make it very far.

"Taking heavy fire. The enemy is everywhere," said Samantha.

"Jack?"

"Same here in the front—we are being overrun. The Viper hit has slowed them down, but there are just too many."

* * *

Captain Alex Preston was listening to all mission communications. He said to his first officer, "This is bad. Send in the other two Vipers. Direct the Vipers on-site now not to worry about picking up hostages. Their only job now is combat support. They can't land to pick anyone up under these conditions."

AWACS vectored the two new Vipers to the site. The pilots went to maximum thrust, and the two aircraft bolted into supersonic flight. In a few minutes, they would be over the target.

* * *

"Viper One, this is Red Fox. I need you to hit the backyard while we exit the site," said Commander Rayman.

"Roger that." The Vipers returned and headed to the rear.

"Sally Crab, I need you to be ready to join us in the backyard on my command. We're leaving the site."

"Roger," said Sally Crab.

CHAPTER 5

Rayman assigned Bill and Jack to assist the two former hostages. "Elaine, keep the girl with you. Hold her hand if needed. Don't lose her. If she can't keep up, then pick her up and carry her. OK?"

"All right." Elaine knelt down to the girl and explained what they were going to do. She told her to stay close as they ran, and the girl said she understood.

"Bill and Jack, same to you," Rayman said, gesturing to the former hostages the two men were supporting. "If you have to, carry them."

"Yes, sir," they both said.

"Red Fox, this is Viper One. We have fifteen seconds to target."

"Viper One, roger that." Everyone gathered at the door. "Sally Crab, where are you?"

"On my way, sir," said Sally Crab.

Just then, the fighters began to hit the backyard and the sides of the house fiercely for several moments. Then they stopped hovering and returned to horizontal flight.

"Now!" said Rayman as he threw open the back door. It slammed against the wall, and he ran out and into the backyard with his team. At the wall, he helped every member climb it as they used him as a stepladder. Just like in training.

Samantha was the last one over, and she stopped on the top of the wall to help Rayman over with a hand. It was then that Samantha saw two rockets jump into the sky and streak toward the Vipers.

* * *

The communications officer said to Captain Alex Preston, "Sir, AWACS is reporting that both Vipers have been hit. They're on their way back. Viper One is badly hurt—it may not make it. They were hit by fragments of surface-to-air missiles. They rescanned the data and have confirmed that the missiles had the undeniable sig of QW-201 advanced AI missiles."

"What? Where in God's name did they get those?" Captain Preston said to no one in particular. "Also, have Rescue and Recovery stand by," he said to the first officer.

"Yes, sir."

"Inform the two Vipers of the missile threat. Take evasive AI countermeasures. Be aggressive. I don't want any more fighters getting hit."

"Yes, sir," repeated the first officer.

* * *

Once they'd cleared the wall, the SEAL team took off running parallel to the beach. They were ten blocks away from the beach; right now they were running just to get away. Rayman was searching for a spot where they could be lifted out.

Both support aircraft had to leave from injury and were flying back to the carrier. The birds were gone and the sky had cleared.

"Viper One, this is Red Fox. We need extraction support," said Lieutenant Commander Rayman.

"Red Fox, this is Dark Sky. Viper One is six minutes out. Copy?" said Captain Peterson of the USS *Reagan*.

"Dark Sky, roger. Do they have our location?"

"Red Fox, this is Dark Sky. Yes. Mapping has you on visual."

Rayman scanned around as they ran. They were hampered by the two former hostages, but the two were running as hard as they could. The girl was no problem; she could easily keep up with them, despite her injuries. She did, however, hold Elaine's hand as they ran.

"Where's Betty Crab?" asked Rayman. He searched again. Nothing. "Betty Crab, report in."

"Sorry, Commander, I got hung up a little. I'm coming."

As they reached the backyard of another house, he scanned behind them. Nothing. Suddenly Betty Crab emerged from between two houses about half a block behind them.

She scampered to and fro, firing her gun like crazy. She had placed herself between them and their attackers, and she was slowing them down, helping to keep the distance between them and the bad guys.

"I see you, Betty. Great job."

"Thank you, sir," she responded. "I'm doing my best."

"Turn left; it's a straight shot to the beach. I hate to use the beach—everything's an easy target—but the Vipers can quickly land and extract people on the flat terrain," said Rayman. They turned ninety degrees left and headed off for the beach. "Copy that, Betty Crab?"

"Yes. I'll be there."

Rayman shook his head as he ran, trying to suppress his worry. The problem with the beach was that they would be completely exposed to enemy fire. On the other hand, they could easily get picked up.

There was only one way to find out.

CHAPTER 6

"Viper One, Red Fox. We are headed to the beach. Can you be ready to receive three when we arrive?"

"Red Fox, roger. But be ready—we can't sit on deck for long," said the Viper pilot.

"Understood, thanks."

The Vipers dropped low over the ocean and went subsonic, flying just above sea level. Viper One would fly in at sea level, land, and pick them up. Viper Two climbed vertically in a steep ascent. While they hovered, the weapons officer would keep them occupied at another area of the beach. Hopefully, the enemy would be confused and misjudge what part of the beach the SEALs were at.

The team ran up to the edge of the beach. Jack, Sue, and Sam dropped behind a sand dune and began suppression fire as Elaine, Rayman, and Bill carried the three injured hostages.

"Viper One, this is Red Fox. We're in position," said Rayman.

The team was amazed at how quickly the Viper appeared from nowhere. It flew in from the ocean and set down almost right in front of them.

Quickly the former hostages were loaded into the Viper. Elaine strapped the girl into her seat, but when she tried to pull her hand out of the girl's hand, the girl clutched her even tighter. Elaine ran her other hand through the girl's hair. "You'll be all right. These people will take good care of you." Elaine moved in quickly and kissed the girl's forehead and then backed up out of the Viper's way.

Farther down the beach, they could hear the Gatling gun of Viper Two firing away.

Passengers secured, the Viper lifted off. When it was two feet from the ground, the Viper moved out over the ocean, slowly climbing in altitude. Then it went supersonic and was gone.

"Exit," said Rayman. "Don't wait for anyone. We will regroup one mile at sea."

Elaine dropped to her knee. "Sally Crab, get on," she commanded.

"Yes, sir," said Sally Crab, jumping onto Elaine's back and securing herself. "Secured."

Elaine activated her jet pack, then lifted off the beach and headed out over the water. Bill, Jack, and Sue followed. Where was Betty Crab? "Betty Crab, report location."

Samantha scanned down the beach, but the crab was nowhere in sight. Samantha had decided that there was no way she would leave without her.

"Two blocks behind you on the beach."

Samantha finally saw a small object down the coastline. It was Betty Crab.

Viper Two was continuing to harass the enemy from a distance. Samantha and Rayman activated their jet packs and darted up to Betty Crab behind a sand dune. Samantha knelt in front of the crab for one second, and Betty Crab ran to the top of the dune and jumped for Samantha's back. She landed on Samantha—not correctly, but good enough.

With Betty Crab clinging to her back, hanging on for life, Samantha fired her jet pack and launched herself over the dune and out to the ocean to join up with the others. Betty Crab tried to climb into her proper place but couldn't safely get there. Rayman didn't want to waste any more time on Betty Crab with his team hovering over the ocean, so he tied a line around Betty Crab.

Commander Rayman smiled his crooked smile as he tied the other end of the line around Samantha's waist. "Well, Samantha, I guess you're not a rookie anymore."

Samantha smiled back. "No, sir. I guess not, sir."

Betty Crab was hanging on to Samantha as best she could. If she slipped, the rope would catch her and she would just have to make the rest of the trip to the carrier, dangling on a rope swing.

The Navy SEALs were heading back over the ocean to the USS *Reagan*. Mission accomplished.

Day One

CHAPTER 7

Earth Orbit
City of Liberty

"I'm so excited!" Megan wrapped her arm around her uncle's arm and pulled herself close to him. "Thanks for coming, Uncle Mat. I know you don't like to fly."

"You're welcome." He gave her a big hug, like he had done when she'd met him at the spaceport. Megan's mom and dad couldn't be here, but he could. And was.

"Look at how many chairs there are for everyone on the podium. I think everyone who works in the White House is here."

"Everyone's going to be here," said Mat.

"No kidding. I wonder how many chairs there are."

The speaker's platform had been built near the center of Freedom Park and faced the largest open space of grass with trees clustered about in twos and threes. The platform was three feet high and had steps leading up on both sides. In the back of the platform were three long rows of metal folding chairs. In the front center of the platform was a podium for the speaker.

"How many people do you think are here?" asked Megan.

Mat scanned all the people gathered to listen. "At least a hundred thousand." He shrugged. "Lots."

Megan had selected a spot in Tier Two near the edge, so they had a good view of the speaker's platform. It was odd and beautiful. Sitting above the treetops with a view downward into the park, you quickly became accustomed to this new reality. It was a three-dimensional space. Walking around Tier Two was like being on the ground. Then you looked over the side of the tier, and there was another ground flowing underneath you.

Liberty, the first and only orbital city, was located in a medium orbit. A high orbit would have been preferable, but the cost of flying there dictated a lower orbit. The city was built like a bicycle tire: artificial gravity was created by rotating the city around the hub. The city—the tire part of the city—had two ribbons or belts. The bottom outermost belt served as the agricultural belt. This ag belt was made from lunar material, and it served two purposes.

The primary job, and the actual reason it existed, was to block harmful radiation. Without this lunar material blocking the radiation, it would kill everyone. The second purpose of this lunar belt was agricultural. The designers decided that since they already needed the lunar material to block radiation, they might as well get the most out of it— so the lunar dirt was used as farmland.

The second ribbon formed the city proper, which contained the real estate of the city. This was the land on which buildings were built. Weaving through this ground level was a second tier, Tier Two, a platform two or three stories above the ground. Tier Two was a second ground level containing smaller buildings. It created a three-dimensional land space.

The seats in the back of the platform began to fill up quickly. TOD cars were arriving with dignitaries at the edge of Freedom Park, and groups were being escorted to the speaker's platform by police officers dressed in their best blues. The Washington elite were walking through the park escorted by more police officers. The dignitaries were arriving now and taking their places on the platform.

The city of Liberty had no cars and was divided into regions. To allow travel from region to region, four monorail lines ringed the city near the outer two walls. One monorail line went clockwise and the other counterclockwise. Tier Two was designed as the transportation tier; the ground level was pedestrian. To travel within a region, a Transportation-on-Demand system, or TOD, was used. TOD cars were similar to automobiles: small vehicles about the size of golf carts that the engineers claimed were able to seat five (four in reality). The TOD pathways were about ten feet in width.

To access these vehicles, a citizen walked to a "TOD Spot," a circular brick two feet in diameter—a stepping stone. Simply stand in a TOD Spot, and a personal transit vehicle quickly arrived to pick you up. That was TOD.

TOD was very popular. The key to its popularity lay in the fact that TOD cars were safe and fast. Very fast. You would get in and tell the car where you wanted to go, and pretty soon you would be there. No traffic, no waiting in line. It was a little like an elevator, only it was horizontal. Beyond TOD, everybody hoofed it.

Mat watched the Speaker of the House arrive with his

wife. They walked up holding hands. The monitors showed a close-up of the Speaker and his wife as they waved to everyone in the park before ascending the steps of the platform.

The president and his family were the last to arrive. The speaker's platform was full; almost all the metal seats were taken.

"Look at the First Family," said Megan.

The president was holding the First Lady's hand, and their two teenage kids, Sarah and Michael, were following them.

"The president does have a nice family," said Mat. "Well, it's about to start."

"What do you mean?" asked Megan.

"The president and his family are the last ones here, for security. His presence means that the speeches are about to begin."

"Well, I feel sorry for Sarah. She's like a sophomore in high school, I think," said Megan. "And I think Michael is in the eighth grade. Fourteen years old. Something like that."

"Why do you feel sorry for Sarah?" asked Mat.

"I mean, just think about it. She is the daughter of the president. The average guy she might normally meet and date in high school isn't going to just walk up to her and ask her out."

"OK. Maybe."

"A lot of guys are shy, especially in high school. Asking the daughter of the sitting president out on a date—who would do that? What normal guy would have the courage to do that?"

"She will survive it," said Mat.

"And then if she does go on a date, what about the Secret Service?"

"What about them?"

"Uncle Mat, you know that they are going to be going on that date too."

"You have a point there. I sure didn't want any adults around when I dated in high school."

"Who would?" she said. "And then there's college. I bet she'll have the Secret Service around all the time. If it were me, I'd say no thank you. I mean, what kind of a life is that?"

"Speaking of dating, Megan, how's your boyfriend?"

Megan lowered her head so that she had to roll her eyes up to look at Uncle Mat. "I don't have a boyfriend."

"What about that Bill guy?"

"I never dated Bill. I don't date jerks."

"Then there was that other guy . . ."

Megan interrupted him. "Oh no. Don't even think about it. You don't want to go there, Uncle Mat." Megan shook her head and poked a finger into his chest. "Don't go there."

Mat started to say something, and Megan raised her head. Her eyebrows formed two high arches on her forehead—akin to cocking a gun and chambering a bullet. "Where is your girlfriend, Uncle Mat?"

Mat just looked at Megan and didn't say anything. The world thought that Sheriff McKenna was standing next to his niece, Megan: an intelligent, attractive woman who was in her first job since graduating college. But Mat McKenna knew better. He knew he was in the presence of a python. Anything he said could result in her tightening her grip on him, slowly taking away his ability to breathe until he was gone.

"What about Amber? I've been to the office enough to see how she looks at you. She likes you, Uncle Mat. You could ask her out." Megan crossed her arms.

Mat had to get out of the swamp. Now, while he was still breathing. "Stop it. Amber is a deputy. She is a lot younger than me. And you're mistaken about those looks you imagine she gives me. You can tease me, Megan, but leave everyone who works for me out of it, OK?"

"OK, I guess. Just promise me that you will keep your eyes open."

"I promise."

The president and his family walked up the steps of the platform and took the last remaining seats, in the center front row. Before sitting, he and the First Lady shook hands with half the people already sitting. Others they waved to and acknowledged with a word or two. Then the family sat down.

Mathew McKenna counted three large screens along the side of the park, each showing a view of the speaker's platform. There were also screens set up on Tier Two.

They had come here three hours earlier, then pushed some people aside, cajoled some, and bribed many with homemade cookies in order to get a little closer. It wasn't as close as Megan had wanted. She had envisioned leaving four hours early and getting a spot a lot closer—but she was happy. And if she was happy, then Uncle Mat was happy.

They had a picnic, of sorts, in the middle of a crowd, and they waited like everyone for the event to start. Mat

McKenna would never have thought of doing anything like this.

"Just think, Uncle Mat, the ten-year celebration of Liberty, the first and only orbital city in the history of mankind. It seems like Liberty has been here forever, and it seems like it just happened yesterday."

She wrapped her arm around Uncle Mat. "Thank you so much for coming. I'm so excited. Just think, right down there is the president of the United States. I will never get this close to a president ever again."

Mat nodded. She really was excited.

The screen showed a close-up of the First Lady when she first stepped onto the stage. A woman about Megan's age with her boyfriend, standing next to Megan, pointed to the screen and said, "That's our First Lady." Her boyfriend nodded. Megan and the woman exchanged looks. "She looks good," she said to Megan.

"I know," agreed Megan. "Look at her. What a beautiful dress. And those shoes. Can you believe those shoes?"

Her new friend agreed. "Everyone will want those shoes now. You watch."

They both laughed. Megan said, "Red and white shoes with that deep ocean-blue dress. Red and white shoes! I guess it's Patriots Day. Only she could pull that off."

"And look at those heels. They have to be at least five inches!" said Megan's new friend.

"At least! More like six inches. No two- or three-inch heels for Samantha," said Megan.

"I hope I look like that when I'm in my forties."

"Me too," agreed Megan. She said to Uncle Mat, "She's

the most popular person in the White House."

The crowd noise dropped as the mayor stepped toward the podium. Then, when she reached the podium, everyone applauded.

Mat surveyed Freedom Park, taking it all in. Behind the speaker's stand were four police officers and three Secret Service agents. Onstage were three more Secret Service agents. Two sat next to the First Family; one sat directly behind the president's seat. To each side of the speaker's platform were two police officers and one Secret Service agent. He glanced around the park. Along the perimeter were half a dozen police officers. Crowd control.

Liberty was a gun-free city. He had read that for this event, the city and the president's security detail had to each make concessions. He had no idea exactly what that meant, and nobody would say. It was said that this was "the safest venue short of the White House living room to make a speech."

He did know that he'd been forced to leave his sidearm behind. He was not even allowed to bring it on the spaceliner when flying out from Orlando International Airport. He'd handed his weapon over to Amber, one of his deputies, who was kind enough to drive him to the airport.

Farther to his right, about fifteen yards away, was another Secret Service agent. Mat reasoned that there must be other Tier Two agents on the other side of the park.

The mayor of Liberty was currently speaking, not that anyone actually cared. Mat didn't. He and Megan watched the large screen to their right. It showed the mayor wrapping up her speech. And to their downward left was the mayor herself.

Mat nudged Megan and pointed at the mayor. "She's right down there, you know." He smiled. "You don't have to watch the monitor. You can actually see her." He pointed again. "See? She's right there."

"I know." She punched him in the arm, and he rubbed it as if it hurt. She was watching the television coverage on her tablet as well. She rotated between looking at the speaker, the monitor, and her tablet.

Mat studied the people around them. At least half the people who came here to see the speakers in person were watching the monitors, not the speakers. *That must say something.*

Then the crowd erupted. Cheers, throaty yells, and high-pitched whistles filled the air. The mayor was done speaking! The mayor was sure that the yells were for her, but Mat was pretty sure they were because her speech was finally finished.

"Yay! The mayor's done!" yelled someone near them, and everyone on the tier laughed. The cheers became louder. The mayor's speech was over; this called for a celebration. Mat gave away their last bag of homemade cookies to a couple standing next to them to celebrate. Mat and Megan watched as the bag was passed around until the last of the cookies was gone.

"I'm so glad we made those cookies and brought them," she said into her uncle's ear.

"I'm sure they are too," he said, pointing to the people eating the cookies. They laughed.

The president of the United States smiled as he stood up from his chair, and the crowd exploded. This was what they had waited for. The mayor faced the president as he

approached the podium. President James Devane extended
his hand, and he and the mayor shook hands vigorously
while talking privately in public for several minutes. Then
President Devane stepped to the podium, resting a hand on
each side.

The mayor retired to her assigned seat behind the
podium on the platform. She was surrounded with political
dignitaries. On her right was the Speaker of the House.

"Congratulations!" said the president. The crowd went
nuts. "I'm so glad . . ." He paused. ". . . and honored to be
here with pioneers like you."

The cheers were so loud he was forced to stop, and he
stepped away from the podium with a small half step as the
crowd cheered loudly.

Mat was glad he was there. Megan was so excited. It was
an event. It was like a rock concert, only this wasn't a rock
concert. He understood. She wanted to be part of something
big. It wasn't about seeing political celebrities or listening to
speeches. It was about being part of a movement. A part of
history. Now that he was there, he was glad to be sharing
this moment with her.

He had known that he had no choice but to be here.
Listening to politicians give speeches didn't strike him as a
fun way to spend an afternoon. Yes, technically, he too was
a politician. But not really. No he wasn't. That was a
technicality. Running for office was just required for the job.
That's all. Not the same thing.

I'm a sheriff, not a politician. Really.

Anyway, now that he was here, he too could feel *it*.
Whatever *it* was.

Mat tapped on Megan's shoulder. She was watching the president speak on her tablet, and she raised her eyes to him with a smile and asked, "What?"

He pointed down to where the president stood on the platform below. He knew that he was being a little bit of an ass, but so what? What's an uncle for?

"I know!" she said after she hit him again. She returned to watching her tablet, but Megan made sure that Uncle Mat saw her stop and watch the president for just a moment. Then the moment passed, and she was watching everything on her tablet again.

Mat decided that she just couldn't help it. She was used to her whole world coming to her through her tablet—that and her phone. Or perhaps the proper order was her phone, then her tablet.

Anyway, he decided he would leave her alone for a while. OK, not really.

CHAPTER 8

Megan whistled loudly and brought her hands together repeatedly in a loud, slow clap. The audience clapped and cheered at every conceivable moment. *At this rate, the speech will last forever,* thought Mat.

Pop, pop, pop, pop. The clapping continued, but Mat McKenna's muscles tensed—a trained reaction from twenty years of military service, including several tours of combat duty.

The Secret Service agent to Mat's right was gone. There was a man there though, holding some object in his right hand. The man took two steps to the terrace wall. He raised the object up and placed it on the wall. It was a rifle.

At that moment, Mat spotted the agent. He was still there, on the ground, crumpled. Motionless.

The people on the platform were looking at each other and shrugging their shoulders. A few scanned the area, searching for the source of the sounds.

Mat grabbed Megan and shoved her to the ground forcefully.

"Uncle Mat?" she groaned.

Mat lay on top of her. "Stay down."

Pop, pop, pop, pop. The clapping stopped. The entire security detail around the speaker's stage crumpled and folded to the ground. It looked like all the Secret Service agents had been hit. Most of the wounds were fatal; many were instantly fatal.

Pop, pop-pop. The cheers from the crowd stopped.

Pop-pop-pop, pop-pop. The shouting stopped. The snipers had carefully eliminated their targets on the speaker's platform. The area around the base of the stage was swept clean.

Pop, pop. It was as if someone had just placed the cursor over the mute button and clicked. Everything went silent.

Pop-pop-pop.

Then came the screams.

* * *

From the comfort of a restaurant adjacent to Freedom Park, Yassin watched everything from the monitors on the wall. He patiently waited for his cue, listening as the crowd reached a loud moment of cheering. That was what he was waiting for.

He smiled at Shakira. She was beautiful. He loved the way she turned heads when she walked into a room full of men. She wore deep red lipstick, blue jeans, and a black, sleeveless, well-fitted knit shirt. Her hair was black as night, and her brown eyes could speak a language more complex than any verbal one created by man. She knew the effect she had on men, and she used it to her advantage—and to her pleasure. Especially her pleasure.

Yassin picked up his comm and said, "Go." He set the

comm down and picked up a french fry from his plate and dipped the fry into the thick red ketchup from Shakira's plate.

"Help yourself," she said.

"Thank you, I will." He bit the fry in half.

* * *

The female terrorist patiently waited with her male partner. Both wore comm pieces with almost invisible mic wires coming out of the earpiece to the sides of their cheeks—standard issue for all of them—and everyone heard the "Go" command in their own standard-issue comms. The shooters counted off four seconds. The others, two-person teams comprising a woman and a man each, moved immediately on the command.

Her small, feminine fingers wrapped around the black handle of the knife hidden at the back right side of her waist underneath her T-shirt. She angled her body sideways as she stepped forward between the couple blocking her from the Secret Service agent, her target. She used the weight of her body to drive the blade deep into the agent's throat. The agent's heart was pumping massive amounts of blood out of the wound; he was unable to yell as he stared into the soft brown eyes of his assailant.

She smiled back at him gently. Then she expertly moved to his side, slipping under his arm and driving her knife deep into the side of his chest. His heart was pierced by the blade. He collapsed, quietly, and was dead.

She sheathed the knife back at her waist. People moved away from her, gasping in horror. The smile lingered on her face as she returned their looks.

Her male partner lowered his bag to the ground and casually withdrew two parts of a rifle from it. He snapped the barrel into position and locked it in place. The rifle was now ready.

It was then that the two terrorists heard the first *pop*. With his rifle in his hand, he walked to the edge of Tier Two, his partner at his side with a pair of binoculars. She was there to help him find targets quickly.

* * *

President Devane stopped speaking. He patiently stood at the podium, waiting for the right moment to continue. The question of what those sounds meant was beginning to enter into his conscious thought.

The agents sitting next to the First Family performed as they were trained. Standing tall, they withdrew their hand weapons and searched for targets. Those agents were quickly targeted and dispatched.

Several agents dove on top of the First Family, shoving the kids and the First Lady underneath them. Those agents were among the first to understand. Using their bodies as shields, they protected the First Family as best they could.

Secret Service agents are trained differently than other officers. Trained to stand tall and return fire. To be visible. They are taught to become the target and draw the fire away from the president.

The agent who had been sitting behind the First Family rushed toward the president, who was ducking behind the podium. The agent's body violently collided with the president and drove him into the ground as forcefully as he could manage. The power of the collision almost caused the two men to tumble over the side of the platform.

The agent positioned himself on top of the president, surrendering his body willingly as a shield, to preserve the life of the president of the United States.

CHAPTER 9

Megan's eyes were wide. "Uncle Mat? What's happening?"

"Stay down," he repeated. The shots were coming from everywhere in Tier Two, both from his left and his right. Gunfire was heard coming up from ground level, from no place in particular and from everywhere throughout the park.

Some people ran out of the park, anywhere, just to get away. Located around the perimeter were men with weapons. Guns. The bloody bodies of murdered police officers lay scattered around the perimeter, grotesque and distorted shapes lying on the ground, their bodies destroyed by explosive rounds of ammunition. Many in the park dropped to the ground. Some fell to their knees; others lay down where they stood. Some lay in the fetal position with their arms covering their neck and head. Others just stood and cried, too afraid to do anything. The screams were deafening.

Sheriff McKenna leaned in toward his niece and spoke into her ear so she could hear him above the crowd. "Stay with me."

Megan got up to her knees, and Mat grabbed her hand. Together they ran, hand in hand, bobbing and weaving through the panicked crowd, until they reached the back of the tier.

"Megan, I need you to go back to your apartment. I'll join up with you later."

"No! No, Uncle Mat, don't go."

"Megan, go back home. I'll be there later." Mat gave his niece a hug. "Go."

He pulled away from Megan and weaved through the crowd, trying to keep a tree between himself and the two shooters. He pulled up behind the tree, then glanced around him. There were people lying on the ground, covering themselves with their arms. A few went to the retaining wall to see for themselves what was going on down in the park.

The majority of people on Tier Two were fleeing for the back. He was close now, fewer than ten yards away from the shooter. He realized there were two terrorists, not just the one he had seen shooting. The shooter had a partner, and his partner was a woman.

He'd gathered himself and stepped away from the tree when the woman terrorist began a sweeping view around Tier Two. Mat pulled himself back behind the tree, exhaling slowly. If she saw him, he could be a dead man standing. He waited, his back pressed against the tree, forcing himself to count to three. Slowly he leaned out and peeked around the tree.

She hadn't seen him. She was looking out into the park with the binoculars again. Around the shooters, people were fleeing in terror. There was no one between himself and the two of them.

To hell with this. He stepped out from behind the tree and began to run toward the shooters. Four steps away, he selected the spotter and moved toward her.

Somehow she sensed the danger, sensed his presence. The female terrorist stared at him over her shoulder. Her eyes were crisp, clear, and the color of hatred. They gazed at each other for a moment, eye to eye. One was armed, and one was not. One would live. The other die.

Mat took another step as he charged her; then with one hand he grabbed her waist, and with the other he grabbed her between her legs. The terrorist's hand fumbled at first as she reached for the handle of her knife. In one smooth, continuous motion, Mat raised her into the air and flipped her over the retaining wall. Her hand gripped the knife's handle, and she pulled it out clumsily as she flailed in the air, falling. She hit the ground with a thud, still holding the knife. She hadn't even screamed. She was dead.

Mat placed his left hand on the top of the retaining wall to maintain his balance and faced the other terrorist, who was still aiming at targets over the wall. The shooter angled his head toward his partner. The terrorist was kneeling in a firing position, his rifle resting on the top of the wall, when he realized his partner was gone. The shooter stared directly at him with a question on his face.

Mat lunged into the terrorist, who was still on one knee. The shooter attempted to stand, but he fell backward, and Mat ripped the rifle from his grip as he fell. The terrorist landed ass first on the ground in a sitting position, his legs sprawled out in front of him. It was like someone had pulled the chair out from underneath him.

Mat spun the rifle around in his hands and shot the man while he was on the ground. It was over; the terrorist was dead.

Sheriff Mat McKenna went to the body of the slain Secret Service agent and knelt beside him. He suddenly jerked in surprise when he felt a hand grab hold of his shoulder. He lunged to the side, pivoting around to confront this new threat.

"Uncle Mat! What are you doing?" asked Megan.

What the hell? Megan! He grabbed her upper arm and shook it. "Dammit! You scared the hell out of me." He clenched his teeth as anger and relief fought for dominance.

She was crying. "Uncle Mat, don't leave me!" she pleaded, tears running down her face. "I'm scared."

He wrapped his arms around her and embraced her as a father would.

"Don't leave me, Uncle Mat. Please don't leave me."

He pulled back to look at her while still holding her tightly by the shoulders. "I'm not leaving you."

Sheriff McKenna had no time to waste. He knelt next to the dead Secret Service agent and removed the man's handgun. He discovered an extra magazine the agent had on him. Then he stripped the shirt from the agent and removed his ballistic vest.

He handed the vest to Megan. "Put this on."

She began to put it on over her T-shirt.

"No. Under your shirt."

Megan froze.

"Now. Take off your shirt, then put the vest on. Megan, we don't have all day. Just do it."

She pulled her shirt over her head as fast as she could. She was wearing a bra but clearly still felt exposed, embarrassed. Mat could feel her embarrassment. He could see it in the color of her face, the way she looked away from him. But he needed her to wear the protection under her shirt. He didn't want the terrorists shooting at her to know she had a bulletproof vest. With Mat's help, she put the vest on and slipped her shirt back on over it.

Mat put the handgun under his belt in the small of his back. He then moved to the dead terrorist. He took the knife and sheath from the dead body and put it on, then picked up the dead terrorist's rifle and assumed the position that the terrorist had moments before.

"Uncle Mat, there's another pair of shooters over there on the other side." Megan pointed across the podium to the other side of the park.

Mat gazed at his niece a moment, then to where she was pointing. Sure enough, there were two other shooters. He glanced back to his niece. *She's my brother's daughter.* Across the park was another man-and-woman sniper pair. Using the scope, he focused on the spotter. He gently squeezed the trigger.

The head of the woman in his scope suddenly jerked backward, and she disappeared behind the wall. He then slid his aim over and targeted the man leaning against the wall next to her. He held his breath, focused, and squeezed the trigger gently. A small puff of red and white smoke filled the air around his head, and the man drifted out of sight behind the retaining wall.

Megan scanned the area with the pair of binoculars she

had found lying on the ground.

"Megan, stay down. Get below the wall and stay out of sight. I don't want you looking for targets." She was ignoring him, and he felt anger rise inside him. Then he realized she wasn't looking for targets. What was she doing?

He set the rifle down. Megan was looking at the speaker's platform through the binoculars.

"Can I have that?" he asked. "And get down."

She handed the binoculars over to her uncle. He raised them to his face and viewed the speaker's platform.

The platform was a massacre. The carnage was horrific. The chairs were a chaotic jumble; beneath the chairs were dozens of murdered dignitaries sprawled out among pools of blood. The bodies and the chairs were tangled together in a bloody mess. It looked like someone had made scrambled eggs out of people and chairs. Two bodies lay sprawled over the side of the platform, their arms hanging down toward the ground. The platform was a mangled, twisted mass of metal chairs, arms, legs, and bodies.

The president was still alive, with a Secret Service agent lying on top of him. The agent was also alive. Behind the platform, the First Lady was on the ground. She was covering her two children with her body, and another Secret Service agent was on top of all of them.

No one else was moving. Agents and police officers who had surrounded the platform were sprawled out on the ground in a bloody ring. None of them had survived the assault.

Mat lowered himself behind the wall and laid down the binoculars.

Megan said, "The president is alive. So are the First Lady and their kids. I think everyone else is dead." She looked at her uncle. "How could the terrorists miss the First Family? Especially the president. How could they miss him? He was standing at the podium. He was wide open, the easiest target of all."

"They didn't miss. They want the First Family alive," said Mat.

Megan silently mouthed, *Oh my God.*

CHAPTER 10

Terrorists with weapons were everywhere. Most were located around the perimeter of the park, at least the parts he could see on this side. There were lots of them. The terrorists could be at the platform any time they wanted.

He faced his niece. "Megan, go back to your apartment. I'll join you as soon as I can."

"No. The terrorists are everywhere. I'm staying with you. No, Uncle Mat."

McKenna lowered his voice. "I need you to go back to your—"

"*No.* I'm coming with you," she interrupted.

McKenna quickly scanned Freedom Park with the binoculars. He had no time; the terrorists were sending teams up into Tier Two, and several were already on the way up to where they were. "Follow me."

Staying low behind the retaining wall, they made their way to the stairs that led down to ground level. At the top of the stairs, he stopped and pressed himself against the wall. Megan was behind him, making herself as small as she could.

"If any shots are fired, drop to the ground. Understand?"

"Yes."

He whispered to her, "There are two coming up the stairs."

The terrorists were walking briskly side by side. Each carried a semiautomatic weapon in his arms. Mat noted that the shooting had almost stopped; the gunfire was sporadic. He took the gun he'd taken from the Secret Service agent and confirmed that the safety lock was off. *Thank God I took Megan along on a couple of hunting trips.* She knew how to use a weapon; he had seen to that.

He handed the sidearm to Megan. "Don't shoot unless it's totally and absolutely necessary. We don't want to draw attention to ourselves. OK?"

"OK," she said. "I understand."

He withdrew the military knife he had taken from the corpse of the terrorist and wrapped his fingers tightly around the thick black handle. His knuckles were white. *Are you kidding me?* He loosened his grip and let the blood flow back into his hand. He steadied himself, forcing himself to be calm, and then he regripped the knife. If he waited too long and let them clear the top of the stairs, the terrorists might spot them in time to react, and he and Megan would be dead. If he attacked too soon, they would have too much time to react and easily shoot him and Megan. Either way, he and Megan would be dead.

Behind him, he could feel Megan tightening up. His big fear was that he would bring the terrorists down on them. He needed to eliminate these two quietly. He focused on the sound of their footsteps, mentally measuring the distance of their voices as they climbed the steps, talking and laughing with each other. His mind narrowed. The muscles in his legs tensed. He watched the top steps next to him. He waited. He saw the leg of the nearest terrorist break into view when his foot reached the top step. Nikes. The terrorist wore black Nikes.

He burst upward, releasing all his pent-up energy. In two steps, he was on him. The man faced him. Their eyes met and locked. With his left hand, Mat moved the terrorist's right arm up and slammed the blade of the knife into the side of the man's chest, just to the front of the armpit. Deep inside the man's chest, the blade sliced into his heart. The terrorist looked stunned, as if he wasn't fully comprehending what had just happened.

Like a machine, Mat withdrew the blade and pumped it into the man's chest. Again the blade sank into the man's heart. The terrorist's eyes went wide and his mouth froze open. He knew he was dead. Blood filled his chest cavity and his lungs. His heart beat sporadically in spite of the trauma. His blood vessels constricted, his body working desperately to maintain pressure. Then he passed out and collapsed on the top step. As he lay on the ground, blood spilled from his mouth. He was dead.

The other terrorist stepped away from Mat, his gun held across his chest. The terrorist raised his weapon, but Mat stepped over the body on the ground and toward the terrorist, with his knife gripped tightly in his right hand.

Then *pop-pop-pop* sounds came from behind Mat, and he saw the chest of the terrorist hit three times with bullets. Bloody material exited from the terrorist's back. Then the man's knees buckled, the legs became limp, and he fell in place, landing in a clump on the cement next to his dead comrade.

Breathing heavily, Mat said, "What? Why did you shoot?"

"It was absolutely, totally necessary," she said. "No one threatens us with a gun."

Hard to argue with that, he thought. Mat gazed upon his niece. He glanced around to see if anyone had heard the shots and was coming to investigate. Not that he could tell, but who knew? Mat reached over and grabbed one of the terrorist's legs, but Megan didn't move. "Megan, I need help," said Mat.

She leaned over, about to grab a leg of the other terrorist, but she stopped, her eyes pleading with her uncle.

"Megan, you did what you had to do. Take dominion of your emotions. We're fighting for our lives." Mat used his matter-of-fact tone, devoid of emotion.

Megan's eyes closed for a second when her hand touched the corpse of the man she had shot dead. Then the moment passed and her grip tightened, and together she and Mat dragged the two terrorists behind the wall, hiding them as best they could. Then Mat removed a knife and handed one to Megan.

"No," she said, shaking her head.

He shoved it closer to her. "Take it."

"No, Uncle Mat. I can shoot, but I don't know how to kill with a knife. I can't do that."

"All right, but put it in your purse anyway."

Reluctantly she took the knife. "I'll put it in here instead, OK?" She placed the knife in their picnic bag.

He studied the two bodies. It appeared that every terrorist had been issued one assault rifle, one military knife, and one extra magazine. He swung one of the assault rifles over his shoulder. Then he thought better of it and took it off. If he entered the park with it, he would be an instant target.

Megan handed him the handgun instead, and he tucked it between his belt and his blue jeans in the small of his back. He carefully peeked around the top of the wall. Good. Every terrorist was still busy doing their own jobs, too busy to notice that some of their people were missing. That wouldn't last much longer.

"Megan, I have to go now before it's too late. I need you to go home."

"No. Don't leave me."

"I'm going to the speaker's platform. You're going home. I will be going to your place a few minutes behind you. We will join up at your apartment. I don't have time for this. Go home."

After a moment, she said, "OK." She clearly hated the idea, but she understood.

"We *will* meet up later," said Mat.

"I love you, Uncle Mat."

"I love you, Megan. No matter what happens, don't forget that."

"Come back to me," said Megan.

"I will."

Sheriff McKenna watched as Megan fled from the park.

CHAPTER 11

Sheriff McKenna walked down the steps onto the ground level of the park. He ran with scattered elements of the crowd, weaving his way toward the president, doing his best to blend in with the panicked crowds. It was obvious that the terrorists felt safe, in total control. *Not yet—on both counts,* he thought.

By now, the park was thinning out. People were leaving the park, fleeing in all directions. Many of the people who had fallen to the ground and covered up were now up and running away. In another two minutes, the park would be empty.

Mat jogged in a zigzag pattern, using the people in the park to cover his intentions. He ran so it would appear that he was running past the platform, toward the rear, but he was working his way toward the First Family. Seven terrorists were at the platform.

The First Lady and her two children, Sarah and Michael, were standing behind the back of the platform on the ground. Standing with them was one Secret Service agent. They were shoulder to shoulder, huddled together; three terrorists with assault weapons surrounded them. President

Devane was standing onstage near the podium with a Secret Service agent next to him. They were surrounded by four terrorists.

The Secret Service agent standing with the First Lady and her kids threw down her weapon. A second later, the scene was repeated for the president's agent. Now both agents were unarmed. Two terrorists approached the president.

One of them spit in the president's face, and another struck the agent in the gut with the butt of his rifle; the agent doubled over and fell to the ground. Another man sauntered up to the fallen man. The agent covered his face with his arms just before the kick landed on his head.

The platform wasn't far from Mat. And as one of the three terrorists surrounding the First Lady grabbed her daughter, Sarah, and yanked her toward him, Mat knew he would have to make his move soon. Whatever it was.

"You touch her and you die," said the First Lady calmly to the terrorist holding Sarah.

The man laughed. "Oh really?" He grabbed Sarah's blouse at the V of the neck and ripped down on it. He laughed louder. He motioned with his arms open to his friends next to him. "I don't think I'm dead." All the terrorists laughed with him.

One of the terrorists next to the first lady noticed Mat jogging past the platform a few yards away. "You there! What are you looking at?" said the terrorist to Mat. He raised his weapon and aimed it generally toward Mat. "I'm looking at a dead man, I think." He laughed and faced his comrades, who were laughing with him, congratulating each other on their joke.

Mat stopped abruptly, withdrew his weapon, aimed, and squeezed the trigger. A red dot formed where the bullet entered the terrorist's forehead. Mat moved his aim to the next man to his right and fired again. The terrorist dropped his weapon and grabbed his chest, then fell forward facedown into the dirt. Dead.

That's when the First Lady stepped up to the man holding her daughter and punched him directly in the throat. He let go of Sarah and staggered backward, grabbing at his neck. His windpipe was crushed, and his body instantly went slack from the shock to the spinal cord. He hit the ground, gasping for air through bubbles of blood in his throat.

Of the three terrorists surrounding the First Lady and her children, two were dead. The third was dying.

Mat fired at one of the terrorists on the stage.

The First Lady bent down and grabbed one of the semiautomatic weapons from the body of a terrorist. Bill Dougan, the agent lying on the deck, gathered all his strength and tackled the president, driving both of them off the rear of the stage and into the air.

The First Lady swept the deck with semiautomatic fire until no one was standing. Secret Service Agent Cass went over to the president and pulled him underneath the rear of the stage while Agent Dougan grabbed the two kids and pulled them over to their father. Mat took hold of the First Lady by the arm, and together they joined everyone at the rear of the stage.

"Thanks, whoever you are," said the First Lady. She extended her right hand to the stranger who had saved their lives.

Mat only gave the First Lady a quick glance. "Sheriff Mathew McKenna, Shady Oaks, Florida." Then he reached out and grabbed the body of the nearest dead Secret Service agent. He pulled his knife, and in one violent motion, ripped her shirt off. Agent Cass gasped, her mouth open.

Mat removed the agent's ballistic vest. He spoke to Cass as he reached out with the vest to give it to Sarah. "Put this on." The First Lady took the vest and helped Sarah put it on.

Now Agent Cass understood, and she grabbed one of her dead friends and pulled her to the platform. She ripped off the shirt and removed the vest. The president took the vest and quickly helped his son Michael put the vest on.

"Take their weapons too," said Mat.

Mat grabbed another vest from another dead agent. He pulled off his shirt and soon had the vest on and his shirt back on over it. He slipped on a holster for his Secret Service sidearm and holstered his weapon. He now had three extra magazines, which he pocketed.

"We have to get going." He pointed the opposite way from where he had come. "That way."

"Why that way?" asked Agent Dougan.

"Why not? Does it matter? Just go."

Agents Cass and Dougan corralled the First Family together.

Mat and the First Lady studied each other. Finally she said, "What?"

Mat pointed to her high-heel shoes. "You gotta lose those, ma'am."

"Oh. Yeah." She pulled off her shoes.

He said to each member of the First Family, "Run as fast as you can. Don't stop for any reason." They all nodded, their eyes wide.

The First Lady was already sporting a Secret Service handgun and holster and an assault weapon. Sheriff Mat McKenna grabbed one of the rifles from a dead terrorist lying next to him.

Mat said to Agents Cass and Dougan, "Get them out of here." He pointed to Cass. "On the count of three."

"One," said Cass.

"Two—"

Sheriff McKenna bolted from the back of the stage, running as fast as he could toward a clump of bushes and trees. He angled to the left and dove into the bushes like an Olympic diver, headfirst. He raised his rifle and fired at the terrorists rushing toward them from their left. Two of the terrorists were hit and fell to the ground, mortally wounded. The others scattered for the trees and hit the ground for cover.

"Three," said Cass.

Dougan was in the lead, then the teenagers, then the president and First Lady. Agent Cass was last. The park was empty now, as was Tier Two, except for the army of terrorists. The First Family ran as fast as they could, heading for a wooded area at the side of the park. The First Lady fired her weapon to her right as she ran, forcing the terrorists to slow down. Cass did the same but to her left. Together they made it difficult for the terrorists to advance.

When the First Family ran past Mat, he got up and chased after them. Mat attempted to fire his semiautomatic weapon at their pursuers, but it jammed. He dropped it and continued on.

As Agent Dougan approached the tree line, he stopped and returned fire at the terrorist closing in on them. Dougan took a bullet in the head and collapsed. Cass and the First Lady, Sam, fired their weapons until they were empty. They had served their purpose, and they threw them aside as the First Family broke into the tree line.

Mat glanced at Dougan, lying on the ground, as he ran by. The head wound was ugly; at least he'd died instantly.

Mat felt three bullets strike him in the back. It felt as if he had been punched, and he could feel the bruises already. The ballistic vest had done its job. If he survived this, he was going to need a long, hot shower, maybe a sauna, and definitely a cold brew.

No, make that a keg. Maybe some rum too.

He ducked under a large low-hanging branch and disappeared into the trees.

CHAPTER 12

Cass caught up to the family and led them through the woods and out the other side. They ran out of the park and headed for a shopping plaza.

Cass spotted a Blair department store and headed straight for the front door. Blair was one of the mall's anchor stores. Mat ran up to the door and followed the family inside. They were all there: the president, the First Lady, Sarah, Michael, and Cass.

In the plaza, the terrorists were fanning out. "No time to talk; we have to keep going," said Mat.

"We can't go back that way." Cass moved away from the door. "I think we're trapped. They're surrounding the plaza. There are lots of them."

"Follow me." Mat journeyed into the interior of the store. The store was empty; no one was inside. Everyone had fled, including the employees, not that he blamed anyone. He came to an escalator that was still on, and he charged up the moving steps. The president, his two kids, and the First Lady followed. Cass brought up the rear.

Just yesterday Mat had been there with Megan. They'd shopped for hours, and Mat had given his opinion on everything from tops and dresses to shoes. He'd been there with his niece looking to enjoy life; now he was here looking just to live.

"Do you know where you're headed?" asked the president.

"Yep." He was heading up. They weren't going to like what he was planning. But they didn't have to like it—they only had to do it.

Mat ran around the perimeter of the floor until he came to a door that said *Employees Only*. He entered it and within a minute had located an employee's stairway in the far corner. He pushed open one of the double metal doors, and they charged up the stairway.

In the distance below them, they could hear the terrorists entering the store.

The group traveled three floors and then came out onto the building's rooftop.

"Oh crap!" exclaimed Cass, looking around. She placed her hands on her hips. "We are definitely trapped now."

The president said to Mat, "Is this where you wanted to go?"

"Yep." Mat jogged over toward what would have been the rear of the store. "Stay with me."

They looked around at each other, then headed over to him. They were at Tier Two elevation, except that the Blair department store was not connected to Tier Two. They could see Tier Two several buildings down, but they had no way to get there from this rooftop.

"Did you think this would get us to Tier Two?" asked Cass.

"Nope."

The First Lady glanced around the rooftop. "There's nowhere to go."

Cass said to Mat, "This isn't even Tier Two. You do know that, right?"

"Banking on it," said Mat.

"We're screwed," said Cass under her breath.

Mat walked over to the far edge of the roof near the side of the city wall. They weren't very far from the wall—the wall that separated the city from space. The only thing between them and the wall were the two monorail lines.

Mat backed up about ten feet from the edge, jogged to the edge of the building, and jumped into the air.

Michael and Sarah watched with their mouths open. The First Lady gasped.

CHAPTER 13

Michael Devane ran to the edge of the roof. Had Mat really just jumped off the building? He dropped to his knees and, with both hands on the edge of the roof, slowly peeked over the side.

"Michael, careful," said the First Lady.

"Holy shit!" said Michael. He was the first to the edge.

"Michael."

Michael grudgingly acknowledged his mom, and she gave him a disapproving look: *Language.*

Everyone rushed to the edge of the roof and leaned over to look.

"No way," said Agent Cass.

Attached to one of the support columns for the monorail track were metal U-shaped bars that served as both handgrips and ladder steps going up the column to the top of the track. They were there to give maintenance workers access to the monorail track. Mat was swinging from one of these steps. He got his foot on a step, and the swaying stopped.

After he had secured himself, he faced everyone. "All right, who's next?"

They all stared at him. It slowly became apparent to everyone what he was asking them to do.

"No. You have to be kidding," said the First Lady.

"I'm not kidding. Do you want your children in the hands of the terrorists? If not, then I suggest you get moving. Now. We don't have time to argue. You have two choices: join me or join the terrorists. Your choice."

Sarah began to cry, but she walked to the edge and studied the distance. It wasn't far—only five feet—it was just high above the ground. The fact that it was so high was what made the jump difficult. You could almost reach out and grab a person by the hands. Almost.

Mat said, "Sarah, you're next. You can do this. Just jump to me and I will grab you." Sarah was the key. If she did it, they would all do it.

Tears flowed from Sarah's eyes. They were drenched in fear.

"Sarah," Mat repeated. "You're next. I will catch you. Just do it. The quicker you do it, the quicker it will be over."

"She will never do it," whispered the First Lady.

"She will if she wants to live."

Mat and Sarah eyed each other as she stood at the edge of the building, looking at the distance and the height. He lowered the tone of his voice and began to use his coach voice. "Sarah. Your turn. Let's go. Don't make me come back and throw you over."

Sarah had no doubt that he would do exactly that. She raised her hands up to her cheeks and began crying harder. She walked away from the side of the building until Mat could no longer see her.

The First Lady and her husband together shook their heads. "Impossible, Mat."

At that moment, Sarah darted toward the gap. Placing one foot on the very edge, she pushed off and jumped into the air toward Sheriff McKenna.

Mat was about to say something when suddenly Sarah was flying in the air toward him. He lost his grip for a second he was so startled, but he grabbed the ladder again with his left hand just as Sarah arrived. His right arm wrapped around her waist in a tight embrace. Sarah grabbed the handrail with both hands and got a foot onto the ladder, silently crying until she realized that she had made it and was OK. Then suddenly she was crying and laughing all at the same time.

Mat steadied Sarah on the ladder. "Now that wasn't so bad, was it?"

A huge smile flashed across her face. Mat had his arm tight about her waist.

"Are you OK? You got a firm grip?"

"Yes, I think so."

Mat motioned with his head to the top of the monorail. "Climb all the way up."

"I will." Soon Sarah was sitting on top of the monorail track. "Michael, you can do it; it's easy."

Michael went next. He made it, joining his sister on the track. With the kids across, everyone else fell into line quickly. One at a time, Mat grabbed them and helped them when they landed. In less than a minute, it was over. They were all on the monorail.

"No one say a word. Stay quiet. Follow me." Everyone

slowly stood up, and off they went. Mat, Sarah, Michael, the president, the First Lady, and Agent Cass were all slow-jogging it down the top of the monorail track. At eighteen inches wide, the track made a perfect jogging trail.

"I guess you can say we're taking the monorail out of here. Literally," said Michael.

"Very funny, Michael," said Sarah.

Everyone laughed quietly. It was so unreal: the First Family jogging down the monorail track.

They had jogged for less than two minutes when Cass suddenly shouted, "Down—everyone get down!"

CHAPTER 14

Washington, DC

Amy Henderson grabbed her purse on her way to the front door. It had everything she needed, including her tablet and phone. She reached out for the door handle when suddenly she stopped. With her hand in the air, she turned completely around.

Faith stood behind her with her blankie trailing on the wooden floor. Floofy the lion was there too. In her other hand, she held a stainless steel pot dangling at her waist.

Amy bent down and wrapped her arms around her baby. "Faith, I have to go. I want you to get lots of sleep and drink lots of liquids. Can you do that for Mommy?"

Faith coughed several deep-throated, abrasive coughs. When she was done, she looked up at her mother. "OK, Mommy." Faith's eyes were red and hot, and her voice scraped the inside of her throat.

Amy placed the back of her hand against Faith's forehead. She was burning up.

"Lots of sleep and drink lots of liquids, and Daddy will fix you some chicken noodle soup. OK?"

Faith's eyes drifted to her daddy, who nodded at her

encouragingly. "OK, Mommy. Come back soon." She coughed for several minutes, raising the stainless steel pot in both hands and gripping it tightly. The pot was hers, just in case she felt like she was going to throw up again. It seemed to make her feel better just to hold it.

Amy hugged her husband goodbye. "I don't know when I'll be back."

"We'll be fine. I've already called into the office for the day, and I'll call in again tomorrow. I can work right here at home for a couple of days. I'll be here with the kids for however long it takes. Go. We'll talk later. Just go."

Amy went out the front door and ran to the black limo that was waiting at the curb. One of her aides was waiting at the rear of the limo. As Amy ran up, she opened the back door and Amy jumped in. Her aide leaped in after her. The limo pulled away from the curve as the door was being closed.

"So what's this about?" asked Amy.

Her aide's mouth opened slightly, her eyebrows elevated. "What? What did you say?"

"What's this about?" repeated Amy.

"Haven't you been watching television? Haven't you talked to anyone?"

"No. I've been directed to the White House by Beth Cook, assistant chief of staff to President Devane. She said a limo would be at my door in less than two minutes, and here you are."

"You don't know?"

"Know what? My daughter is sick. I haven't done much of anything except watch her. I *was* going to watch the president's speech, but I was with Faith, reading to her in bed. I figured I would watch a replay of his speech later."

Her aide picked up her phone and started streaming the news. Then she handed the phone to Amy Henderson, the national security advisor. "Watch this."

CHAPTER 15

Everyone lay quietly on the monorail tracks. Loud voices were coming from behind them. Through the tree branches, Mat watched a group of terrorists walking around the rooftop of the Blair department store, shouting and pointing at each other. For the moment they had not been spotted. He could hear a lot of yelling and saw a lot of shrugging. Then they were gone. They had left the roof.

Cass pulled herself up to her knees and studied the rooftop again. She waited a second. "I think it's clear." Cass stood up.

Mat lifted himself to his knees. "Yeah, they're gone."

The group was soon jogging down the track, Mat leading them a little faster this time. A quiet minute passed. Then another. The Blair department store was fading into the distance.

"Look!" The First Lady pointed behind them, and they all stopped jogging and looked back. Six terrorists were again on the store's roof.

Mat saw one of the terrorists point toward them, and every terrorist on the roof turned and looked at them. Mat felt his muscles tighten. Any thought that this was going to be easy vanished. One of the terrorists jumped off the roof and was soon standing on the top of the monorail track. Mat felt his blood freeze as he reinforced his determination. So now they knew where they were. So what? The terrorists still had to catch them.

"It looks like they found us," said Mat. "Keep moving." He picked up the pace. He didn't want to go so fast that someone would slip, but they had to move faster. It had taken the terrorists time to realize where they had disappeared to. The race was on again.

Several quiet moments passed with everyone lost in their own thoughts. The group was jogging to stay ahead of the terrorists when Sarah spoke up. "Sheriff, how do you know that a train isn't going to come?" she asked.

The response was plain on everyone's faces: *Good question.*

"What makes you think I know that?" Mat answered.

"What?" said Cass. "You mean a train could come? I figured you knew what you were doing."

"I know what I'm doing. I'm taking a calculated risk."

Michael laughed. He found that hilarious for some reason.

"So what happens if a train comes?" asked the president.

"We jump," said Mat.

Everyone paused for a moment to look at the ground far below them. Then they were jogging again.

"Oh my God," said Sarah.

"Holy shit!" exclaimed Michael.

"Michael!" said the First Lady. "Your language. You need to watch it."

"Jumping would be like a death sentence," said Michael.

"We are *so* not jumping," said Sarah.

"There is no way you can land and not break bones," Michael continued. "Lots of them."

"Yeah, assuming you somehow survived. If a train comes, we're doomed," said Sarah.

"There is another maintenance ladder for the tracks not that far away," said Mat. He pointed toward it as he jogged.

Everyone stopped to see how far away it was. Cass finally spotted it in the distance. "That's close? You call that close?"

"No, I didn't say 'close.' I said 'not that far.'"

Mat figured that since they were now motivated, he would pick up the pace. "C'mon, keep up with me." He increased his jogging to a slow run. He was still not going so fast that he thought they might slip, but they didn't want to be up here when a train came. And they all knew that a train would eventually come. He glanced behind him and saw everyone was keeping up.

Mat held the pace. No one was saying anything; all was silent as they ran down the top of the monorail track. Quiet moments passed by where the only sounds were those of leather dress shoes on the monorail track.

The silence was shattered when Cass yelled, "Behind us!"

CHAPTER 16

"A train!" exclaimed Cass.

On the other monorail track next to them was a train. It was almost upon them, heading in the same direction they were running. It whisked by with a quiet *whoosh*. It was four cars in length, including the engine. They felt the breeze as it passed them.

The people in the train didn't even seem to notice them; most just sat there in their own worlds, though Mat saw a couple of people suddenly point at them with their mouths open as they passed by. And then the train was gone.

The train told Mat something he didn't know. There were two monorail tracks on each side of the city, next to the two city walls, for a total of four monorail train tracks. The tracks made a giant circle running along the circumference of the city. On each side of the city was a track that went clockwise and another that went counterclockwise. The train that just passed them was going in the same direction as they were, which meant the train that ran on their track would be coming toward them, head-on.

At least they could see the train coming. It wouldn't suddenly appear from behind them as they ran. *That is good to know,* thought Mat.

Everyone jogged steadily.

The train, somehow, seemed to have relaxed everyone, but it also gave them new energy. It scared them at first, then as it passed by, it made them laugh.

"We are over halfway there," announced Mat loudly.

"Great," said the president. "Keep running, everyone. Michael and Sarah, you doing OK?"

"Yes, Dad," said Sarah.

"I'm OK," said Michael.

"How about you, Sam? Are you doing all right?"

The First Lady answered, "I'm doing fine."

"Cass?"

"I'm fine, Mr. President."

From time to time, both Mat and Cass glanced behind them to monitor the progress the terrorists were making. They were closing the gap, but slowly. Fortunately, they'd had a good head start. Mat led them as fast as he felt he could, sticking to a slow running pace. Even without the terrorists chasing them from behind, he was worried about someone slipping and falling.

The president was a jogger, the First Lady a cyclist. He wasn't too concerned about them; they were in good shape and used to the physical exertion. He wasn't worried about Cass either. He knew that as a Secret Service agent in the presidential detail, she was required to be in shape. She had to keep up with the president when he jogged every day. The kids, that's who he was worried about. He just didn't know what condition they were in. His fear was that they would get tired and make a misstep—and a misstep up here meant death. So far, they seemed to be holding up well.

"How close are we now?" asked the First Lady.

Mat took a guess. "About three-fourths, I'd say."

"Yay," said the First Lady in her happy voice, and Mat knew this voice wasn't meant for him. "I think we got this one, Michael and Sarah!"

Both Michael and Sarah answered their mom with a "Yay!"

"The family that runs on the monorail together . . . stays on the monorail together. Or something," said the president.

"What?" said Sarah. "Dad, that is so . . . stupid." She laughed.

"Well, I'm not staying on the monorail," laughed Michael. "But you can, Dad, if you want."

"Look!" screamed Sarah, pointing into the distance.

Mat had already seen it. Breaking into the field of vision from the curvature of the tube was a monorail train headed toward them. There could be no doubt: this train was on their track.

They all thought the same thing. Terrorists coming at them from behind, the train coming at them from in front. If one didn't kill them, the other would. How could they survive? What chance did they have?

CHAPTER 17

Amy Henderson, NSA, ran down the corridors located deep below the White House. These were the corridors of countless movies, assumed to exist by everyone. These were the hallways of legend and lore.

Amy arrived at the entrance to the PEOC. The room went by many names. It was called the Vault, the Tank, the War Room, and for those in the know, the President's Emergency Operations Center or PEOC for short (pronounced *pea-ock*). It was manned twenty-four seven by specially chosen personnel from all branches of the military services.

Amy picked up the phone at the entrance and spoke to the duty officer sealed inside and requested to be let in. He immediately obliged. They had been expecting her—no, waiting anxiously for her. Amy stepped back as the large, heavy steel door opened outward toward her. She slipped inside, and the door was closed and then sealed behind her.

Amy surveyed the operations center. This was where the

staff worked every day. Inside this twenty-by-thirty-foot room were phones located along the walls in small communication stations. An array of monitors lined the walls, streaming information from any and all available sources, including television and the many internet broadcasting services available worldwide.

Around the room was a series of communication posts, each standing about three feet high, and on each post was an AI comm cylinder four inches high and two inches in diameter. These cylinders allowed PEOC personnel to talk to a wide array of agencies and advisors from across the world. The AI systems could provide any data requested. Each comm was linked to a specific default monitor behind them on the wall and could display the data in multiple formats. To access the AI, an officer talked to the comm as if it were a person, and it responded through its built-in speakers. It could patch you through to another person or answer any question.

Off to one side of the operations center was an executive, or presidential, briefing room. This presidential briefing room had a designated entrance specifically for the president and his staff. In the middle of the room was a large mahogany conference table with enough padded wooden chairs arranged around it to accommodate twenty people. In the middle of one side was where the president sat. On the wall behind the president's chair was the presidential seal, displayed for everyone to see; along the wall were more chairs where additional advisors to the president could sit close to him.

The walls were painted a neutral cream, the carpet was a

deep dark blue, and the floorboards and the inset ceiling were trimmed in rich dark wood. Overall, the room was functional with a hint of class. State-of-the-art communications technology was hidden inside those walls. More monitors were located on and around the conference table, and in the center of the table sat a single AI comm cylinder three inches high and two inches in diameter.

This lone cylinder was the communications hub for the room. Speakers and microphones were located around the room, and if one knew where to look—and looked diligently—it was possible to see them. This comm could display the data on individual laptops or on any of the built-in monitors. It could, if requested, take an image from one laptop and echo it to any of the monitors or to any other PC in the room. The presidential conference room was where the action took place, where historic decisions were reached in times of national crisis.

The screens around the room were filled with images of the assault on the speaker's platform. Each network displayed the same images over and over again. Amy Henderson spotted who she was looking for and walked briskly over to Scott Chao, the secretary of defense. "What can you tell me?" she asked him.

"Not much, actually," answered the secretary of defense as Stevenson came over and joined them.

"What can you tell us? Has anyone been able to get in touch with the president yet?" asked Amy.

"No," said Stevenson, the director of the CIA.

"The president's detail?"

"No."

"Anyone? The mayor? The Secret Service? Any authority from Liberty? Anyone?"

"No," said the secretary of defense.

Stevenson added, "All we have is what we know from the news outlets, and they are still broadcasting."

Amy saw a person manning one of the comm stations turn toward her group. She walked over to her. "What have you got?"

Major Sally Cox said, "I have the Situation Room on the comm. They have an analysis update."

The Situation Room is designed to be an information hub for the president and his senior staff. It was created after the Bay of Pigs disaster. President Kennedy ordered the creation of the Situation Room so that future presidents would have accurate and reliable information to make critical judgments on. This is the place where intelligence information is organized and synthesized.

Amy spoke to the nearest comm stationed on a post next to the major.

"Situation Room, this is Amy Henderson, NSA." Amy cleared her throat. She didn't want to ask this question, but she needed to hear the answer. "What do you have?"

"The president was assaulted while making his speech at Liberty. We believe, based on seat assignments and the images of carnage, that the Speaker of the House is dead. The Senate majority leader and minority leader are dead. The mayor is dead. Virtually anyone and everyone on the platform has been killed. The entire White House staff that was traveling with the president, we believe, are dead. We received phone video from a witness that shows a small group fleeing the podium into a nearby wooded area. In this group, we have identified the president and the First Family with a ninety-one-percent probability.

"Two Secret Service agents have also been identified: Laura Cass and Bill Dougan. Both Cass and Dougan were at the podium at the time of the assault, so that fits. One person fleeing with them has still not been identified. We just don't have very good images of him. The data we have comes from a person who took a video with their phone and transmitted it to a friend in Kansas before the communications between Liberty and Earth were taken down.

"It is our belief that at this moment the president and his family are alive, along with two Secret Service agents. We believe they are fleeing or hiding. If they were dead or captured, it's likely that the terrorists would have made an announcement."

"Anything else?" asked Amy.

"No."

"Thanks." The comm line dropped. "Hi, I'm Amy Henderson," she said, turning and extending her hand to the major.

"Hi, I'm Major Sally Cox from airlift operations. I came here from the Eisenhower Executive Building. I thought you might need some help with air transport operations."

"Thank you, Major," said Amy.

Amy turned to the secretary of defense. "Scott, we have to assume that this is a decapitation event. Where are the vice president and the secretary of state?"

"The vice president is in Australia headed to the airport

to fly back to Washington. The secretary of state is in Japan."

"Major Cox, bring them both home now. I want fighter escorts assigned to both of them. Make sure that the security details with them have been notified of the potential threat."

"I'll notify the Pentagon ASAP."

Amy said to the comm cylinder, "Ms. Vice President, you there?"

"I'm here, Amy," said Sandy Ross.

"I understand that you are headed back to Washington."

"Correct. I'm here in Australia, five minutes away from the airport. I should be back to Washington in seven hours. What's the latest?"

"We believe that this could be a decapitation event. You will be flying home with fighter escort. The secretary of state has also been ordered home and will also receive fighter escort."

"What is the latest intel?"

"We believe that the president and First Family are still alive and at large."

"Thank God," said the vice president. She continued, "Amy, I want you to bring back all cabinet officers. I want them ready for a briefing when I arrive."

"Yes, ma'am," said Amy. "Ms. Vice President, there is one more issue for you to consider."

"What is it, Amy? Let's hear it."

"I recommend that we go to DEFCON 3, Ms. Vice President," said Amy.

"I concur, Ms. Vice President. We should go to DEFCON 3 and be ready to go to DEFCON 2," said Scott Chao, the secretary of defense.

Silence. "Do it. Keep me posted on any additional information."

"Yes, ma'am," said Amy.

The comm dropped.

Scott Chao notified the Pentagon. The orders for DEFCON 3 went out, with a standby order for DEFCON 2.

"All right, Major Cox, bring all cabinet officers home."

"Yes, ma'am."

Amy placed her hand on the back of Major Cox's chair. "Did you know that the last time we went to DEFCON 3 was during the attacks on 9/11? We went to DEFCON 3 worldwide."

"What about the Cuban Missile Crisis? What happened then?" asked Major Cox.

"We went to DEFCON 2 during the Cuban Missile Crisis, but that was just for North America. It wasn't worldwide," answered Amy.

DEFCON, short for Defense Condition, ranges from one to five. It represents a state of military readiness: the lower the number, the greater the threat. DEFCON 1 is feared. No president has ever given the order to go to DEFCON 1. It means an attack is imminent. It could mean nuclear war.

Amy watched the monitor showing a replay of the hit on the president. In the back of her mind was the Twenty-Fifth Amendment of the Constitution of the United States, which deals with succession to the presidency.

Amy moved away from the monitor and stared at the comm cylinder for a moment. Then another moment. She shifted her weight from foot to foot. Her silence began to draw the attention of the others as everyone in the room saw that she was uncomfortable. Her body language, the subtle tics of her face, the way she leaned, adjusted her weight. Everyone near her looked, compelled to stop and watch. What was she up to?

Amy rallied her thoughts. She had a duty, and she leaned forward toward the comm. "Get me the assistant attorney general in the Office of Legal Counsel."

There were a few moments of silence, then a voice came over the comm: "This is Andrew Peters of the Office of Legal Counsel. How can I assist you, Advisor Henderson?"

"I want you to prepare for us the needed information and documentation for the temporary transfer of executive power to the vice president under the Twenty-Fifth Amendment."

"Temporary transfer of power?"

"Yes. Report to the Situation Room. Be prepared to move us forward on that point. ASAP."

"You got it."

"Do I need to inform you that time is of the essence?"

"No, ma'am. I will be at the Situation Room as soon as I am prepared."

"Thank you." Amy dropped the comm. The Twenty-Fifth Amendment allowed for the temporary transfer of power to the vice president in the case that the president was incapacitated. When the president was able to execute the duties of his or her office, he or she would be returned to power. Amy knew the concept, but she had no idea how it actually worked. That's why they had lawyers—and in

Washington, there were lots of them. Everywhere.

Her mind drifted back to her daughter, Faith. Faith had the flu. She felt ashamed to be thinking about her daughter at a time like this, when so many people had died. People she knew, people who were her friends. That wasn't always easily said when you worked in the White House. People often pretended to be your friend; she had made real ones. And now some of them were dead.

She watched a screen image of the assault and slaughter on the stage. The corner of her mouth hinted at a quiver, and her eyes held back a river. *Oh my God. If Faith hadn't gotten the flu, I would've been there in Liberty with the president. That would've been me. I would be dead. Faith would have no mommy.*

CHAPTER 18

They ran at full speed for the ladder, but it was still at least a minute away—the train was getting closer with every step.

"Hurry," said the president. His voice was solid, sounding confident but urgent.

They were running now, at a full sprint down the track. Mat prayed that no one would slip, especially not one of the kids. A part of him said that he should be more concerned about the president, but he wasn't. There was no room for error. No margin for a stumble. A twisted ankle meant a twisted fall to death.

Mat ran hard, his arms pumping at his sides, and he realized for the first time how tired and out of breath he was. But he ran. *At least Megan is safe.*

Not a word was spoken. The train was closing in on them fast.

The First Lady tried not to think about it, but it was hard. Hard not to think about her children getting splattered on the windshield of an oncoming train. Hard not to think about herself and her husband.

The president was grateful that his family was in front of

him. They had a better chance of getting to the ladder before the train got there.

Then Michael stumbled. The First Lady watched as her son lost his footing and hit the track, sprawling out completely. He bounced and slid on the path. Somehow she grabbed his shirt and pulled him toward her as she dropped to her knees, one hand with a fistful of shirt, the other on the side of the track to help maintain her balance. She drew him close to her with a powerful pull, and he came to a stop in his mother's arms. She helped him to his feet.

The president ran up to his wife and helped her up. "Go!" he said to them both. "Run!"

Mat was the first to arrive at the maintenance ladder. He ran one step past it, then he stopped and turned around. His back was to the train.

Sarah got to Mat first, and he reached out and Sarah grabbed his hand. "Go down," he said to her. He helped her keep her balance as she swung her feet around the side and onto the metal U-shaped ladder. She climbed down several steps and came to a halt.

Michael and the rest of them were farther behind than he'd realized. He was unaware that Michael had fallen. Now he guessed that something had happened. The train was getting closer; even though he wasn't facing it, he could see the train in Michael's eyes. "Run. Keep running. Faster! You'll make it," he yelled to Michael.

Michael's eyes darted up toward the oncoming train. He ran to Mat at full speed, almost knocking him right off the track. Mat grabbed Michael like a baseball catcher on his knees. Placing one hand on the track behind him for balance, Mat caught himself and Michael. "Good job! Now go down, quickly."

The pupils in Michael's eyes were the size of quarters. The corner of his lips quivered. Mat grabbed his hand as he had Sarah's. "Don't look at the train. Look at me," commanded Mat. "Go down."

Michael stared at Mat, then swung himself around and went down.

The First Lady was next, followed closely by the president. Cass was next in line. She began to say something, but Mat cut her off, barking, "Go!" In Cass's eyes, he saw raw terror.

He knew the train was on them. Mat dove down the ladder as if diving into a backyard swimming pool. Then his feet were knocked sideways by the train, and he felt himself tumbling. He reached out for a rung of the ladder, any rung. Miraculously his right hand felt steel, and he gripped it with all his might as his body tumbled past his hand.

Whoosh. The train blew by.

His body swung around and slammed into the concrete column. The air was driven out of his lungs from the force of the impact, but he held on. It took a moment for him to come to the knowledge that he was hanging by just one arm. He reached up with the other arm and grabbed the handrail with both hands. Cass and the president grabbed him and pulled him firmly against the column. Mat fumbled briefly but finally got a foot onto one of the ladder's rungs. He coughed until he regained his wind.

Sheriff Mathew McKenna smiled as he saw the rear of the train moving away.

We did it.

"Thanks," he said to Cass and the president.

"I can't believe we did it," said the president. He reached over and patted Agent Cass on the shoulder as he smiled at his family.

Suddenly, as if the thought had hit everyone all at once, they all clambered back up the ladder several rungs to get a better view. Crowded at the top of the ladder, they all watched the train as it moved away down the track. Everyone wanted to see the same thing. Everyone had the same questions.

What about the terrorists? The train was now headed right for them!

They all watched as the terrorists on the track pivoted around and began running back for the rooftop, but the rooftop was too far away. There was no way they could make it.

As they watched, one man slipped off the edge of the track. He screamed until he hit the pavement below. Then he was silent. The others were sprinting as hard as they could; one of the terrorists pushed a man out of his way because he wasn't running fast enough. He too tumbled awkwardly to his death.

Then the train was upon them, pushing them all right off the track.

"Genius!" said Michael.

Everyone sighed in relief. They all climbed down to the ground.

The president said to Mat, "Why do I think you knew that would happen?"

"I wouldn't know," said Mat. A knowing smile showed faintly on his face.

The First Lady crossed her arms. "OK, Sheriff, give it up. What did you know?"

He smiled. "I was here yesterday with my niece. We shopped in the Blair department store. I think we shopped all the stores, actually. I noticed the ladders placed periodically on the columns."

"So you knew there was a maintenance ladder on a monorail column behind Blair's?" said the First Lady.

"No. But I knew there was the one here that we climbed down. There's another one farther down the track. The ladders are located equidistant, so there should be one behind Blair's, based on distance. But no, I didn't actually know about it at the time. I just figured there should be one there."

"And the trains?" asked the First Lady.

"The trains cycle through about every twenty minutes. When we'd first reached Blair, I saw a train go by. That gave us about sixteen minutes to make the next ladder. I figured we could make it."

"You son of a bitch," said Cass. "You could have told us that."

"Yep, I could have," said Mat. "That leaves one observation."

"What's that?" said President Devane.

Cass and the First Lady looked at Mat.

"I'm a little surprised that the monorail trains are still running," said Mat.

"Good point," said Cass. "Why haven't they shut the trains down?"

"I think there are a couple of reasons why. They never planned for a terrorist strike. It never entered into their thoughts or planning at any level," said Mat.

"And what's the other reason?" said Cass.

"The mayor, the police chief, all the department heads and senior managers were all at the event. The leadership of the city is gone. No one knows who's in charge. At least not yet."

CHAPTER 19

The president said, "I would say let's go to Air Force One and get out of here." He placed his arms around his two kids and pulled them next to him. "But I have a bad feeling about this. They have an army. And clearly they've been planning this for a long time. They aren't going to just let us go to Air Force One and fly home."

"Agreed," said Cass.

"Where to then?" asked the First Lady.

All eyes stopped at Sheriff McKenna. "Well, I'm going to my niece's apartment. You're welcome to come. You should be as safe there as anywhere. At least for now."

"I like it," said Cass. "We have to go someplace. Then we can regroup and learn what's going on."

President Devane said, "Then it's settled. We'll go with you to your niece's place."

The First Lady agreed. "Lead the way, Sheriff McKenna."

* * *

Mat led them in a tubular direction, moving parallel with the ring. The same direction they were headed while on the monorail track. The monorail ran in a tubular path. After a couple of minutes, Mat came to a TOD Spot and stepped on the circular stone. He waited for a few seconds, and an empty car came around a turn in the road and stopped in front of Mat. They all climbed into the car.

Michael had to wait and climb in last. He was forced to sit in his mother's lap. Sighing, he pointed to a notice in the car that read *Limit 5*.

Mat leaned into the back seat to face Michael and teased him. "Maybe I should arrest you since you were the last one in, making six in this car."

Michael smiled back at him.

"Car, map," said Mat.

"My pleasure," said the car, and a map popped up on the dash in front of him. It showed where they were in relation to the roads in this region.

"Go here." He tapped an area in the far corner of the region on the opposite side of the tube.

"My pleasure," answered the car as it pulled away and headed down the small road. It turned toward the wall and went up a ramp to Tier Two, the transit tier. It then accelerated to standard speed and headed for its destination.

They had to exit this area. For now, it appeared that they had eluded the terrorists. Maybe. But who knows?

The car came to a place where Tier Two had a crossway path, a path that traveled side to side or wall to wall. The car turned onto that road, and they traveled across the tube to the other side, then turned ninety degrees and continued on a tubular path—parallel to the city ring—again.

"So, Sarah, what do you want to be when you grow up?"

"I want to be a neurosurgeon."

"A neurosurgeon? Really?"

"Yes. I'm hoping that I'll be accepted into Johns Hopkins University."

"You must be very smart then."

"Yep, I am. I'm a brainiac." She smiled at him with her arms crossed and her head tilted deliberately at a shallow angle. He didn't know her that well, but he knew that she was telling the truth and teasing him all at the same time. He smiled back.

"How about you, Michael? Do you know what you want to be?"

"Uh-huh. I want to be an astronaut. A starship captain exploring new worlds or maybe leading an effort to colonize a new planet in another solar system."

"You must be smart too. But we don't have starships. And we can't fly to other solar systems."

"Not today, but maybe in twenty years we will," he answered.

The TOD car pulled into a small plaza and stopped, and they all piled out in the reverse order that they had piled in. Hoofing it, Mat continued in the same tube direction. He soon found a set of stairs and traveled back down to ground level. He stayed close to the wall as they entered a new region of the city. After five minutes, they came to a small park. There he followed a jogger's path into the heart of the small, winding wooded trail.

Eventually the group came to a park bench, and Mat stopped and sat down. With everyone standing around him, Mat got up from the bench and motioned for someone else to sit down. Cass, the First Lady, and Sarah all grabbed seats on the bench. Michael sat down on the grass, and Mat decided to sit down next to him. The president seemed to like the idea, and he sat down next to Michael also. He patted Michael on his knee and winked at him. Michael smiled back at his dad.

Mat pulled his phone out from his pocket. Then he pressed a few buttons and held the phone up to his right ear.

"Megan?"

"Hi, Uncle Mat! When will you get here?"

"As soon as we can. It'll be at least an hour. But we're on our way."

"We? Wait—what?"

"I need you to do something."

"Sure, name it."

"Grocery store close to you?"

"Of course."

"Get some groceries: lunch meats, bread, fruit bars, fruit drinks."

"OK. But what's up? What's going on?" she asked.

Mat ignored her question. "Pizza place near you?"

"Yes."

"Good. Order three large pizzas and pick them up on your way back home from shopping." Mat glanced at the two kids. "Make one of the pizzas a cheese."

The First Lady smiled at him and gave him a thumbs-up sign.

"Sure. What's up? What's going on?"

"Megan, you still in your apartment?"

"Of course I am."

"Megan, you should be halfway to the grocery store by

now. Go. Don't waste time. Get it done as fast as you can and get back home. OK?"

"OK."

"Bye."

"Wait. Uncle Mat! Uncle—"

Mat killed the line. "All right. Before we go anywhere else: Mr. President, Michael, you need to lose your ties," said Mat.

The president removed his tie. "Done. I know where this is headed." He nodded to Michael. Michael removed his tie too.

"Next, lose the suit coats."

The president stood up and removed his suit coat. Michael gave him his coat, and the president walked over to a garbage can and shoved them in, along with the ties. When he was finished, he came back over to the group and sat back down next to Michael.

They emerged from the park with no jackets or ties. Mat found another TOD Spot, and they climbed in the car again.

"Where would you like to go?" asked the car.

"Just go, I'll direct."

"OK." The car took off down the path.

"Make this left," said Mat.

As the car zipped along the path, Mat spotted something. "Car, is there a stop here?"

"Yes, there's a plaza stop. Would you like me to stop?"

"Yes."

"My pleasure." The car traveled another twenty seconds, took an exit into a side road, and stopped at the shopping plaza. Everyone climbed out of the car.

"What's up?" asked the First Lady.

They all followed Mat to a bench under some trees. He retrieved his phone from his front pocket and put it in notebook mode. Quickly he compiled a list of their jeans, T-shirt, and shoe sizes on his phone.

"We need to get you some new clothes, and now is the best time. Agent Cass and I will go; no one knows us. You need to stay hidden."

"Good idea," said Cass.

After thirty minutes, Cass and Mat emerged from the plaza, each with several large bags. They all went to a bathroom where they washed themselves as best they could using paper towels. Quickly they slipped on their new sets of clothes. The clothes they'd been wearing were in terrible shape by now. For some of them, their clothes were just dirty; for others, they were covered in blood and filth.

Now cleaned up and dressed anonymously, they were on their way to Megan's. They hopped into another TOD car and exited on Tier Two at a monorail station, where they boarded a monorail train. Then they all sat down and finally relaxed.

Michael poked Sarah in the arm. "The monorail is more enjoyable when you're *in* the train."

Sarah leaned over to Michael. "And safer too."

The First Lady smiled at her husband, and the president reached over and took the First Lady's hand.

CHAPTER 20

M at knocked on the door twice. Before his fist could strike the door for the third knock, it suddenly opened.

"Uncle Mat!" Megan jumped into his embrace, and he carried her inside as they hugged. Everyone else followed him into Megan's apartment.

He set her down. "Megan, let me introduce you to President Devane." She shook his hand with her mouth open. "And this is the First Lady, Samantha Devane." Samantha shook Megan's hand. "And their two children, Sarah and Michael."

Sarah and Michael smiled and waved.

"And this is Secret Service Agent Cass."

"Hi," said Cass as they shook hands.

"Thank you for letting us come into your home," said President Devane. "It's very nice of you."

Megan stood staring at the First Family, stupefied, until Mat nudged her in the shoulder. She gathered herself quickly. "It's my honor," she said, her cheeks growing red. Megan looked a little overwhelmed. And why not? The First Family of the United States was in her apartment!

Mat said, "We have one shower, and we might not have much time. I have no idea what to expect. I don't know if you noticed this, but we need showers."

Everyone agreed he was right.

"Megan, if you don't mind, show the First Lady where the bathroom is."

"Sure," said Megan.

Soon everyone was gathered around the monitor in Megan's living room. The news was on.

The report began with a replay of a press conference with city officials stating that martial law had been declared and a state of emergency was in effect. Everyone was directed to stay inside their homes, and all businesses were ordered closed. Only grocery stores were allowed to be open. The TOD system would remain up, but the monorail system was down until further notice.

"They look pretty young," said Mat softly to himself as he looked at the city officials in the press conference.

"They do look young…," said Cass as she stood next to Mat. "…and green."

"Yep," said Mat.

"They kept the TOD system up," said Cass.

"They have to. Without it no one can go anywhere. There are no cars. People still have to eat. They still need to drink water. The toilets still have to flush. Some things have to remain up and running," said Mat.

The news report was showing the devastating attack at the park. They listed the people who they believed were killed: the Speaker of the House, the Senate majority leader, the minority leaders in the House and Senate, and scores of senators and congress people from both parties. The list included the mayor as well as the deputy mayor; the power structure of the city would never be the same. The list of believed fatalities also included the head of the city council, the police chief, and many local dignitaries and political power brokers.

The list was devastating. However, missing from the list was the president of the United States and his family. Where were they? No one knew.

The reporter said, "The spaceport has been taken by the terrorists. All flights to and from Liberty have been canceled." The news reporter continued, "They hit all three police precinct offices. Bombs. And they assaulted police headquarters. Everyone inside was killed. It was a slaughter."

The news report showed the police headquarters. It *had* been a slaughter. Bodies lay everywhere. The reporter noted, "Only the terrorists had lethal weapons. Police have suffered a massive loss of life." The images were clear: the building lay in ruins.

They learned that all telecommunications between Liberty and Earth were shut down. If you were on Liberty, forget calling Mom on Earth. But the local phone net on Liberty remained working. All local broadcasting within Liberty remained up. All the major global nets broadcast only what the terrorists permitted. Clearly the terrorists wanted their story told, and they intended to use the global news networks to their advantage. It was also clear that they had control of Liberty.

In closing, the reporter stated that the remaining police were regrouping at this very moment with city officials at the control center, in accordance with catastrophic event preplanning protocol. Of course, that was only a rumor, an unconfirmed report at the moment. However, it made sense.

Then the news cycle began all over again, repeating the same information. Different people and different faces, all saying the same things over and over and over.

Mat raised an eyebrow. He said nothing. Then he walked to a cabinet, grabbed a stack of plates, and set them next to the pizzas on the kitchen table. He motioned the two kids over to the table. Soon everyone was eating. Everyone was starving.

As they ate, Mat spied Agent Cass sitting alone in a corner of the kitchen. He slid an empty kitchen chair around toward her and pulled up next to her. He felt for her. The burden she was carrying was chiseled into her face. Her burden was unique. Historic. Protecting the First Family was her responsibility. It appeared now that she could very well be the last surviving Secret Service agent on this detail. That duty, all of it, now fell solely to her.

"So, what are you going to do?" asked Mat.

"I don't know." She sighed. Her face was hollow. She shook her head slowly. "I don't know."

Mat nodded.

She looked at him.

Silence.

"So, what are you going to do?" asked Cass.

"Well, I'm going to eat some pizza. Then take a shower. Then probably eat more pizza." He handed Cass a plate with a slice of pizza on it. "I recommend that you do the same."

Cass smiled. "And then what?"

"Then we do whatever we have to do," said Sheriff Mathew McKenna. He took a bite of pizza. He was starving, and the pizza was delicious.

CHAPTER 21

Sheriff McKenna walked out of the bathroom, drying his hair. He was the last one to shower.

The First Lady asked, "How was it?"

"Cold," he answered.

She laughed. "That's what I figured. That's what you get for insisting on being last."

Mat filled his cup with coffee and surveyed the cardboard pizza boxes. There was a third of the cheese pizza left. The pepperoni-sausage pizza was gone. A third of the supreme pizza remained. He grabbed a slice of the supreme. It was his favorite anyway. Cass, Sam, and President Devane had gathered around the kitchen table.

"We need to decide what we are going to do. What have you learned, Cass?" asked President Devane.

Mat listened, but he didn't join them at the kitchen table. He stood back from the group and leaned against the kitchen wall: close enough to listen, far enough to not be part of the president's group.

The First Lady noticed. "Sheriff McKenna, you're more than welcome to join us in this discussion. I'd like to hear your thoughts on the matter. Pull up a chair and join us."

He smiled at the First Lady. Megan was in the living room with the kids, watching a movie on the large monitor in her living room. He said to the First Lady, "Thank you, ma'am. I'm honored." He walked over and sat down on the last kitchen chair, pizza and all.

"Please, just call me Sam." She spotted Megan. "Megan, that goes for you too. Just call me Sam."

"OK, Sam," said Megan.

"Thanks for joining us," said President Devane. "And you can call me James. All my friends call me James."

"Nope. I appreciate that, Mr. President. But the people elected you the president of the United States. Out of no disrespect to you personally but out of respect for the office and the people of the republic, I'll call you Mr. President or President Devane. I might even be talked into President James. But I think that's as far as I can go, especially today, Mr. President. But thanks anyway," said Mat.

"As you wish, Mat. I'll do my best to live up to that honor."

"You already have, Mr. President. Just get your family home safe." Mat took a bite of pizza.

"Pizza?" asked Cass, shifting her eyes meaningfully between Mat and the president.

He nodded. "Yep." Mat knew that Cass didn't approve of him coming to the meeting while eating a pizza, but his inner voice told him to draw this line with Cass. It created space between him and Cass, and he wanted the space.

Cass showed him a frown.

The president addressed Cass. "Here's what I understand. I want you to correct me where I'm wrong."

"All right," said Cass.

"The Secret Service comm doesn't work."

"Right."

"About fifteen minutes ago, all phone systems within Liberty went down. People in Liberty cannot call each other anymore," said the president.

"Right."

"We cannot communicate with Washington or anyone on Earth, for that matter."

"Correct."

The president paused to take a bite of his pizza.

Cass said nothing.

"The local television networks are still up within Liberty, but all the nationals are down. The terrorists are feeding the national networks whatever they want, so the world only knows what they are being told by the terrorists."

"That's correct," said Cass.

"Every major police precinct was hit. Police headquarters was obliterated. You may be the last surviving Secret Service agent on this trip."

"Yes," she said. The quiver in her voice betrayed her pain.

"All the other dignitaries who were with us on the stage are dead."

She hesitated. "Probably. I'd say yes." She paused. "Someone might have survived, but I don't see how."

"That includes the entire White House contingent that made this trip."

"Yes."

"The terrorists hit the celebration at the park and then they took control of the spaceport."

"Correct, sir."

The president studied the First Lady. Then he took a long drink of soda. He rocked back and forth in the kitchen chair for a moment in thought.

Finally, the president said, "How did they miss us?" He cleared his throat. "I mean, my wife, the First Lady. Our children. Me, the president of the United States. How did they miss us?"

"I don't know, sir," said Cass. "I guess we were just lucky."

There was silence until Mat intervened. "They didn't miss you, Mr. President."

"What? I don't understand," said the president. "Could you explain that, if you don't mind?"

"They wanted everyone else dead. They wanted you and your family alive. That's what gave us an edge. That's why we were able to escape. It's also why Cass and I are still alive; they couldn't shoot us without risking killing you. Agent Dougan survived the assault originally because of his proximity to you; he was only killed when it was safe to kill him. He was killed when he was no longer close to any of you."

The president and First Lady nodded their heads as one. Cass's right eyebrow rose.

"I believe there was another factor as well. Frankly, they were overconfident. They thought they had it in the bag, and they got sloppy. You shouldn't be here. You and your family should be prisoners waiting for public torture. Agent Cass should be dead."

"And what about you, Sheriff McKenna?"

"Well, just call me Mat." He waved to everyone. "I'm just a small-town sheriff from Shady Oaks, Florida."

Sam smiled.

"Of course, there is one thing you should know about the hardworking folks of Shady Oaks, Florida."

"What's that?" asked the president.

"We don't care too much for perpetrators."

The First Lady said, "What are we going to do now? One option is to stay here."

"OK. What's another option?" said the president.

"Well, we could proceed to the control center. Link up with law enforcement," said Cass. "Before the comm went down, I heard fragments of conversations suggesting to me that they were thinking of moving operations to the control center. The entire police force at Liberty has not been eliminated, and it would be logical for the survivors to do that. But I have to admit that I don't actually know what they are going to do."

"What's the control center complex?" asked the president.

"It's where all major internal systems are controlled, like agriculture and transportation systems like TOD and the monorail. By protocol, the city is preplanned to operate emergency operations from the control center. Of course, they were thinking of defending against asteroids or some catastrophic structural failure, not a terrorist attack. It's only an educated guess, but I think operations are moving to the control center."

"And you think that's where the city's emergency operations will be? You think that is where the police will be operating from?"

"Yes, sir. That's my opinion."

"Hmm. OK." The president leaned back in his chair. "Any other options?"

There was silence.

"Mat?" asked the president.

"I think that pretty much sums it up. You have two basic choices. The first is to stay in hiding, here with Megan or wherever. You hide, and you hope that there is an intervention of some kind to rescue you and the city. The second option is more active: you attempt to reorganize with city officials and coordinate a response to counter the terrorists."

Everyone nodded. "Agreed. Those are the only two options we have," said Cass.

"The problem with option one, hiding, is that I don't think an intervention has much chance of success. They control the city. They have all the time in the world," said Mat.

Cass spoke up. "And the problem with option two is that, I assume, it means going to the control center. We don't actually know for certain that they are even regrouping at the control center complex. That's an unconfirmed report. I believe it to be true, but I don't know that."

The president added, "And the part about coordinating a response. Like what, exactly? They have the weapons. The police have nonlethal force, and not much in that regard. I'm not sure what kind of a response there could be."

"Of course, we could leave the kids here with Megan, and we could go to the control center," said the First Lady. "That's kind of a combination of both options. I think that's about it. Those are the only choices we have."

"Yes," said Cass. "I think that's it."

"Thank you, everyone," said President Devane. He pushed his chair back, stood, and walked over behind his wife's chair. "Give us a few minutes to think about this."

* * *

"All right everyone. This is what I've decided," said President Devane. "We are going to go to the control center. If we have to, we can always go back into hiding. We need to make a genuine effort to do what we can to assist those responsible for the safety of the citizens of Liberty. Maybe they will have some emergency means of communicating with Washington."

"Does that include Michael and Sarah?" asked Cass.

The First Lady nodded to her husband, and the president answered, "Yes."

"Sheriff McKenna, I sure would like to have you join us, though I understand if you prefer to stay here with your niece," said President Devane. His voice became grainy and cracked as he continued, "You saved my family today." His eyes were red. "I will never be able to repay you for what you did today. Thank you."

"You're welcome, Mr. President. Just doing my job."

Sam's eyebrows punctuated the question: *Are you coming?*

McKenna spoke. "Neither one of us knows what's safe and what isn't. My gut says not to leave Megan, and I've learned to trust my gut, so I won't leave her. It also says you're going to need me. So I'm coming. Megan and I will both be coming." He had already discussed this with Megan, who'd agreed. She wasn't going to let Uncle Mat leave without her.

"That's all right with me. I understand exactly; the terrorists control the city. That's why we won't separate from Sarah and Michael," said President Devane.

"We have some more things to do before we leave," said Mat.

"Like what?" asked Sam.

"What do you have in mind?" said Cass.

"Well, we have to change the way some of you look. I'm sure you've seen this in the movies many times," said Mat. He took another bite of his pizza.

"What are you saying?" asked the First Lady. "We are still waiting to hear what you want."

He swallowed. "I can't make your hair grow, but we can cut it shorter. It's about the only thing we can do to give you all a different look."

Her hands went to her hips, and her head fell slightly. "I knew you were going to say that."

"Anything else?" asked Cass.

Mat said, "The First Lady, the president, Agent Cass, and Michael and Sarah. All of you need haircuts."

"No, I'm not getting a haircut," said President Devane. "It's the Second Article of the Constitution of the United States. Presidents don't have to get haircuts if they don't want to. I'm a lawyer, but you can check it yourself."

"Yes you are," said Mat.

"Excuse me, I said no. I don't want one. Besides, it feels like surrender."

"Everyone knows what you all look like. Especially you,

Mr. President. You and I both took oaths of office. Right now that oath requires you to get a haircut to make it difficult for the terrorists to identify you. I can't even imagine how bad it would be for the country if you were taken captive. You're also a husband and father. Do I need to spell out in detail what the terrorists are likely to do to your children—and what they would likely do to your wife—if they are captured?"

"Good point."

"I would think, Mr. President, that you would want to do everything in your power to protect your family and your country. A haircut is a simple thing. Think about it."

Everyone was quiet. The president and First Lady gave each other knowing looks. The president said to McKenna, "I'm first. I've been wondering what I would look like in a butch."

"And I'm next!" said the First Lady.

Michael and Sarah clung to each other. Their mouths were open.

The First Lady patted her husband on the shoulder. "You're the first president in history to get a haircut in the line of duty."

"I'm not getting a haircut," said Agent Cass.

"You're getting a haircut," answered Sheriff McKenna.

"I'm not a member of the First Family. Why would I need a haircut? And who are you to tell me what to do? No offense, really, but small-town sheriffs don't tell Secret Service agents what to do, OK? Do we understand each other? I don't tell you what to do."

"You think this assault is well organized? Do you think it

was well planned? Do you think they got over fifty terrorists with semiautomatic weapons into Liberty on a whim?"

Cass was silent. She stared at Mat.

"How long have you been assigned to the presidential detail?"

"Two years."

"I bet they have pictures of every agent that might be with the president. I bet they have yours. Do you want to take a risk that they ID the First Family because someone recognizes you? Do you want to take that risk? Is it your risk, or theirs?"

"Point taken. I will get a haircut," said Cass.

CHAPTER 22

The group exited the monorail and quickly found a TOD Spot, flagged a car, and hopped inside.

"The control center complex," said Mat.

"My pleasure," said the car. And they were on their way.

Megan was watching the news on her phone. "Quiet, everyone."

They all stopped talking.

"What's up?" asked Sarah.

"They just announced on the news that an emergency procedure to close the regions of the city is underway right now. The monorail will no longer be running." Megan paused. "We might have been the last people to ride on the monorail."

"What?" asked Mat.

"The city's sectors are being closed. Partitioned off as part of some kind of emergency protocol."

"Can I see that?" asked Cass.

Megan handed Cass her phone, and Cass watched the broadcast for a few minutes. She said to the president and First Lady, "This could be excellent news. Megan got it right: Liberty is sealing the city's sectors."

The president and First Lady exchanged glances at each other. The president's brow was scrunched up like he was curious and irritated at the same time. He said to Cass, "What's happening?"

"The city's sectors are being closed."

"Just what in the hell does that even mean? Can you enlighten us, please?" His voice was sharp, but not like a knife, like a piece of broken glass. Jagged and angry. Dangerous. And tired, very tired.

"Mr. President, the city is designed so that it can be sealed off into three separate, independent sectors. A structural failure in one sector wouldn't endanger the integrity of the other two. Each sector even has its own water and air."

"Understood."

"The city can be divided into three subcities so a catastrophic failure is hopefully isolated to just one sector. It's like the city becomes three cities. When the event has been resolved, the sectors can be unsealed and the city returned to normal. This was designed with the idea of an object striking the city and penetrating the infrastructure. It's a little bit like a submarine sealing off compartments to keep water from rushing into the entire sub and dooming it, only this is done to keep the air inside from leaving and dooming the city."

"So why is this such wonderful news?" said Sam. "Explain to me why the authorities are doing this."

Cass explained, "I believe that they are doing this to trap the terrorists inside the sectors that they are in. They actually accomplish two things at once with this one move: they limit the mobility of the terrorists, trapping them inside the sectors, and they protect the citizens in the other sectors that don't have terrorists."

"So we isolate the problem and deal with it piece by piece, sector by sector."

"Exactly. Break a big problem down to smaller ones, and solve the smaller problems one by one. Classic problem solving," said Cass.

"And exactly where would they do this from?"

"This can only be done at the control center complex, Mr. President."

President Devane continued, the edge in his voice gone, "It all fits. The rumor has, in fact, now been confirmed. The authorities have regrouped at the control center complex. And they have started taking countermeasures to deal with the terrorist threat."

"Yes, I agree with that assessment completely," said Cass.

"The police and the authorities are now taking steps to reestablish control and are starting to implement countermeasures."

Cass nodded, "Yes, Mr. President. I think that's safe to say."

"Cass, are we in the sector that has the control center?"

"Yes, sir."

"Great! It's about time. Finally some good news. Maybe, just maybe, there is a light at the end of this tunnel."

"Yes, sir. I'll feel a lot better once we get to the control center."

"Me too," said the president.

The president said to McKenna, "You sure are quiet,

Sheriff McKenna. Is there anything you would like to add or say?"

"Nope."

"Where did you learn about this protocol, Agent Cass?" asked Michael.

"Studying the city and aspects of its operations potentially relating to the security of the First Family was required for all agents assigned on this trip. No one expected that the emergency sealing of the sectors would happen— but this is why we study."

CHAPTER 23

The elevator came to a stop at the fourth floor, and the doors opened. The environmental control center filled the entire fifth floor of the building. Agent Cass stepped out of the elevator into the hallway, followed by President Devane, then the First Lady. Sarah and Michael stayed close to their mom, and Megan and Mat exited the elevator together last.

The elevator was set into a wide hallway about twelve feet in width. The floor was covered with a dark, rich blue carpet except for the area directly in front of the elevator, which was made up of large stone tiles. The elevator was located in the center of the wall. Mat could hear voices coming from the hallway to his right, though no one was visible. He listened hard, but he couldn't make out any of the words. Mat scanned the hallway. In the far right corner was a red exit sign. Stairs.

It was pretty much like any office building he had ever been in. He was glad he didn't work in one. The group, led by Cass and the president, moved toward the right. Megan waited for her uncle, and together they followed behind Sam as the group walked down the hallway. On the wall adjacent to the elevators were the restrooms. As they walked down the hallway, the voices became louder. They passed a small pantry to the right. The pantry contained a sink, and next to the sink was a coffee and hot water station.

President Devane and Agent Cass quickly headed for the conference rooms where the voices were coming from. Trailing behind them were the First Lady, Michael, and Sarah. Mat and Megan were in the rear. Megan tugged on his arm and smiled at Mat, and he smiled back. Or he tried to anyway. He wondered if his niece could sense his discomfort.

President Devane walked up to the open door of one of the middle conference rooms. A large wooden table ran down the middle of the room. Three large paintings hung side by side on the far wall. The individual paintings, when viewed together, formed a larger picture.

At the head of the table was a man wearing a grayish-blue pinstripe suit. Seated at the table with him were six other people, three to his left and three to his right. They were dressed casually in blue jeans and khakis. There were two women in the room, also in jeans. It was obvious to Mat that they had interrupted a conversation this man was having with the people around him. In front of him on the desk was an open laptop and, next to the laptop, a communications device.

The man at the head of the table stopped talking and lifted his head toward the intruders. "May I help you?" he asked the president. His eyes became bright, and he raised his eyebrows. He picked up his comm from the table. He raised a finger in the air and said to the president, "Excuse me. I'm sorry, this will only take a moment." He then pressed a button on his comm and spoke into it quietly.

Finally he lowered the comm and pushed away from the heavy conference table. The others sitting around the table all rose. They seemed less friendly now.

The man walked up to President Devane and extended a hand. "Hi."

The president took his hand and they shook.

"How may I help you?" he asked the president.

The suit hung from his body expertly, clearly showing the quality of the tailoring. The material was finely detailed. Mat figured he could replace his entire wardrobe with the cost of that one suit.

"May I speak to the person in charge here?" asked the president.

The man studied the entire entourage. His eyes paused a split second on the two kids, and he lingered on Mat for a moment. He then glanced around at the people in the room with him. Some of them flashed smiles back at him.

"Yes, you may. In fact, you are. I'm in charge."

"Great."

"And who might you be?"

"I'm President Devane." He motioned to his wife. "This is my wife, the First Lady of the United States, Samantha Devane."

"How very nice to meet you," the man said, extending his hand to the First Lady. His pupils went wide for a second, and color flushed through his face. "I'm stunned."

"And these are our two children, Michael and Sarah."

"I can't believe this. Hi, Michael. Hi, Sarah."

Michael and Sarah nodded dutifully.

"This is our friend Cass." The president placed a hand on Cass's shoulder. "And out there in the hallway behind us are Sheriff Mathew McKenna and his niece Megan."

The man studied them closely. After a moment, he said to the president, "I'm so embarrassed. I didn't recognize you at first." He leaned to one side to see past the president and motioned to a man in the cubicles, who nodded back. He motioned again, and the man bowed his head once. He was wearing a black T-shirt with a skull and crossbones on the front. The man in the skull-and-bones T-shirt waved to several other men sitting around him, motioning them to come over to him. Mat watched as they bent down and disappeared behind the cubicle walls. Soon everyone in the cubicles was watching the strangers standing at the entrance of the conference room. In several of the cubicle areas, entire groups stood up to watch them.

The man in the fine suit then focused his attention back on the president. "This is truly a pleasant surprise. I am so embarrassed," he said.

Three people emerged from the next conference room down: a woman who appeared to be of mixed Asian and Caucasian descent and two men, one at each side. The men were dressed casually in khakis and T-shirts. Mat was instantly drawn to the woman. His inner voice was unsettled.

The three stood just outside the doorway of the conference room, looking at them. The woman was five nine, maybe five ten. Shoulder-length, shiny, silky, coal-black hair parted down the middle. Well proportioned.

Athletic build with round hips. She wore a flower-print blouse with bright colors and blue jeans. She had a thin, black, leather tablet case that she wore like a purse, and he noticed that she wore athletic sneakers.

She had fine feminine features. Even though her eyes were red and puffy, Mat could see that they were a deep, rich brown. They were soft and alert, intelligent. The woman was beautiful. But clearly something was wrong.

Tear tracks were running down her cheeks. The two men stood stiffly at her side, one of them holding her by the upper arm. The one on the left gave Mat a smile. A small, smug thing it was. The three of them made an awkward group. She didn't belong here, and they didn't belong with her. The other man with her noticed Mat's attention and smiled at him. The woman didn't.

President Devane's face was flush with warmth and openness. "Nothing to be embarrassed about. Actually, it was nice not to be recognized for a change."

The man laughed. "I mean, in blue jeans and a T-shirt. And your hair. You got a butch." He examined the president closely. "Now I can tell it's you, now that I'm looking at you." He laughed again. "You are indeed the president of the United States. I recognize the family now." He took a deep breath, then said, "I just can't believe this."

Then he turned and said to the First Lady, "You look charming in short hair."

"Thank you," she said.

While everyone was watching the president and First Lady, Mat was watching the man in the cubicle who had bowed his head earlier.

"And who might you be?" asked the president.

"I'm Yassin, the president of the Muslim World State. You just saved us a lot of trouble having to find you." He laughed. It was a joyous laugh, full and filled with mirth. Everyone in the conference room laughed out loud with him. One of the men in the conference room clapped his hands together in pleasure.

The color rushed from the president's face. His face was bleached white.

From the conference room behind Mat emerged three men with semiautomatic weapons. One man came up to grab Megan by the arm. Another walked up to Mat and pointed a gun at his head.

The third terrorist went toward the president. Yassin smiled at him as he casually walked up to them. "Karl," said Yassin, "let me introduce you to the president of the United States."

Karl raised his weapon at him and laughed.

Yassin spoke to everyone around him. "See, I told you we would find the First Family."

The three men stood in the cubicles with semiautomatics in their hands. Now McKenna knew what they had grabbed. The man who had motioned to the two other men, Skull and Bones, walked up to the First Lady. He raised his weapon and pointed it at her as he approached.

Megan gasped in surprise when a terrorist walked up behind her and forcibly grabbed her upper right arm. Another terrorist approached her on the other side, smiling broadly as he eyed Megan top to bottom. Clearly they liked the view; Megan was an attractive woman. The two terrorists nodded to each other approvingly.

Mat saw Megan's muscles tighten, the humiliation in her face. Then Megan slapped the closest terrorist across the face. Her hand left a print on the left side of his face. The man clenched his fist and moved to strike back.

CHAPTER 24

Everyone froze at the sound of the slap, and Mat knew it was time. With his left hand, he grabbed the barrel of the gun pointed at his head. At the same time, with his right hand, he grabbed the handgun holstered under his left arm and shot the man behind Megan in the head. In a continuous motion, he shot the man whose rifle he was holding. The bullet struck the terrorist in the chest. Both terrorists collapsed where they stood. In under one second, two shots had been fired and two terrorists were dead. Megan fell to the ground, covering herself with her arms as best she could.

The First Lady did not hesitate. She reacted the moment she saw Mat move, as she'd been trained to do many, many years before. She grabbed the gun she had holstered and, with both hands holding the weapon, fired. The bullet struck the man at her husband's side.

Mat pivoted around 180 degrees and fired two shots past the First Lady, toward one of the men holding the woman with the bright floral shirt. The bullet impacted the man where his neck and body met. He dropped his weapon and reached for his neck as he collapsed. Mat fired again, striking the other man in the right shoulder. He winced in pain and dove for the cover of the cubicles.

The woman's eyes lit up. She glanced at the dead man lying at her feet. Then she gasped, suddenly realizing she was free, and ran toward Mat. She tripped over something on the ground, stumbled, and fell, but she regained herself quickly and crawled the rest of the way until she reached Megan and Cass.

Skull and Bones quickly covered the two steps between him and the First Lady. As Sam pivoted, Skull and Bones struck her in the jaw. She fell in a slow spin to the ground, where she sprawled out on the floor at Skull and Bones's feet.

Cass grabbed the president, who was now free, by the right shoulder and drove him powerfully toward Megan, then past Megan, stopping in the corner of the room in front of the stairs.

Skull and Bones knelt down to his feet and grabbed a groggy First Lady and forced her up. He pulled a handgun from his waist and pointed it at her.

Mat dove to where the president had been before Cass had taken him to safety, tackling Yassin as he was attempting to flee into one of the conference rooms. Mat quickly lifted the man to his feet. He held him by the neck and pointed his gun at his head.

The chaos in the room suddenly and unexpectedly stopped. Everyone was breathing heavily, evaluating the new circumstances. Three terrorists lay dead on the floor, and one more was seriously wounded.

Two important facts were clear to everyone in the room. The first was that Skull and Bones held the First Lady at gunpoint in front of him. A small red trickle of blood was forming at the left corner of her mouth. His left arm was around her neck. His right held a handgun pointed at her head.

The second fact was that McKenna had Yassin in front of him. His back was toward Megan and the stairs, and he faced the terrorists in the room. Mat held Yassin around the throat with his left arm and pointed his weapon at Yassin's head with his right hand. Mat and Yassin were the mirror image of Skull and Bones and the First Lady. Both pairs faced each other, not saying anything.

"Aaziz," said Yassin.

Skull and Bones—Aaziz—smiled back.

Yassin, his leader, understood that smile. While he obeyed Yassin's orders faithfully, Aaziz didn't like Yassin very much. Everyone knew that Aaziz had doubts about Yassin. Yassin was too soft. Aaziz felt that he should be in charge, and this appeared to be his moment. Maybe he could capture the First Family *and* have Yassin killed in the process.

"Aaziz, don't kill the First Lady unless you have to," ordered Yassin.

Aaziz showed indifference at first, then bowed his head slightly to acknowledge the directive. The other terrorists in the room, hiding behind the desks, seemed to notice his reluctant agreement.

Next to Sam was her son Michael, and next to Michael was Sarah. Each was held by a terrorist, their arms behind their backs. The woman wearing the flower print was behind Mat and sitting crouched low next to Megan. Cass was protecting the president, who was between Megan and the door to the stairwell.

I hope no one comes up the stairs, thought Mat. If anyone came up the stairs, it was over.

Mat had their leader, and they had the First Lady of the United States. It was the classic standoff, only it wasn't. Then Mat heard something behind him, and his worst nightmare came true. If things hadn't been bad enough, they had just gotten worse.

A single terrorist armed with a semiautomatic was opening the stairway door behind Cass and the president. As he stepped into the room and swung the door slowly open, his weapon deliberately moved toward the president. In seconds, the door would be open all the way and the terrorist would have Cass and the president dead to rights.

The First Lady watched the men who held Michael and Sarah. She knew that all of them, herself included, were as good as dead. She would have preferred to die fighting. She knew that fighting, whatever the odds, gave them their only chance at living. She had let her children down. Her eyes met her son's. If only they could have a chance to fight.

Police officers and Secret Service agents underwent extensive scenario training—what to do if this or that happened—which included hostage training. However, from time to time, events unfolded in ways that have never been practiced. Life sometimes found a way to defy anticipation. This was one of those times. Something happened that no one had ever thought of. Everyone's attention was on the single terrorist walking into the room from the stairway.

Michael, standing next to his mom with both hands twisted painfully behind his back, leaned his head over to the side and bit into the flesh of Skull and Bones's biceps. It was the arm that held the gun pointed at his mom's head. Aaziz screamed from intense pain and surprise.

Everyone was in shock, looking at Michael and taking in the turn of events. Yassin seized the moment and jumped backward into Mat, and both of them tumbled to the ground. Cass then reacted efficiently, pushing the president sideways away from the gun swinging toward him. She had a split second to shoot before the terrorist would have his gun pointed at her. She fired one shot, striking him easily in the chest. He fell facedown into the room, dead; behind the terrorist, the door was stained with crimson mist. The door to the stairs slowly closed automatically behind him.

Mat rolled up to a knee and fired a shot at the man behind Sarah as the man behind Michael dove into the cubicles for cover. In the confusion, Mat lost sight of Yassin. Two seconds later, he spotted him running past the elevator for the offices on the other side of the floor.

Sam spun around and drove her fist into the lower gut of Aaziz. He doubled over in pain. She then grabbed his hand, twisted it, and pitched him into the cubicles. Aaziz crashed onto a desk, and everything on it, including a computer monitor, went flying into the middle of the room. When he hit the floor, he rolled under the closest desk for cover.

Cass stood and fired shots into the cubicles at anyone with a gun. The cubicles were a target-rich environment.

The First Lady grabbed Sarah, Mat ran forward into the room and took hold of Michael by the arm, and the four of them ran to join everyone gathered at the stairway door. They ran low so that they were hard targets for the terrorists and so that Cass wouldn't accidentally shoot them as she fired rounds over their heads and into the cubicles.

When Mat, Sam, and the two kids arrived, terrorists were emerging from the other side of the building past the elevators. Yassin had gathered the forces at that side of the room. Yassin was about to come at them from the other side of the elevator. Cass knew she had to keep the elevator hallway clear, so she changed her strategy. She stood up in the corner and began firing shots past the elevator to keep the Yassin and the soldiers pinned down.

Mat stood up and fired a volley into the room while backing up to Cass. "Cass, get 'em outta here."

"Roger." She grabbed the president and went out the exit into the stairwell, and everyone followed.

CHAPTER 25

The woman saw Cass take off, and she stood up and faced the cubicles and shouted as loudly as she could into the second floor, "Run for your lives! Now! This is your chance! Everybody run! *Run!*"

The fourth floor suddenly came alive as people who were being held prisoner by the terrorists began to run toward the elevators and the stairs. It was almost as if a bomb had gone off, and the people were the pieces of shrapnel flying around. Mass confusion was everywhere.

The president leaned forward toward Michael and Sarah. "Stay close to me. No matter what. OK?"

"OK, Dad," they said.

With her weapon in front of her, Cass charged down the stairs. Michael and Sarah followed right behind Cass; the president was behind them. Megan and the woman followed next. The First Lady and Mat remained at the exit for just a second, firing down the hallway, trying to keep their pursuers at bay, until Mat heard the elevator ding. He paused and glanced down the hallway the short distance to the elevator.

Mat asked the woman, "What's your name?"

"I'm Mary Lu Hayashi," she said.

Her eyes were even more beautiful up close, even though they were bathed in fear.

"I'm Mat. Stay with us, Mary Lu Hayashi, and we'll get you out of here," he said.

"Everyone just calls me Mary Lu."

"OK, Mary Lu." Mat gently moved Mary Lu toward Megan and Sam.

"Mat! C'mon," said Sam, standing inside the stairway door.

Six soldiers burst out of the elevator. One of them spotted him and pointed his gun directly at him, and Mat fired two shots and dove for the stairs with Sam. Bullets ripped into the side of the wall where he had been standing.

They reached the third floor, and the stairs came to a stop, forming a small square platform. Past the third-floor exit door, the stairs continued down after turning 180 degrees. Megan and the woman were waiting for them at the third-floor square platform. Together they continued running down the stairs, trying to catch up to Cass and the others.

Sam said between breaths, "We have one thing going for us."

"You mean that the terrorists are idiots."

"Yes. They almost had us again," said Sam.

"How could they leave the stairway open?" asked Mat.

* * *

Aaziz was beside himself. He picked himself up and walked over to Yassin. "How could you let them escape again?

That's twice now that we had the First Family and they have gotten away."

"They haven't gotten away yet. Our men are in pursuit; we may have them yet. If not today, tomorrow. If not tomorrow, the day after. They are trapped inside Liberty. In that sense, we have them already," said Yassin.

Aaziz was not convinced. He repeated, "They have escaped from our grasp twice now."

"Aaziz, I have work to do, if you don't mind," said Yassin. He walked back to the middle conference room.

Aaziz stood and watched for a moment, his arm still bleeding. Then he slammed his left fist on a desktop and walked away to get his right arm stitched and bandaged where he had been bitten.

Yassin couldn't believe it. Aaziz had the First Lady in his grip and he'd let her get away! Not only that, he had let her strike him and throw him onto a desk. Now he had men chasing them. At least now they knew where the president and his family were, and with any luck they would capture them soon and be on schedule again.

Yassin walked into the conference room, where Shakira was waiting.

"Yassin, be careful with Aaziz. He has ambition larger than the universe and an ego that's even bigger," said Shakira.

"I know. As long as he and his troops obey orders. Now is not the time to struggle against each other," said Yassin.

"He blames you for letting the president escape from the park. Just be on your guard around him, my love."

He placed his arms around her. "Thanks for your concern. Let me assure you that I will deal with him."

* * *

When Cass reached the second-floor platform, Michael, Sarah, and the president were right behind her. Cass stopped for a second, looking up the stairwell for the others.

"Keep going," said the president. "We can't let them trap us on the stairs."

Cass could hear them coming down the stairs. *He's right.*

She began to run downward with President Devane, Michael, and Sarah right on her heels.

Bam! echoed in the stairwell. Cass knew what it was: the second-floor doorway had just slammed against the wall when it was thrown violently open. She reached the 180-degree turn of the stairway.

"Keep going," she said to the president and the kids as they ran past her.

She knelt behind the stairway handrails and fired just one shot as the first soldier broke into view. He took a strike in his upper thigh and fell down several stairs before coming to an agonizing stop.

But Cass did not wait to see the result of her shot. She was already running. The soldiers dropped to kneeling positions, expecting more shots, but there were none from downstairs.

* * *

Sam, Mat, Megan, and the woman had just turned a corner in the stairs and were halfway between the second and third level when *Bam!* echoed from the second floor up to them.

Sam and Megan abruptly stopped. Mat and the woman took another step, then they stopped as well. They all knew what the noise was. They had heard a gunshot from below. Just one shot, but Sam and Mat recognized the sound; it had been a Secret Service weapon.

Cass.

Then they heard the sound of shouts, orders from the soldiers, then dozens of footsteps heading up toward them.

"Go up," said Mat.

Mary Lu shot a glance up and down the stairs. She grabbed Mat by the arm. "I work here. Follow me." She sprinted back up the stairs, taking two steps at a time, Mat, Megan, and Sam chasing after her. When they approached the third-floor landing, Mary Lu stopped. Three soldiers were coming into view from above.

They had soldiers coming at them from above and below. Mat had only two choices with no time to think about it: either charge up or charge down. Since he was four steps away from the third-floor landing, he charged up. Mat fired two quick shots at the soldiers coming into view from above.

On the third shot, his gun clicked—he was out of ammo. One bullet had struck a soldier in his side. He stumbled and fell, grabbing at his wound. Sam rushed by Mat, firing her gun upward. He dropped the magazine, reached into his pocket, and slapped another in place. The other soldiers stopped and fell into defensive positions with their weapons raised. Mary Lu and Megan passed Mat and went into the third floor of the building, and Sam and Mat followed.

The third floor was empty. Mat sprinted after Sam, who

was sprinting after Megan, who was chasing after Mary Lu.
Mary Lu ran down a short hallway, then she suddenly made
a right turn. The hallway went several more feet and came
to an end at a wide spacious area with couches, tables, and
chairs. There was a huge photograph of the Amazon River
filled with rich, deep shades of green covering most of the
wall. Several five-foot-high statues of archaeological looking
artifacts were scattered around the large open space.

Mary Lu stopped in front of another hallway leading out of
this open area, where Megan, Sam, and Mat caught up to her.

"Why is this floor empty? What's on this floor?" asked
Megan.

"Agriculture, Parks, and Recreation," said Mary Lu.

Megan guessed, "The terrorists have no use for the
people who work here, so the employees here were able to
get away."

Mary Lu nodded. "Exactly." She pointed down the
hallway. "This way!"

Suddenly Megan, Mat, and Sam understood. It came to
them all at the same time—this was an external hallway
crossing from one building to another.

Connecting two buildings together.

Mat nodded. "OK. This way," he repeated. "Lead the way."

Mary Lu ran down the external crossing with Megan,
Mat, and Sam at her side. They could hear the troops behind
them as they fanned out onto the floor, searching for them.
They were no longer there. They must be in another
building. How long before the soldiers realized where they'd
gone? Mary Lu led them to another stairwell. As they
approached the stairs to go down, they heard loud shouts

behind them in the building next door.

The soldiers had figured it out. But by now they had gained a lot of ground.

Mary Lu opened the stairwell door for them, and they headed downward.

"Stop!" she said.

Mat, Megan, and Sam froze, not knowing why she'd barked that command. They faced her with question-mark expressions.

"Not that way. Up," she said.

"What?" asked Sam.

"Go up!" said Mary Lu again.

There comes a moment, Mat reflected, when you act on faith, on instinct, on gut, on anything you wish to call it. You just do it. This was one of those times.

What the heck.

Mat and the others ran up the stairs. When they came to the top, the fourth floor, Mary Lu stopped. They could all hear soldiers opening the stairway door one floor down. Standing in the stairwell, Mary Lu quietly opened the metal door to exit onto the fourth floor. When they were all on the fourth floor, she slowly closed the large metal door behind them as softly as she could.

She led them across the building. On the other side of the floor was a small stairway leading down. This was not an emergency stairway; this was a nice, carpeted stairway. They traveled down to the third floor, then exited a main door and found themselves on Tier Two.

* * *

Cass ran down the stairs as fast as she could; she could feel her blood pumping through her veins. She came to ground level, exited the stairs, and found herself outside on the street. President Devane, Michael, and Sarah were there waiting for her. Other than the four of them, the ground level was empty.

"Follow me," said Cass, and she took off across the street to the next building. She realized that she needed to change her thinking. She needed to think like a local.

OK, she thought. *Go crosswise and get to one of the city's walls, then go along the circumference of the city toward an adjacent region. Maybe we can find a shopping complex away from the control center.*

They reached the building, and suddenly Cass pivoted ninety degrees and headed crosswise. They broke into a full sprint. Get away from the control center; that was priority one, two, and three.

After running for a few minutes and passing through several buildings, Cass stopped and leaned against a wall. President Devane, Michael, and Sarah caught up to her and stopped as well.

"Dad! What about Mom?" asked Sarah between deep breaths.

President Devane lifted his eyes to Agent Cass. His hands were on his knees as he tried to catch his breath. He had the same question. He waited to hear the answer.

Cass said, "I heard them go back up. I think they exited on the third floor. I heard them fire weapons, and I heard troops chasing them out of the stairs. As far as I know, they're alive."

"Dad, we have to go back for Mom," said Michael. Sarah's eyes pleaded.

President Devane was firm, short. "No." This was his all-business, I-want-no-garbage-from-you tone. His kids understood that tone well.

"But Dad," said Michael.

The president gave Michael and Sarah the look.

Michael and Sarah began to cry. They turned their eyes away from their dad.

He grabbed both of them and shook them gently. "Look at me," he said, and they reluctantly raised their eyes to him. "Your mom is a trained Navy SEAL, and she has Sheriff McKenna with her. If we go searching for her now, we will endanger her life. Do you want to lead the terrorists straight to your mom?"

"No," they said.

"I need you to believe in your mom. We will find her when the time is right. When it is safe. OK?"

"OK."

"Now we have to go." He hugged both of them. "She'll be fine."

"OK, Dad."

President Devane wasn't sure if they believed him or not or if he believed it himself. But they had to move. Now. "Cass, let's go."

"Yes, sir." They headed off again in a sprint.

CHAPTER 26

Mary Lu led them out on Tier Two for two blocks, then they took the stairs to ground level. When they arrived, Mary Lu ran to an office park. The soldiers were still chasing them.

Mat, Sam, Megan, and Mary Lu ran up to the double-wide glass door of the business. Whoever they were and whatever they did, they must have been good at it, because their building had two floors. Mary Lu opened one of the large doors, and the four of them went inside. They stood on a large tiled area ending at a front desk and a hallway that went to the right and to the left.

The tile was partially covered with a throw rug. Mat knew little about throw rugs, but he bet this one was expensive. In the open space in front of the reception desk were two trees in two-foot-high round planters. Two plush chairs were placed next to each tree. In the center of the throw rug was a couch. A glass coffee table stood between the couch and the reception desk, magazines scattered across the top.

They all stopped and stared at one another. They all had the same question. Go right or left? Sam led them to the right. Down the wide hallway they went. Soldiers were heard entering the building farther down from where they were running. Two soldiers had followed them into the building and were heading toward them.

The soldiers and Mat spotted each other at the same moment. Mat fired a shot at one of them, but both soldiers dove behind one of the large tree planters.

"We can't go back," said Mat. He fired again. His bullet struck the tree square in the trunk.

Toward the far end of the hallway, the sounds of troops were getting louder.

One of the terrorists rose up from the pot to shoot at them and Mat fired back. The bullet struck the tree in the base where the trunk and soil met. The trunk fractured, and dirt and wood splinters flew into the face of one of the terrorists.

It was not a good tree day. Mat saw him cover the eye that was closest to the tree. He cried out in pain.

"Sam?" asked Mat.

Sam pointed to an intersecting hallway going deeper into the building. "This way."

The four of them ran down the hallway into the back of the building. They spotted a carpeted stairway and began to charge up it in leaps and bounds onto the second floor.

The floor was like two different areas. To the left was a hallway leading to a bunch of offices. The right side was composed mostly of cubicles. Against the far right wall was another single row of offices.

OK, forget the cubicles.

They ran to the left as quietly as they could. When the

hallway came to an *L* shape, they followed it all the way down to the last office on the outer wall. They could hear the terrorists shouting directions, coming up the stairs. Sam, Mat, Megan, and Mary Lu entered the office, and Mat closed the door. The office was large and spacious.

The desk had a modern design, large and white. A cabinet sat against one wall with an array of personal pictures. Against another wall was a chestnut-colored built-in bookcase with just about everything one could imagine sitting on a shelf except books. In a corner was a small table on wheels that had been converted into a coffee center.

"We're trapped," said Sam.

"Like hell," said Mat. Above the desk was a window. Mat examined the window. There was no latch or anything; the window was designed to never be opened.

Mat grabbed a statue off the desk and handed it to Megan. "Use this to break the window."

Mat reached down and grabbed the desk. Sam saw what he was going to do, and together the two of them shoved the desk halfway toward the door.

Megan smashed the statue against the window and shattered the glass. She used the statue to clear the entire windowpane of shards as best she could. Mary Lu grabbed a towel from the back of the desk chair and threw it over the bottom of the frame.

"Don't wait for us," said Mat.

Again Sam and Mat shoved the desk toward the door. This time they made it all the way and pressed it tightly against the door. The door opened into the office, so the desk would slow them down. Mary Lu was first. She climbed out and hung from the window, then dropped. Megan went next. Mat shoved the chair against the desk and then the coffee center. He heard the terrorists running down the hallway toward them.

He glanced up to the window just as the First Lady climbed out and dropped to the ground. The terrorists were opening each office door as they came down the hallway. Their office was the last one.

Mat reached the window. *Bam!* The door opened an inch and slammed into the desk. There was a lot of loud shouting behind the door. *Bam!* The sound reverberated inside the office. Then came the sliding sound of wood on carpet.

Mat climbed out the window and hung from the windowpane with both hands, swaying gently to and fro. He let go and dropped to the ground. Above him, a terrorist leaned out the window with a gun in his hand. His head burst open in a cloud of red, white, and gray. Then the man fell forward and slumped against the windowpane, dead, his chest half in and half out the window. His right arm dangled down from the window, his left arm lying underneath his body.

Mat fell against the wall. In the yard, crouching with her knees bent, positioned next to a tree, the First Lady was holding her weapon out in front of her with both hands.

"Let's go!" said Sam to Mat.

He needed no convincing, and he ran to the tree and joined the First Lady, Megan, and Mary Lu. Then they were off running.

"Hold up," said Mat after they had run two buildings down. Everyone stopped. "We need to find a place to hide."

"But where?" asked Sam.

"Follow me," said Mary Lu. Her voice was soft but firm. Confident. She darted away.

Mat, Megan, and Sam looked at each other. No one said a word. They chased after Mary Lu. They entered a building and emerged out the other side. They traveled across the pedestrian way and through several more buildings. She led them into a building on one side and exited the other side. She was leading them toward the far corner of the sector but in a zigzag pattern.

They entered a large five-story building, an office complex with many tenants for many different companies and organizations. The building was empty, just like all the buildings they had run through.

Mary Lu traveled up one floor to the second floor, slowing to a walk as she headed down the corridor. She stopped in front of a double-wide glass door and waited until they were all there.

Barnes and Associates said the black lettering on the door. Behind the lettering was a logo of modern abstract design, containing an image of a large tree with a strong trunk and a large green canopy. A jagged grass line ran underneath the lettering to the tree.

"Nice logo," said Megan.

Mary Lu pushed against the glass door and it didn't budge. She pulled off a chain necklace and inserted a small ID wafer into a slot in the door. She pushed against the door again, and this time it opened. She removed her ID passkey from the door and put it back around her neck. They all walked inside the office, where they were greeted by an empty reception desk large enough for two or three people to work at. Behind the desk were three empty chairs. Two monitors rested on the desktop. Otherwise, the desk was clean and empty. On the corner walls behind them were six plush chairs, three per wall, with a large wall lamp in the corner between them. No tables. On one wall was a picture of a falcon in flight. It appeared that the falcon was about to grab his prey, but no prey was shown in the picture. The artist left that to the imagination of the viewer.

Mary Lu walked slowly past the reception desk and down a plush hallway to the interior of the office.

"Have you been here before?" asked Mat.

"No."

She opened a couple of doors as she went, pausing to peek inside. The hallway made a ninety-degree turn and continued on.

"If you have never been here before, how did you have a key to get inside?" asked Mat.

"I have a universal key," she answered.

Shortly, the hallway opened up into a large area divided into cubicles. She walked past those and opened another office door and peeked inside. This time she walked in. They followed her into the office, and she closed the door.

"Is this it?" asked Sam.

"Yes, this is it."

Mat glanced around the office. It looked good to him. "We'll be right back," said Mat. He tapped on Megan's shoulder. "Come with me."

They left the office. Soon they returned, pushing two large chairs into the office.

"I wondered what you were up to," said Sam.

Everyone claimed a chair and sat down.

"Why did you pick this place?" Mat asked Mary Lu.

"Location. There is no safe place here in this sector, but this location is near the sector wall and farther away from the control centers and spaceport. Not far from here are the stairs leading down to the agricultural belt. This place should be safer than most."

The room became quiet, everyone lost in their thoughts. Mary Lu sat alone and quietly began to cry. Not a bawling or uncontrolled sound, but a sad, mournful one. The tears traveled smoothly down her face.

Mat pulled up next to her. "Hi, we haven't been introduced. I'm Sheriff Mathew McKenna from Shady Oaks, Florida. Just call me Mat." He extended his hand and she took it.

"I'm Mary Lu, chief engineer of Liberty. I'm in charge of engineering maintenance here at Liberty."

"This is my niece, Megan."

Megan shook Mary Lu's hand. "Hi."

"Hi, Megan." Her voice was soft as a whisper.

"And this is the First Lady of the United States, Samantha Devane," said Mat.

Sam came over from where she was sitting. "Hi, Mary Lu. Just call me Sam."

"OK, Sam."

The room grew quiet again as everyone went back to their chairs. Mary Lu closed her eyes, and the tears quietly flowed down her cheeks.

"Is there anything we can do for you?" asked Megan.

"No. But thank you," said Mary Lu.

Silence.

Mary Lu finally spoke again. "They killed everyone who wasn't deemed essential. They had them form a line. They were on their knees with their hands tied behind their backs and tied to their ankles. Then they shot them. Slowly. One at a time. Execution style. They made us all watch. I knew them all; at least half of them worked for me."

"I'm so sorry," said Sam.

The First Lady waited a moment. Then she said, "We have to go back and look for my family."

"No," answered Mat. His answer was immediate. "If we search for them, we could lead the terrorists right to them. Looking for them will put them and us in more danger."

"We have to go back to them."

"Not this moment, we don't." Mat was firm, no hint of wavering. It was out of the question.

"But my kids—"

"Will be safer if we escape. The terrorists now have a much more complicated task: they're searching for two groups now, not just one. Our presence will require that they split their effort by half."

"But—"

"You might save your kids by *not* looking for them. Understand? We will look for them later."

"How?"

"I don't know. But we will. When the moment is right, I will help you get them. I promise."

* * *

It was after midnight now. Everyone was tired, but no one was sleeping. Mat left the office, their home base, and walked down the hallway. Megan followed him, as did Mary Lu and Sam.

Mat said, with a hint of a smile at the corners of his lips, "I can't believe all of you followed me out here."

"We wanted to see what you were up to," said Sam. "We figured you were probably up to no good."

Mat walked up to the coffee counter. "Well, I'm glad you all joined me, actually."

"Why's that?" asked Mary Lu.

He picked up a box of vanilla coffee creamer and handed it to her. "Because there is more here than I can carry."

He grabbed a box of artificial sweetener and handed it to Megan. Then he unplugged the hot water thermos and handed it to Sam. Finally he unplugged the drip coffee maker and picked it up, and they all followed him back to their base. He set his coffee maker on the shelf he had cleared. Megan handed him the thermos, and he set that next to the coffee maker. Soon the new coffee and tea center was done. He found a pitcher and filled it up with water, then grabbed a stack of napkins and brought those into their room as well.

"So what happened?" asked Mat.

Mary Lu asked, "What do you mean?"

"About Liberty having the sectors closed."

"The terrorists did that."

"The terrorists sectioned the city? Why? Why would they do that? How could that possibly help them?" asked Mat.

"I don't know." Mary Lu paused, thinking. "I have no

idea. But I do know that they ordered it done. I was there," said Mary Lu.

"I have a bad feeling about this," said Sam.

"No kidding. One thing's for sure: they didn't do it for a good reason," said Mat.

No one replied; everyone looked exhausted.

"It's getting late," said Mat. "Is there anything else we need to do before we try to get some sleep?"

They shrugged at each other.

"No, I don't think so," said Sam.

Mat rose and walked to the door. "I'm going to take one last look around."

"Good idea," said Sam.

"I just want a better feel for where we are and to make sure we don't have any unwanted neighbors," said Mat.

Everyone got up and left the room. They cruised around the floor, locking the exterior doors to the office complex with Mary Lu's security pass and unlocking all the office doors in case they needed to use one. After a few minutes, they came back to the room. They slid a desk in front of the door and made sure they were ready to break the office window to flee if necessary. Then they all picked a spot and lay down to get some sleep.

CHAPTER 27

A gent Cass ran down the walkway with President
Devane and the kids following. They darted right and
went down a narrow path between the two buildings.
Distance. They needed distance. Because the sectors were
sealed, they were trapped in this sector. They needed a place
to hide. They came to a small shopping plaza located among
some apartment complexes. The advantage the designers of
Liberty had was that without cars, there were no parking
lots. There were walkways—lots of walkways—and small
areas with trees and park benches.

Cass surveyed the shops. The soldiers were nowhere in
sight, at least not yet. But they would be soon. *Does it matter?
Just pick one. Pick a store, any store.* She moved behind a
grouping of trees and led them to a small gift shop. She
opened the door, and they all entered together.

An elderly woman was at the counter. She had shoulder-
length gray hair. Her blouse buttoned down the front with
a floral pattern with a white backdrop.

Agent Cass scanned around. No one was in the store.
Thank God.

"Hi! I was just about to close," the woman behind the

counter said to them.

"Can we stay awhile?" asked Cass. She heard the desperation in her voice. It surprised her. She believed herself to always be in control. It was something she took pride in.

"Martial law has just been declared. Only the grocery stores are allowed to remain open. Everyone has been directed to close down," she said.

"When did that happen?" asked Cass.

"Maybe an hour or so ago. I already sent all my employees home."

The woman studied them closely for a moment. "I suppose you can come in. I'm Angie. Welcome to my store, Angie's Gift Shop."

The president saw the look in Angie's eyes and knew that she knew who he was. President Devane extended his right hand to Angie. "Hi, Angie, I'm President Devane. This is my son Michael and my daughter Sarah." He motioned to Cass. "And this is our friend Cass."

Cass shook the woman's hand. "Angie, we really do appreciate what you are doing for us and for the country." Cass had wondered if he was going to introduce her as a friend or as a Secret Service agent or at all. In presidential functions and gatherings, agents didn't exist. They were just present, like air.

"Hi. I thought that was you," said Angie. "Of course you can stay as long as you like." She went to the front door and locked it, then flipped a cardboard sign around so that it said *Closed*.

Agent Cass walked to the storefront and carefully peeked out the front window. She was there for several minutes, watching and observing as three terrorists ran into the plaza. They stopped and wandered around in circles for a moment, and Cass pulled back away from the window as far as she could and still see. The terrorists took off running farther down the path until they were out of sight.

The terrorists had no idea where President Devane had gone.

Cass nodded to the president. "We're all right."

"Angie, could you do us a favor?" said President Devane.

"Sure, what can I do for you?"

"Please don't tell anyone we're here. You never saw us. OK?"

"OK," she said. "I'll do whatever I can."

"Is there someplace we can hide?" asked Agent Cass.

"You mean, like, in here?" she asked.

"Yes."

"Of course there is. Follow me." She walked to the back of the shop. She stopped and waved an arm. "Will this do? You can hide in here for now. I also have a small break room you could use."

"Thank you," said the president.

Cass stepped up to Angie. "Angie, mind if I ask you a few questions?"

"No, go ahead."

"How many employees do you have?"

"Well, there's me and Cheryl. We both work here full time, and we have four part-timers. I try to keep two in the shop most of the time."

"Thank you. Sorry to be so nosy."

"Mr. President, your family can stay with me until this

blows over, or whatever. Stay as long as you like. It would be my honor," said Angie. "You can stay here at my gift shop or, if you would prefer, at my home. I have an apartment not very far from here. About ten minutes by TOD."

President Devane placed his hand on Angie's shoulder. "Thank you, Angie. There is a good chance that we just might take you up on that. But we haven't had a chance to do much thinking lately. Give us a few minutes to think about our options."

Angie leaned a little closer to the president. In a soft, grandmotherly voice, she said, "I like the haircut." She smiled.

He nodded his thanks.

* * *

"What are you thinking, Cass?"

Cass glanced over at the two kids.

"They're old enough to handle the truth. No secrets. I won't lie to my family. Talk freely. What do you think? Should we stay here? Or go to Angie's home or something entirely different?"

"There is no sure bet."

"Understood."

"I think Angie's home is our best bet, at least for now. The problem is getting there. I think we should do it tonight or first thing in the morning. If there is traffic, then we can take a TOD car. Otherwise, we hoof it. We cannot stand out. We can't be the only ones riding a TOD car."

"What is it?" he said, noticing her discomfort.

"Well, there is another option that you should consider."

"Go on?"

"You could ask Angie to take the two kids with her, and we could meet them there."

"So Angie could take Michael and Sarah to her home, and we would join them at her home but get there separately."

"Right," said Cass. "You should consider it."

"All right, I'll think about it." President Devane paced around the storage room. Everyone watched him. Even Michael and Sarah knew better than to bother him when he was like this.

He came to a stop and lifted his head to Cass. "No. Michael and Sarah will stay with us. If they go with Angie, they will place her in danger. It might be safer for the kids, but who knows? But we do know that it would definitely be more dangerous for Angie. We can't do that. We can't place her in more danger than absolutely necessary."

Cass nodded.

"We will get up early tomorrow, see what TOD traffic is like, and come to a decision on how to leave for Angie's."

President Devane raised his arm in front of him. "Watch, wake me up at six tomorrow morning. Do it gently."

"Done. Soft alarm set at six," said his watch.

"Angie, we have decided to take you up on your generous offer. But we will spend tonight here and leave for your place first thing tomorrow morning."

"Wonderful," she said, excited. "Let me show you where it is."

"Angie, you can't let anyone know. You can't tell anyone that we were here. If you do, you will be in grave danger. Do you understand?"

"Yes, I won't tell anyone."

"If the terrorists find out, they will probably kill you. Understand?"

Angie gulped. "Yes."

CHAPTER 28

Washington, DC
White House
The President's Emergency Operations Center (PEOC)

Vice President Ross arrived at the White House and went directly to the PEOC. Accompanying her were the vice president's chief of staff, the assistant to the vice president, and a military aid to the vice president.

Ross leaned forward in her chair and said to the national security advisor, "Amy, proceed with a quick summary of what is known."

Amy nodded. "Yes, ma'am. Since the initial assault, the terrorists have seized control of all communications from Liberty to Earth. All our information and analysis is based on the news feeds coming from Liberty, which the terrorists control. We only know what they want us to know. Everyone should keep that in mind.

"Here's what we have. The president and First Family survived the initial assault in the park and escaped. That is based on the phone video we intercepted. We believe that they are still at large. That's based on the fact that the terrorists have not announced their capture or deaths. We also know the terrorists have taken control of Liberty. They control the spaceport. All transportation to and from Liberty has been shut down. No one comes or goes. We estimate that the terrorists number roughly one hundred. This is just an estimate based on the early video evidence and the knowledge that a separate force took control of the spaceport.

"So we know that there were actually two initial assaults: one against the president and the other against the spaceport. We estimate that the assault on the spaceport occurred within a few minutes of the assault at the park. Given the distances, they had to be separate forces."

"Is anyone claiming responsibility for this terrorist attack?" asked Vice President Ross.

"Yes, ma'am. The Muslim World State has taken responsibility. They demand the usual. The removal of the United States from the region of the Middle East. They demand that we sever all ties to our allies in the area," said Stevenson, the director of the CIA.

"The Muslim World State takes claim. Is it credible?" asked Ross.

"Yes it is." A picture popped up on the screens. "This was taken from the news videos of the assault. We have confirmed that this is Yassin Bakur. He's the president of the Muslim World State, he created them. We had no idea that they had this kind of backing, that they were capable of pulling something like this off. As far as we knew, they were a relatively small organization."

"Tell me about this Yassin," said Ross.

"We don't know much. He graduated from Harvard. He

was a B student. After graduating, he spent some time in China. Several years ago he created the Muslim World State. They've done a couple of suicide missions in Israel. Nothing major."

"Harvard?" said Ross.

"Yes, ma'am. He comes from a wealthy family."

"Great."

"Yassin has a reputation for being smart, calm, cool, and radical. He likes women. It's our understanding that he's a real lady's man."

"Anything else on him?" said Ross.

"It's not likely this is a suicide mission for him," said Stevenson. "But one can never know."

Another image popped up on the screen.

"This is Aaziz Hammoudi. He's the opposite of Yassin. He has a reputation for being a hothead. He's dangerous as hell. His own people are afraid of him. His older brother, who practically raised him, was killed in a terrorist operation in Iraq. The Navy SEALs killed his brother. He's capable of anything."

"Thank you," said Ross. "I appreciate all of you coming to this meeting. I requested immediate options from Scott Chao, the secretary of defense, upon my arrival. Secretary Chao, please proceed. What can we do?"

Secretary Chao said, "Our options are thin. Practically nonexistent. Everyone wants to know—can't we just send in the Marines?"

Everyone in the room waited for the answer.

"No, actually, we can't." Secretary Chao took a drink from his coffee mug. "We have no vehicles to launch an assault in a space environment. Even if we fly up two hundred combat Marines and dock them at Liberty, there would still be no way to get them inside the city."

He pressed a button on his laptop, and an image of Liberty popped up on the monitors around the room. He pressed another button, and the monitor showed a close-up image of a spaceliner going through a docking procedure.

"The docking bays have independent docking doors that are under the control of the terrorists. We would need somebody on the inside to open the door, somebody with proper security clearance. I personally don't believe that a spaceliner would be permitted to get close to Liberty. That's just my opinion. The reason I believe that is simple: the terrorists have been planning this for many, many years. They are probably prepared for us to try some form of forced boarding."

"So there's nothing we can do?" said Sandy Ross. "Is that what you are telling us?"

"No, I didn't say that." He shook his head. "The docking bay doors are designed for exit and entry from spacecraft only. Liberty has an array of docking hatches located around the city."

He pressed another button on his laptop, and a line of little red dots appeared around the city. "These red dots are exit hatches. They can be opened externally. They require a security pass, which we have obtained."

Vice President Ross studied the picture of Liberty for a moment, then shifted her focus toward Secretary Chao. "So we need to get an assault team to one of those hatches," she said.

"Yes. That's doable, I think, but complicated. First, there was an assault at Advanced Technologies Design, the manufacturer of the space suits. ATD's manufacturing facility was sabotaged, and the equipment damaged. The FBI is currently reviewing the security cameras to see when it happened. It looks like an inside job. I'll leave all of that to them to explain later. Anyway, the equipment has been damaged, and no new suits can be manufactured for at least thirty days. ATD said that the suits are modular in design, so they are currently attempting to piece together two or three suits for us from the damaged ones."

Amy held up three fingers and mouthed, *Three?*

"Yes, three suits, maybe. If we are lucky. We have also acquired four additional suits that were on display at museums across the country. They should be arriving at Cape Canaveral within the hour."

You have to be kidding, thought Amy. *Six, maybe seven suits? The maximum number of soldiers that we could have fighting the terrorist army would be seven. Seven against a hundred?*

"What about NASA? Surely NASA must have some," asked Amy.

"They do—and all of them are on Liberty. Keep in mind that NASA uses Liberty as its focal point for space-based operations. The astronauts take a spaceliner to the city like everyone else.

"There are other problems. We can't use spaceliners; they are slow and easy to detect. They're not designed to be opened in the vacuum of space. In fact, they are designed *not* to be opened in space. Opening a spaceliner in space would be risky. It has never been done. It's never even been attempted.

"So what does all this add up to? Here is what I propose. We have talked to Boeing, and they are making emergency modifications to the X303 Advanced Global Strike Fighter prototype. We only have one; the second prototype won't be ready for another six months.

"The X303 was designed as an air supremacy global strike fighter capable of flying a wide variety of missions. It actually flies into space, just above the atmosphere, where it can then move anywhere above Earth and drop back down into the atmosphere and strike. It has a standard crew of two: a pilot and a weapons officer."

"Am I wrong, or can it only fly into very low orbit? It can't reach the orbit of Liberty, right?" asked Stevenson, the CIA director.

"Well, yes and no," answered the secretary of defense. "Boeing is stripping it down, removing everything that isn't strictly needed, including the back seat and weapons electronic systems. The goal here is to reduce the weight configuration for two additional crew members. She won't be carrying any ordnance, so that saves over a hundred and sixty pounds. And Boeing believes they can strip enough weight from the weapons systems inside the cockpit for another crew member. Boeing is even removing the back seat for the weapons officer. Boeing says that she will be well within weight parameters.

"The plan calls for the X303 to fly into low Earth orbit twice. The first time, the two-man crew will drop off an extra fuel tank, return home and refuel, fly back into orbit, manually refuel in orbit, and fly to Liberty. It's a stealth fighter, and it could remain undetected for most of the flight to Liberty.

"She will make an unorthodox approach. Instead of slowly rising to the city from a level orbit, the X303 will fly above the city and make a shallow downward approach. She will then fly to an exit hatch in the city proper—the tubular part of the city, *not* the docking bay. She'll be manned by a crew of four, the pilot plus three Navy SEALs. The three Navy SEALs will enter Liberty while the pilot flies back home. So the craft's approach will be faster and at an unexpected angle. I think this just might work.

"We are waiting for Boeing to call us back with the results of their manual refueling tests. The four-person crew is with Boeing now, training for the mission."

"Even if it were to work, what can three SEALs do?" asked Vice President Ross.

"Well, their mission is to get into Liberty and provide recon. Once we know what is happening, we can formulate a plan. It gives us three people to assist with any future assault."

"Does this plan have a realistic chance of success?" asked the CIA director.

"We believe so, yes. The plan does have two things in its favor: speed and size. The terrorists might not be expecting a fast response that's also small and limited. We believe the terrorists will be expecting a large-scale response that would require time for us to develop. A small operation designed to gather intel might just work," said Secretary Chao.

"It seems like a stretch," said Amy.

"It is a stretch, but it's the best we can do. We do think it can be done. Everything is a stretch. No matter what we do, it will be a stretch. The plan is simple. It's basic. Get three SEALs onto Liberty. Think about that. The goal is to get three people onto Liberty. If that's a stretch, then I think that says everything. This plan is about as simple as it gets."

"What about the demands of the Muslim World State? How should we respond?" said Amy.

"We're not going to give them what they're asking for. They already know that. I'll worry about responding later," said Ross.

The vice president stood up, placing a hand on the back of her chair. "Let me think about this mission. Secretary Chao, notify me the moment Boeing completes its testing. I'll have a decision later on this matter. Thank you." Then she left the room to go for a short walk.

Day Two

CHAPTER 29

Mat McKenna lay on his back. Sleep was hard to find during the night. He rolled over onto his side and tried to cover his eyes with his arm. Light was coming in through the window blinds. He gave up and moved to a sitting position on the floor. Propping himself up with his arms behind him, he let his eyes wander around the room. Yep, it had actually happened. He had fantasized that he would wake up in his own bed or maybe a hospital bed. Maybe this was a bizarre dream. But it wasn't a bizarre dream, it was a bizarre reality. *Great.*

He watched Megan, who was lying beside him, and waited. She was lying on her side, facing him. She cracked open an eye and looked back at him.

"That's what I thought," said Mat. "You faker."

She smiled and gave a little laugh. "Uncle Mat?"

He looked at the others, Sam and Mary Lu. They were smiling at him from where they lay.

"I guess it's up to me." He stood and stretched his arms. "It always falls on the man."

"Oh please," said Sam.

"Yep. Don't worry. I'll get it done. You can depend on

me." He walked over to the coffeepot and removed the basket for the grounds, scooped five little coffee cups into the basket, and set it back into the coffeepot. Then he picked up the pitcher of water and poured it into the top of the drip coffee maker. He set the pitcher back down on the shelf next to the coffeepot and flipped the brew switch to "On."

Then he stretched again. "Mission accomplished."

"Wow, you're really talented," said Mary Lu. "You must be a man."

Mat glanced in Mary Lu's direction and gave her a single nod. "Yep."

As they waited for the pot to brew, they all got up and dragged themselves to the bathroom to wash up. Megan opened her little carry bag and handed out the two toothbrushes and one tube of half-used toothpaste. They shared the brushes and the toothpaste and washed themselves with soap, water, and paper towels, then they all drifted slowly back into the office.

Before long, the pot was done brewing and everyone was sitting together drinking coffee. Each person was lost in their own thoughts, coming to terms emotionally and rationally with what had happened. No one said anything, respecting the others' moments of reflection.

At length, Mat stood up and stretched his legs. He glanced at his watch: 11:22. "I'll be back in a few."

Sam, Megan, and Mary Lu made faces at each other in disbelief.

"What? Where do you think you're going?" asked Sam.

Undeterred, Mat walked out of the office and into the hallway. It was obvious that no one was working today. The offices were empty. Everyone was staying home as directed. Who could blame them? Travel from sector to sector was impossible now that the sectors were sealed. Unless you lived in the same sector as your job, you could not go to it even if you wanted to. And given the circumstances, who would want to?

The First Lady, Megan, and Mary Lu followed Mat out of the office, almost like children. He exited the office and walked over to the stairs, then went down to the first floor. He walked over to the building's main entrance and stopped in front of the elevators. He might have found exactly what he needed—an office directory. He skimmed over it quickly and discovered what he was searching for, then went to the elevator and pressed the Up button.

Megan, Sam, and Mary Lu stood next to him, and they all waited for the elevator. Or, rather, Mat waited for the elevator. Megan, Sam, and Mary Lu waited to see where Mat was going.

"So where are we going?" asked Megan.

Mat gave her a half smile.

A light above the elevator doors came on, and after a second, the doors slid open. Mat stepped inside, followed dutifully by the three women. He pressed the button for the fifth floor, the top floor.

"Where are we headed?" asked Sam. The elevator doors closed, and the elevator went up. "Is this like a game?"

Mat had a poker face. Yes, he was enjoying this.

The elevator stopped.

"We're here. You will know soon enough," said Mat.

Mary Lu laughed. "Why won't you tell us?"

Mat glanced at the floor indicator above the door. The door began to open. The light above the door read *4*.

"What's the big secret?" Sam crossed her arms and smiled at Mary Lu.

Wait. This isn't our floor.

The hairs on Mat's neck stood on end.

Without a word, Mat shoved Megan, Mary Lu, and Sam into the front right corner of the elevator.

"What?" said Sam.

"How rude," said Mary Lu.

The doors opened, and two terrorists were standing directly in front of them with their weapons pointed into the elevator.

Before the terrorists could react, Mat grabbed the barrel of one of the assault rifles with his left hand and pointed it to the side. He crouched low and hit the other terrorist in his kidneys with his right fist.

The terrorist bent over in a shock of intense pain, and Mat stood up and kicked the other terrorist in his crotch with all his might. The terrorist lifted off the ground from the impact of the kick. He fell back down and groaned in agony, releasing his gun as he doubled over and grabbed himself between his legs. He hit the floor hard and landed on his side in a fetal position.

Mat swung the gun around by the barrel until it was in his hands. He pointed it at each terrorist and pulled the trigger, moving right to left. Both terrorists were sprayed with bullets. It was over before Megan, Sam, and Mary Lu took a breath.

Mat stood blocking the elevator door to keep it from

closing. He withdrew his handgun and raised it in front of him, placing his index finger in front of his lips. They listened quietly for a few moments. Silence.

Mat holstered his gun. "It looks like they were alone."

The tile in front of the elevator on the fourth floor was quickly covered with crimson as two thick pools of blood slowly spread out on the floor.

The three women stepped forward to look.

Megan was shaking. Mat hugged her. "It's over."

Mary Lu was quiet. Tears were flowing. Mat wrapped his arms around her and held her tightly. She was crying silently, tears streaking down her cheeks. Was Mary Lu reliving the moment when her friends were executed? He held her and wondered.

Sam stepped out of the elevator and over the bodies. "Let this be a lesson to us," she said in a low, determined voice.

Mat released Mary Lu. He knew what she meant. "Good point."

"We always have to be ready," said Sam.

He then pulled Mary Lu to the front of the elevator, blocking the door. "Don't let the elevator door close. Understand?"

She wiped her face. "Yes."

Mat exited the elevator and stood next to Sam. Megan joined them but did not look at the bodies.

Mat and Sam knelt beside the two dead terrorists and quickly began to strip them of all weapons. They now had two assault rifles and two knives.

Sam and Mat each took a gun and a knife. They offered none to Mary Lu. She didn't complain.

Sam and Mat stood up. Mat stared at the corpses.

"What is it?" asked Sam. "What's wrong?"

Mat pulled his phone from his pocket.

"Phones don't work, remember?" said Sam.

"Yep." He took a picture of each terrorist. Then he handed the phone to Sam. "Hold this for a second."

He knelt down next to the two bodies and removed their wallets. He examined them. Nothing unusual. He handed Sam their photo IDs and had her take pictures of them. Then he put the driver's licenses back into their wallets and their wallets back into their pockets.

"Why don't we just keep the photo IDs?" she asked.

"Because we don't want to leave any hint that law enforcement is involved. Should the bodies be found, let them think someone just killed them."

"Well, we have to hide the bodies," said Sam. "No one should ever find them."

"Right."

They found the garbage receptacle for the floor and dumped the two bodies into it, then covered them with trash. It seemed appropriate.

Having completed his sweep of the floor, Mat walked back to the elevator and pressed the Up button and waited. Megan, Sam, and Mary Lu joined him again, and soon they were on the fifth floor.

He walked down the hallway and found what he had come for. He walked through double doors and entered a large room. The three women followed him in, laughing.

"The cafeteria!" they exclaimed.

He gave a crooked smile. "Yep."

The room was empty. About thirty tables were evenly distributed throughout the room. Corporate pictures were on the wall, showing projects in varying phases of completion the company had worked on. Some of the pictures had corporate employees in them, all of them smiling. Working hard. Working together. Wonderful.

On one side of the wall was a kitchen with an empty buffet in front of it. It had been closed for the celebration. Mat walked into the kitchen and opened first one refrigerator, then another. Soon the three of them had a bucket of potato salad, along with slices of ham, turkey, and salami. They quickly made sandwiches of all kinds and all combinations and put some of the potato salad into drinking cups. They grabbed ice and placed it into plastic bags. Soon they had Megan's satchel filled with food. They found another cloth bag in the kitchen and filled it with soft drinks, fruit drinks, candy bars, and health bars. They cleaned everything up so as to leave it the way they'd found it. As if they were never there.

They returned to their base. It was a spacious office on the second floor. They didn't want to be on the first floor, and they didn't want to be trapped on the upper floors with no way out. This office had something that they required: a window. From one of the tablecloths in the kitchen, they built a rope ladder. This gave them a back way out—they could break the window and exit to the ground safely if needed. They set the ladder in a bundle next to the window on the floor. It made them feel better.

CHAPTER 30

When they were all sitting around the office in their chairs, everyone grabbed a drink and a sandwich and a bag of chips.

Mary Lu set her turkey sandwich down and took a gulp of her Dr. Pepper. "What are we going to do?" she asked. "We can't just stay here and hide and eat, can we?"

"Well, if we could get to Air Force One, we would be able to talk to Washington," said Sam. "Then maybe we could work with them to formulate a plan."

"That's a great idea if you only want to talk once. I bet they would be on us quickly," said Mat.

"I'm not talking about the Air Force One cockpit radio."

"What are you talking about?" asked Mat.

"I mean, the Secret Service has a backup communications system located inside Air Force One. They brought a sat phone just in case something happened with the spaceliner or anything. They prepare for options, lots of options. Being out here in space, they wanted an independent communications line that they could rely on if needed. Something that was completely self-contained. Something that didn't rely on any external systems or personnel. The Secret Service has backup systems for anything they deem potentially critical. That always includes communications; in this case, that *especially* meant communications."

"Makes sense," said Megan.

Mat shrugged. "It doesn't really matter anyway. There is no way we can get to Air Force One. The terrorists aren't about to let us go walking through the spaceport and catch a shuttle to the docking bays."

"True," said Sam.

"No, not true," said Mary Lu. She took another bite of her turkey sandwich.

"What? What's not true?" asked Mat.

She cocked her head to one side and swallowed. "I can get you to Air Force One."

Sam asked, "How? How can you possibly get us to Air Force One, Mary Lu? No offense, but they aren't going to just let us waltz by them."

"You have to change your thinking. This is not like being on Earth. The terrorists *think* that they have blocked all access to the spaceport. They have not. It's simple. Just exit the station—go outside into space. Go to the docking bays externally, in space, outside of the city." She took another drink from her can of soda. "It's easy-peasy."

Mat felt his stomach lurch. He could feel the blood rush from his face. He wasn't afraid of flying. He just preferred to be on the ground. He flew when he needed to. But outside in space, way above Earth? His face went white.

"Are you OK?" asked Sam and Mary Lu together.

Megan reached over and rubbed his shoulder. She

understood. Uncle Mat didn't like to fly. A space walk? She could only imagine.

Mat focused on his job. He thought about the people whose lives were at stake. He could feel the color begin to return to his face, and his stomach began to return to its normal orientation. "I'm fine." Flying here was bad enough. Outside in space?

Great.

Mary Lu continued, "It's not a big deal. Actually, it's not any kind of a deal at all. It's routine. I'm the chief engineer on Liberty. The structure of the city itself requires maintenance—that's my job. I have a small but dedicated staff of engineers and an army of maintenance droids working inside the station and outside, twenty-four seven. They all work just to make sure the station is running properly."

Mat asked, "You have androids working on the outside of the station?"

"Yes. Androids and sometimes people too. Just not as often. Mostly droids. It's safer that way. We let the droids do most of the external work; we just monitor them. Occasionally we send an engineer out." She added, "I have been outside many times myself."

Mary Lu paused. It looked like she could tell they were all impressed.

"Can we use the androids on Liberty to attack the terrorists?" said Mat.

"No. First, almost all the androids are just common service droids. They aren't capable of attacking anything. They don't have the prerequisite programming needed for such a task. My droids, the maintenance droids, are the same. The droids are programmed not to be able to do anything that could harm humans. None of these droids are capable of doing anything like that. These are not military droids. The only exception to that is Andy. Technically, he is capable. But he is specifically programmed not to do anything to hurt humans."

"I understand. I've seen the service droids. I understand what you're saying," said Mat.

Mat, Sam, and Megan could hear the corporate tone in Mary Lu's voice. The kind you get from senior managers, VPs, and corporate presidents. They smiled. They had never heard her sound like this. But then they had just met.

She continued, "The androids do three things. First, they do repairs and standard systems upkeep. Second, they manually check that everything is functioning within accepted parameters. And three, they go to a predesignated area and wait. These are areas inside and outside the station that have been calculated to enable a rapid response in the case of most emergencies. Standard protocol."

Sheriff McKenna stood and walked away from the group, then walked back again. He took a drink of soda and sat back down. "Well, it looks like we have a plan. We exit the station and go into space. Then we travel to Air Force One and get the sat phone. Then we use it to call Washington."

"Sounds good to me," said Sam. "Then we will see what ideas Washington has. You know, the best and brightest." She winked at them.

The room was filled with silence. Smiles formed on their faces. They. Had. A. Plan.

JOHN PARRISH

"So how do we do this, Mary Lu?" asked Mat.

Mary Lu pressed herself back farther into her chair, holding her soft drink with both hands. "Let's talk about this. Mat, Sam, and I are going to go to Air Force One while Megan stays here. I assume that you guys have never worked in zero gravity."

"Correct," said both Mat and Sam.

Mary Lu crossed her legs. The staff meeting had begun. "Let's start with the basics. The suits are modular in construction. The reason for this is production and maintenance costs. The suits are easy to maintain. My team can take a suit apart and put it back together so a faulty part can be easily replaced. The suits are construction suits, what the industry calls hard suits, made of a hard shell. There are several reasons for that: protection from bumping into something, running into space debris, or a construction accident."

Mary Lu paused to make sure she had not lost them. She lifted her soda can and took a long, slow sip, then lowered the can to her lap. "They come in two layers. The first layer is a soft, thin, semihard jumpsuit. This soft jumpsuit can actually hold a seal. It's an amazing piece of nanotechnology. You slip it on and zip it up, then you close the dog collar around your neck. The collar will attach to the hard shell and to the helmet. Don't worry if you forget some of this; I will walk you through it later when we put the suits on. OK?"

"OK," said Sam and Mat.

"Next is the hard outer shell, what everyone thinks of as the space suit. It will also hold a seal, which gives you one hundred percent redundancy. The whole suit is designed for rapid entry and exit. You just step into it one leg at a time, like overalls. Then you put your arms into the hard sleeves and pull it on like a shirt. When you pull it on, the chest plate will be loose in the front. Slip the helmet on and make sure that it locks with the dog collar. The suits are intelligent. Finally, you ask the suit to seal."

She took another long sip of her soda. "When we get there, I will help you. Putting the suit on is easy. Let me repeat: it's very simple. Put the soft jumpsuit on, put the hard shell on the only way you can—feet first—then put on the helmet. Talk to your suit and tell it to seal. It will make itself comfortable for you by adjusting its size to fit your joints: elbows, knees, etcetera. It will report back to you. You do it one time, and you've done it a thousand times."

"I am really glad you joined us," said Mat.

Sam agreed. "Yes, I think we are going to really need you."

"Thank you," she said, and Mat watched her eyes shine as she laughed. Then she continued, "We do have some issues to consider."

"All right, we're listening," said Mat.

"Here's the thing. When you exit the station, a signal alert will be sent to the maintenance facility, and whoever is in the maintenance facility will know who opened the hatch. That would be me since it will be my card opening the hatch. They will know where, and they will know who.

"The terrorists have all the control centers; that includes the maintenance center. If there is anyone in there that understands the systems, they will know when you exit the station. No one comes in or exits without the center being notified. Your average citizen cannot just walk out a door and into space. All of that is controlled."

"Of course, but since you said you could get us to Air Force One, I assumed that you would have the authority to open the exit," said Mat.

"I do. The system knows me, and exiting the station is part of my job. I actually have the highest clearance. But if the terrorists know what they are doing, they will know that I'm leaving. They will know which exit was opened."

"I see your point," said Mat.

"Is there anything that can be done?" asked Megan.

"Yes, there is. Fortunately for us, it's actually a little more complicated than that. We have droids coming and going routinely, doing their standard maintenance checks and whatever work has been assigned to them, so an exit notification isn't an unusual event; they occur daily."

"So what's the problem?" asked Sam.

"If I open the hatch for an unscheduled exit, the system will notify them of that. The system will also notify the operators that I, Mary Lu, have manually opened the exit. It's *not* routine for me to leave the station or override the system. It is possible that the terrorists know how the station works, and if that's the case, they may want to know what's going on with the notification."

Sam shrugged. "OK."

"I'm just saying that you should be aware of the possibility that these events could raise a red flag for the terrorists. They would know the location of the exit."

"We will have to take that risk and be prepared," said Mat.

Sam said, "Agreed. We have no choice. We have to get to Air Force One."

Mary Lu thought for a second. "Well, I think I may have a solution to that as well."

Mat shrugged. "All right, so . . ."

"There's another issue you need to be aware of. We have cameras strategically placed outside the station, so we need to map out your path to avoid potential detection."

"OK, so we follow a map. What about the solution to the first issue, the exit notification issue? What do you have in mind?"

Mary Lu grabbed her leather case and withdrew her tablet. She never went anywhere without it. It was her office, and she never knew when and where she would need it. And she worked all over Liberty. Mary Lu turned her tablet on. Mat, Sam, and Megan glanced at each other with questioning looks. They watched quietly and waited.

Mary Lu smiled at the tablet's camera for a second and was cleared into it. "Issa, I need maintenance. Droid duty, please."

Issa was the name of Mary Lu's tablet. A new screen popped up.

"Thanks," said Mary Lu.

"Anytime," said Issa.

Mary Lu pressed a few buttons on the tablet and scrolled to some new screens. "Ah, here we go." A timetable of the schedule of the external droids popped up. Mary Lu glanced over the information.

"Hmm . . . good," she said, thinking out loud. "There is a way you can exit without them knowing. We have to go to a location where a maintenance droid is performing a scheduled exit from the station. As the droid exits, you would leave with him. I have a droid scheduled to leave a little over three hours from now. That should give us time to get ready before we leave. It departs from exit 8B—that's not that far from here. It will take about an hour to walk there, which gives us plenty of time to get the suits on."

"Sounds good. Let's do it," said Mat.

"Count me in," added Sam.

"I am going to make one change to the plan: I'm going to assign Andy to the task."

Sam asked, "Who's Andy?"

"He is the chief management droid. He is more capable than the standard droid."

"More capable?" asked Mat.

"Yes, specifically, more intelligent. Andy is state of the art in android technology. It's why he is here. Neurotech Inc., the largest designer and manufacturer of domestic androids, believes this city is an ideal proving ground."

Mary Lu entered the classified new assignment into her tablet, and Andy received it instantly. He replied on Mary Lu's maintenance net, an independent communications net for talking to each other inside and outside the station. Only maintenance personnel used it.

"OK, it's done. Andy will meet us there and exit the station with you."

"Aren't you coming with us?" asked Sam.

"No. I think it would be better if Andy exits with you and I stay here and monitor the situation," said Mary Lu.

Mat was surprised. "You're saying you aren't coming

with us? Did I hear that right?"

The First Lady spoke with an edge to her voice. "Andy is coming with us, but you aren't?" She didn't look completely comfortable with Mary Lu making that decision.

"Look," Mary Lu began. "I have as much at stake in this as you do. I'm trapped in Liberty just like you. I need this mission to succeed every bit as much as you two do. And giving this mission the greatest chance to succeed means that Andy goes with you and I stay here and monitor events as best as I can. Andy has capabilities that I don't have. He was designed to function in space. I have abilities here in Liberty that none of you do, because of my position here."

Mat and Sam and Megan all looked at each other, absorbing what Mary Lu was saying.

Mary Lu continued, "Andy going with you, and my staying here gives the mission the greatest chance to succeed. Isn't that what we all want? What we all need? Andy knows the station, and he can lead you to the docking bays without being seen on camera. He has the authority to open the docking bay doors. No one will suspect an android. Andy goes outside all the time. He does supervisory work with the other androids."

"Can't you do it?"

"I could, but Andy has been designed for this environment. If anything came up, he could move much faster than any of us. And that leaves me free to monitor what's happening. If I stay here, we might be able to avoid an incident. If they see Andy outside, it won't raise any alarms. He's supposed to be out there. It's his normal job."

"OK," said Sam, the edge to her voice gone.

"All right. I'm on board too," said Mat.

"Look, I'm just guessing. But my gut says that opening the docking bay exit hatch door will draw attention. If anything will, that will."

"Agreed," said Mat.

"The terrorists might not know anything at all about Liberty's internal workings. Or they might know everything. I know they have the control center complex. One of my employees sent me a text a while back. From what he said, it didn't sound like everyone got out. It makes sense that they would want to keep some people who know how to run the city's systems."

Mat and Sam both nodded.

"I don't have any details. I don't know what's going on inside the control centers. The key thing is, will the terrorists understand what they are seeing on the city's systems? Who knows?

"So they might see Andy and let their guard down. But if they see me, they would be suspicious. They will know right away who opened the door. Androids use an entirely different method to unlock the doors: they talk to the door with their index finger. I'm a human; I use a pass. If I don't have my security pass, the control center has to open it for me."

"Understood," said Mat McKenna. "It's time to go."

CHAPTER 31

"Follow me!" exclaimed Mary Lu. She opened the door, and the four of them stepped out of the office and headed for the ground floor. They had a rendezvous with an exit gate.

Sam and Mat carried the weapons, ready to fight. Megan carried the bag slung over her shoulder. The bag was a book satchel stuffed with four sandwiches, soft drinks, two extra magazines, bandages, paper towels, two extra knives, and even cleaning wipes. It was their office in a bag, everything they might need or want. Anything they thought they might need went into the bag, as long as it wasn't too heavy or too big and the bag wasn't too full. They never knew when they might have to find another place to stay. They had become vagabonds. Vagabonds with a mission.

When they reached the ground floor, Mary Lu moved toward the building entrance carefully. She slowed her pace as she approached the doors leading to the sidewalk. She opened the door and scanned the scene. It was empty—totally empty. There was no one anywhere.

It reminded her of an old movie where everyone had died except for one or two people, left to wander around an empty city. She felt the hairs on her arm tingle as they stood up, as if she were cold. It felt creepy. At least there were no terrorists; for that she was grateful. She pushed through the door and moved right, going along the circumference of the city down the walkway. She tried very hard to become invisible, hoping no one would spot them.

She took a direct route crosswise. Upon reaching the wall, she angled left ninety degrees and went along the circumference. She led them for over an hour in a straight line. Occasionally she weaved in and out of buildings to make sure they weren't being seen or followed.

Finally she came to an abrupt stop in front of a building along the outer wall of the city. Megan, Sam, and Mat gathered around her. On the door in front of them, a small professional sign with silver lettering read *Authorized Personnel Only.*

"We are almost there," Mary Lu said, inserting her security passkey. She pulled the door open and they walked in.

They turned to the right and walked down a long hallway that ran along the circumference. As they walked along the hallway, there were large open rooms and a few large closets. One open area contained a rectangular metallic foam sheet that could patch damaged city walls. In one of the larger open rooms was a collection of structural elements: beams, trusses, connectors, and extra wall segments. These were organized by size, stacked, and sorted. It was a small warehouse. In one of the smaller rooms were power tools in a rack against a wall.

Mat slowed as he walked by. "I have no idea what those

tools do, but they look awesome and huge. And expensive."

Mary Lu faced Mat. "They *are* awesome and huge and expensive."

Sam laughed as she slowed to peek inside. "It looks like a man's wet dream for a garage."

Megan looked like she enjoyed that one. She shoved the First Lady gently with a shoulder to show her approval.

"Have you used any of those tools? I mean, personally?" he asked.

"Absolutely."

Her grin and the way she cocked her head gave her away. "See that one hanging on the hook right there next to that shelf?"

"That small white one with the blue handle? Looks kinda like a drill?" asked Megan.

"Yep, that's the one."

Megan asked, "What about it?"

"I've used that one." She laughed.

Mary Lu walked a few more steps, then entered a door to their right. Inside was a locker room. There were benches in the middle and racks on the walls. And the racks contained space suits—or extravehicular activity suits—but space suits was easier. Along with the racks was shelving with rows and rows of suit components: helmets, gloves, arms, leggings, and suit comms. There were white boxes containing electronic components.

Standing next to the bench was an android.

CHAPTER 32

"Hi, Andy," said Mary Lu. "How are you doing?"

"I'm doing well," he said, looking first at Mary Lu, then glancing over toward Megan, Sam, and Mat.

"Thanks for coming, Andy."

"No problem. Glad to be of help, Mary Lu. Are you going to join me outside this time?" His voice was hopeful.

"No, not this time."

"OK."

"I would like you to meet Mat, Megan, and Sam." Mary Lu raised an arm toward each in turn. "Everyone, let me introduce you to Andy." She raised an arm toward Andy.

Andy was humanoid in form and size. His face had been designed to allow him a full range of human expression—visually, a simplified human face. Andy was a first-generation prototype containing a completely new neuronet. He was one of a kind. His body was similar to an average male, six feet tall with broad, humanlike shoulders. He was designed for work at Liberty. Specifically, for dangerous work in space.

His muscles had been augmented for pure power, though you wouldn't know it by looking. His skin was a metal alloy to deflect impacts from space debris. His hands were of normal humanoid size. His feet, however, were chimp-like. He could walk on them or use them for hands. He had a small hydrogen-powered jet pack built in, in case he got knocked off the city while working outside.

Not sure what to do, Mat extended a hand. "Hi, Andy. Pleased to meet you." He had never extended a hand to a tool before. Wasn't sure why he did this time.

Andy looked pleasantly surprised at the gesture. Usually people treated him as just an AI system, a nonentity simulating human characteristics. He raised his hand and they shook. "Pleased to meet you," he said. People were generally nice to him on one level. They treated him as the embodiment of an AI system. They were as nice to him as they were to watches, thermostats, tablets, the AI systems running their homes, or soda machines.

Sam and Megan followed Mat's lead and extended their hands. "Hi, Andy."

Andy took their hands gently. He said to Sam, "It's a pleasure to meet the First Lady. I've never met a First Lady before."

Quiet filled the room. They were supposed to be in disguise!

"Andy, this is Sam. I think you are confused. This is not the First Lady," said Mary Lu.

"Of course it is. My recognition abilities are excellent, and her voice matches the pattern on file. Her facial features are an exact match, and her eye scan is an exact match also. Nope, this is the First Lady, Samantha Devane. You had to know that, Mary Lu."

"Why did she have to know that?" asked Megan.

"Because Mary Lu knows everything."

Mat patted Mary Lu on the back and smiled at her. Mary Lu smiled back, then stuck her tongue out at him.

Sam covered her mouth casually—or she tried to anyway—as she was suppressing a laugh that could easily be construed as rude. Megan smiled, but she mostly watched Uncle Mat and Mary Lu.

Mary Lu returned to the subject at hand. "Andy, this is not the First Lady. This is Sam."

"No, she is the First Lady. Really, she is."

"No, she isn't. This is Sam," she repeated.

"Mary Lu, I . . . I don't understand . . ."

"Of course you don't, Andy. How could you? But you will. Let me explain it."

"OK," he said.

"There are lots of people looking for the First Lady. You've seen the news reports, right?"

"Yes."

"Liberty has been taken over by terrorists. They are bad people. Very bad. They want to torture and kill people."

"I wondered who they were. Until two hours ago, I've been down. Everyone is afraid of them." said Andy.

Mary Lu stepped closer to Andy. "The terrorists are endangering the lives of everyone in the city. They are breaking the law."

"OK."

"The terrorists have taken control of the spaceport and the control center. They have shut the city down. They've killed communication between Liberty and Earth, and they have sealed off all the city's sectors as if it were an emergency. Andy, you and I are operating on our own emergency protocol. No one else knows that, and we don't want anyone else to know."

"OK."

"This is Mat, he is Sheriff Mat McKenna. He and Megan and the First Lady are with me. We have to act quickly to save lives. I'm going to be depending on you, Andy. Understand?"

"Yes, I think so," he said.

"Emergency protocol. If you have to take an action that results in someone's life being lost in order to save others, you are now directed, by me, to execute those orders."

"I understand."

"That's an order," she said firmly.

"Yes, ma'am."

Mat, Megan, and Sam glanced at each other.

Mary Lu continued, "You have never seen Mat McKenna, Megan, or the First Lady. And you haven't seen or heard from me in fourteen hours. No matter who asks. No matter *who* asks."

"I understand."

"*No matter who asks.* That's an order. I give this order to save lives."

"Yes, ma'am," he answered. "I understand."

"Good. We are going on a mission, and we need your help."

"I would be happy to help. I'll do whatever I can. I don't want people to get hurt."

"I know you don't, Andy. We trust you. Mat and Sam

have to get to Air Force One undetected by maintenance cameras. After you get them to Air Force One, I want you to lead them back here. Undetected. OK?"

"OK."

"Assist them any way you can. They are unfamiliar with the city, and they have never been on a space walk. They don't know how to open gates and exit hatches. They don't know all kinds of small, mundane things that you and I know."

Andy looked back and forth between Sam and Mat. "I understand, Mary Lu. I will help them. You can depend on me."

CHAPTER 33

Mary Lu grabbed a jumpsuit from a hanger. "This should fit you," she said, handing it to the First Lady.

"Thanks." Sam took hold of it with both hands. "It's very lightweight," she observed. "It's much lighter than I expected." The material was soft, smooth, and flexible. It folded easily. It reminded her of a flight suit. It brought back memories and thoughts she hadn't had in many years.

Mat watched Sam's eyebrows rise, and her eyes became distant for a moment. Then the moment passed and she was back.

Mary Lu pulled another jumpsuit off the rack and handed it to Mat. "And this one should fit you."

"One size fits all," he said as he took hold of it.

"No. Actually, they come in three sizes. Small, medium, and large," answered Mary Lu. Then she placed her hands on her hips and faced Mat and Sam. "Well, what are you waiting for? Go put them on. Take off your blue jeans and put them on."

Megan giggled.

Sam and Mat looked at each other, then back at Mary Lu.

Mary Lu grabbed Mat's arm and led him to the other side of the benches. "Put yours on over here, then come back to us when you are ready."

In a minute, Mat and Sam had the jumpsuits on. They handed Megan their blue jeans, and Megan folded the jeans and placed them in her bag.

"Good," said Mary Lu.

Sam said to Mat, "I guess we're really going to do this? Go outside into space?"

"Yep, we're really going to do this."

They each closed the dog collar at the front of their suit.

Mary Lu examined the dog collar on each of them. "Looks good."

She retrieved several comm devices off the shelves. They were very small. They had a wire over the top of the head, two earpieces, and a bone mic extending halfway between the ear and the mouth. She handed one to Megan. "Don't put this on yet."

"But I'm not going outside," said Megan.

"I know, but from now on we will all use these engineering comms to communicate with each other. No matter where we are. They are completely independent systems. They communicate directly to each other. They do not use a net of any kind. This is direct comm-to-comm communication, so there's no chance of the terrorists being able to listen in. Specs required that they be completely independent, designed to function in all conditions."

"So we can use these here inside the city?"

"Exactly. Inside, outside, or both, it doesn't matter. From now on, we use these to talk to each other. Thing is, whenever you talk, you are talking to the entire group." She handed one each to Mat and Sam and grabbed one for herself. She turned on her comm. "Don't worry, I've already turned yours on."

She then took her comm and touched Megan's, Sam's, and Mat's comm in turn. She raised her comm toward Andy, and he touched it with his index finger. "OK, we are now connected into a comm group. Andy is in our as well. Put them on."

They did.

"Everyone hear me?" asked Mary Lu.

They all said, "Yes."

"The signal is scrambled—military spec. Again, just be aware that from now on, when you talk, everyone in the group will hear."

She walked over to the chest and with both hands removed a larger hard-shell suit off the rack. Sam could see that it was heavier. "This one's for you, Sam."

Sam rushed to help Mary Lu by grabbing the space suit quickly. "Thanks." It was heavy but not as heavy as she'd expected. Sam held the suit against her chest to help her hold it.

"We've already talked about this, but let's talk about it again. The suit is hard-shelled to protect against debris collision. The suits are a wonder of engineering. They are very nice—nothing like the bulky suits of the past. Designed for easy, rapid entry into the suit. It's trim in design, not much bigger than a suit of clothes, really. It's basically like a really thick jumpsuit."

Mary Lu looked at Sam and Mat, who were standing in

front of their suits that were sitting on the ground. "Well, put them on," she said.

Mat put his right leg in and then his left. He pulled it up and slipped his right arm in, then his left. The chest plate dangled in front. Sam watched at first and then did the same thing that Mat had done.

Mary Lu walked up to Mat and pulled his chest plate up into position, clipping it to the upper left shoulder. Then she did the same for Sam. She stepped back from them. "Put your helmets on."

Then Mary Lu checked the dog collar and helmet seal on each of them. Everything looked good.

"Now that you have the suits on, I want each of you to say 'Suit on.' The suit will automatically adjust to you and seal. When it has sealed, it will say 'Sealed.' If there is a problem, it will tell you."

They both did as they were told, and their suits reported back that they were sealed, just as Mary Lu had said.

"The helmet has a heads-up display, or HUD. The suit will provide all information to you through the HUD. I don't have time to teach you all the things the suit can do. You will see a picture of the suit in the HUD. The outline will go from red to green when it is on and sealed. The suit should be green now," Mary Lu added, looking at them expectantly.

They both nodded their confirmation.

"The simple schematic will tell you if there is anything wrong with the suit and post any issues on the suit's status. It's an intelligent suit; feel free to ask it questions. The heads-up display also has a map of the city and will show you where you are in relation to the station at all times."

Andy looked at Mary Lu, then at Sam and Mat. It was becoming obvious to Andy that the two humans were going to need real assistance in space.

"Now tell your suits 'Go dark.' We don't want you to be tracked by anyone at the center, and we don't want them to be able to listen in on our conversations."

Again Sam and Mat did as they were told, and the suits answered, "Dark on." The heads-up displays changed to reflect the suits' new operation configuration.

"Time to go," said Andy. "I must follow my maintenance schedule."

CHAPTER 34

Mat and Sam followed Andy as he walked up to the exit chamber door. The chamber was already pressurized. Andy inserted his index finger into the android keyhole, and the door opened.

Mary Lu patted each of their shoulders. "Good luck and Godspeed." She could feel a wave of emotion rushing over her. She fought the tears back. This was a dangerous mission. Her eyes were wet.

Mat hugged Mary Lu and then Megan. "We'll be fine. I'll see you when we get back."

Andy headed for the door, then stopped. He stared at Mary Lu for a moment and then at Mat. He had never seen Mary Lu like this before. She was his boss. He had watched her in business mode, teaching mode. He had laughed with her. This was different. He made a note.

"Be careful, Andy," she said. She put an arm around him. "Come back to me."

"I will."

Megan stood close to Mary Lu as they watched Andy, Mat, and Sam disappear into the small room. It was the first time Mat had ever seen an exit chamber. It was the size of a walk-in closet. On two opposite walls were benches. Handrails were overhead to assist in moving. There were four foot lockers as well.

Mat sat down, using one of the handrails to help, and Sam sat down next to him. He smiled at her. *What had he gotten himself into?* Andy walked to the control panel next to the door leading into space. He pressed a large white button on the panel, and the room began to depressurize.

Every exit had an airlock, a small sealed room for exiting and entering the city structure. A short beep sounded. At first Mat thought a microwave oven was done, but it was the room. It was done depressurizing. Great. Like Pavlov's dog, now he was hungry.

Andy approached the exit door, and Mat and Sam rose to their feet and joined him. Mat watched him as he pressed a button on the pane next to the door. There was a small click, followed by a short, low electric hum, and then the door opened inward.

Mat watched as Andy exited. When he was outside, Andy faced them. Mat went out using a handrail and stopped next to Andy. Sam waited until Mat was safely out, then she exited. Standing next to the external door's control panel, Andy pressed a button, and the door closed and sealed.

At the exterior of the station were three tubular maintenance tracks circling the outside of the ring and three on the inside. These walkways were designed with footing and handrails so work crews could pull themselves along. The spokes, like spokes of a bicycle wheel, led from the rim of the city to the central hub. Every spoke of the city also had a walkway.

The spaceport was located in the rim, so it had normal Earth gravity. However, the actual spaceport docking locations were located at the hub in the center of the ring. Shuttle cars took people to and from the docking location to the spaceport center.

The spaceport was designed like an airport. It contained restaurants, hotels, shops, and arrival-and-departure gates. The primary difference between the spaceport and an airport was that spacecraft docked at the central hub. A passenger couldn't just go directly from the gate and hop onboard a spacecraft. Transportation cars took people from the arrival-and-departure gate to the actual ship located at the hub. The hub comprised three docking rings, each docking ring containing sixteen docking bays. A ship actually attached physically to the city at a docking bay.

In the center of the docking rings was a repair garage, a construction shack. Space probes were assembled there, and heavy repairs on damaged spacecraft were performed there. It was a full-atmosphere environment, so people didn't need space suits, but they did work in zero gravity.

Andy moved on, slower than usual. He kept an eye on Sam and Mat, making sure they were all right, as Mary Lu had requested. The two humans had quickly learned it was much easier if they used the handrails to pull themselves along as they walked. They were on the side of the city wall where they experienced Earth gravity as they rotated with the city's tube. Andy checked his pace to make sure he did not leave them behind.

"How are you guys doing?" asked Mary Lu over the comm.

"Good," said Mat.

"It's beautiful out here," said Sam. "Earth is awesome." Sam gazed at it below them. "Isn't it, Mat? Isn't it amazing?"

"Yep. It is." His tone was flat, mechanical. He wasn't going to look at Earth unless necessary. He felt his stomach rotating. He focused on the path ahead of him.

Mary Lu said, "I know. It is amazing. No picture and no film can capture how it is in real life."

My God, I'll be glad to get back to Earth, thought Mat.

Mary Lu flipped through her tablet and pulled up a map. "Guys, ask your suits for a map."

"What?" asked Sam.

"Just say 'Suit, map.'"

Sam tried it. "OK—suit, map." A map popped up in her heads-up display. "Cool."

"Suit, map," said Mat. A 3D map popped up in his HUD as well.

"It's simple: white dots are people, blue dots are androids, and the red one is you."

"Got it," said Sam.

Even though she was not wearing a helmet, her tablet had the same program that suits used for mapping. She could view anyone's heads-up display. She pressed a few keys on her tablet and highlighted the exit gate they had left. Then she highlighted another exit gate on the docking ring that Air Force One was on. Once they entered the docking ring, they would be about thirty degrees away from Air Force One. It was as close as they could get; each docking ring had only two airlocks, and they were 180 degrees apart from each other.

"I'm going to do one thing now." Mary Lu pressed a key.

Mat watched as two yellow squares popped up on his map. One was close to them; the other was located on a docking ring. "What're those?" asked Mat.

"The yellow squares are the exit gates that you will be using. The one closest to you is the one you just left. The other one is as close to Air Force One as I can get you."

"Thanks," said Sam.

* * *

Andy came to a stop and allowed Mat and Sam to catch up to him. "We're waiting for a camera to rotate around," he said.

After a moment, Andy began walking again.

Silently the three moved forward, step by step. After a time, Andy arrived at one of the spokes that connected the city's ring to the central hub and docking facilities.

Andy came to a stop and faced them. He noted that Mat and Sam were getting better at navigating in the suits; they were only one or two steps behind. "We are going up this spoke to the docking ring. From there, we are going to depart the ring and begin our climb to the center of the station."

"Will the terrorists be able to see us from the spaceport windows overlooking the docking bays?" asked Mat.

"No, just follow my track tightly and they won't be able to. We will be in their line of sight briefly, but we will use the structure of the spoke beams to hide us."

"All right. You lead, Andy, and we will follow. I see what you are doing."

"You're doing a great job, Andy," said Mary Lu.

"Thank you, Mary Lu. Happy to help."

"Andy, when you get to the hub, go inside with them and assist them any way you can."

"Yes, ma'am."

They set off again toward the central hub. The going was harder this time and took more energy. The spoke had a ladder where the U-shaped step served as both a step and a handhold, similar to the monorail ladder. As they got closer to the hub, it became easier to move; the force of gravity was lessening as they became closer to the center of rotation. Mat discovered that it worked best to just use his arms to pull himself forward one step at a time and let his legs trail behind him. Sam did the same. It was about the only way they could move with any kind of speed.

Sam cleared her throat. "Let's hope no one is inside Air Force One when we get there."

"Yep," said Mat.

"What do we do if there is someone in Air Force One?" she asked.

"Improvise."

"I was afraid that was going to be your answer."

All was quiet for a few moments as they slowly worked their way down the spoke shaft of the station, careful to remain hidden from view.

Mary Lu's voice came over the comm. "Are you two OK?" she asked. "Would you like to rest?"

Sam answered first. "I'm fine."

"I'm fine," responded Mat. "How's Megan? Megan, are you there?"

"I'm here, Uncle Mat. I'm here with Mary Lu, watching you guys on her tablet. You guys be careful and come back!"

"We will."

They continued on, slowly working their way down the spoke of the wheel.

"Andy, stop!" barked Mary Lu.

Andy stopped. "Anything wrong?"

"We have an inbound," said Mary Lu to all of them.

CHAPTER 35

"We have a *what?*" asked Mat.

But the image on Mary Lu's tablet left no doubt. She had received a heads-up from one of her employees in the control center. Radar info was coming to her through a back door.

"Liberty is being approached by a spacecraft. It's not far away, and it's closing fast. Too fast. I have no idea what they are thinking. How it got this close without being detected is a mystery to me. I don't know. Maybe we had some kind of a systems failure."

Sam knew. "It's military."

As soon as she'd said it, everyone knew the First Lady was right.

"Of course. The cavalry has arrived!" said Mary Lu.

"Where are they headed, Mary Lu? Can you tell?" asked Sam.

"I think our mission just got scrubbed. Mary Lu, can we get to where they are headed?" asked Mat.

"We need to help them any way we can," said Sam.

Andy broke in. "Mary Lu, I have two people emerging from the station at Docking Ring One, exit port R1B."

Andy echoed the image back to Mary Lu. They watched the terrorists. Just outside the exit hatch, the two terrorists stopped. It was clear that they each held something at their side. Andy zoomed in on them; the two terrorists were positioning themselves to face the inbound spacecraft.

Anchored securely to the station, the terrorists grabbed the objects at their sides with both hands and raised them up. They rested the objects on their shoulders and appeared to be sighting through them, pointing them toward the approaching spacecraft.

"We have to help them!" exclaimed Sam.

"How?" asked Mat. "Mary Lu? Can you do anything?"

"Like what?" she asked. "There's nothing I can do!"

The objects appeared to be surface-to-air missiles, except they weren't. They couldn't be. This was space.

Mary Lu was on the verge of shouting now. "Everyone, I want you to hook yourself to the station. On the right side of your suit is a standard clasping hook. Use it now. Attach yourself to the station. Andy, you too."

Quickly they did as they were told. Andy also secured himself as directed.

A moment passed. Sam and Mat had not breathed. Then two bright lights leaped from the exit hatch and streaked into space. One missile hit the craft, and a split second later, the second one struck.

The spacecraft exploded in a burst of light, and it was gone.

Mat and Sam still had not breathed.

"Oh my God," said Mary Lu.

Sam stared at the glowing red fragments on the horizon. The glowing red and white embers dimmed. And were gone.

Silence.

CHAPTER 36

"The two terrorists are back inside now," said Andy.

Several silent moments passed. The team waited.

"They are still inside the docking ring," said Mary Lu.

They waited.

"OK. They are in a docking shuttle heading back to the spaceport," said Mary Lu.

"Andy, get moving. We have to get to Air Force One," said Mat.

"OK."

The three of them once again began moving down the shaft toward the hub. All was quiet.

Andy led the team on a path that prevented anyone from seeing them through the spaceport windows. After reaching the hub, Andy pivoted the team without saying a word and moved toward the second docking ring where Air Force One was located.

After a while, Andy came to a stop at a hatchway, and Mat and Sam pulled up next to Andy.

"You made it. This is the entrance to Docking Ring Two," said Mary Lu.

Mary Lu moved some images around on her tablet and

sent one to each of them. A map popped up in their heads-up displays. "This is your location in the docking ring." A red light blinked, showing their location. "And this is Air Force One, about thirty degrees to your left." A flashing white dot popped up.

"OK," said Mat.

"There are two ships docked between you and Air Force One. Andy will lead you to this gate." Another light began blinking on their maps. "Andy will open the gate and you'll reenter the city. That's as close to Air Force One as we can get."

"Understood," said Sam.

Mary Lu touched Megan's arm. "Andy, get them inside." She smiled softly at Megan.

"OK," said Andy.

Andy inserted his index finger into the android keyhole and connected to the system.

Mat and Sam saw on the small control panel next to where Andy had inserted his finger an indicator light turn from red to yellow. A black outline of a solid blue rectangle appeared. Quickly the blue began to disappear. When the rectangle was completely empty, the yellow light turned green. The room had been depressurized.

Andy opened the hatch, and the three of them entered the airlock. Andy closed the hatch, it sealed, and he pressed a button on a panel next to the door.

Mat heard a soft *whoosh* as the room pressurized and filled up quickly with air.

* * *

Wadi was leaning back in his chair in the maintenance room, half in a daydream, when he was jerked awake by a small indicator light that had started flashing. The status of the open door and its location popped up onto his display.

"Yassin, someone has just entered the docking bay in Docking Ring Two," said Wadi.

Yassin, sitting in the spaceport diner, studied the monitor showing the docking bays and the spaceliners. There was nothing there. "What are you talking about? I don't see anything. No one has come through here. You can't get to the docking bays except through the spaceport." He paused. "Except through me."

"Yassin, someone has entered the docking bays from an exit hatch. He entered directly from space." He pressed some keys and brought up the information. "I have it here on my monitor. It's just a maintenance android doing a scheduled routine check of the docking bay facilities."

"Are you sure?"

"Yes, the android was scheduled at this time to be in the docking bays. We also know that the android used his finger pass to open the hatch, so it was definitely him. Sorry, Yassin, for the false alarm."

"You did the right thing. Keep me posted if anything else unusual or unexpected happens, but don't be frivolous."

"Yes, sir. I understand. Again, I apologize."

Yassin set the comm down.

"What was that about?" asked Shakira with her come-hither smile.

"It was nothing. A false alarm."

They each took a sip from their soda cans. Shakira set her

can down on the table and grabbed one of Yassin's fries with a daring look in her eye and then ate it. She grabbed her soda and drank again. Then she set the can on the table and studied Yassin. He was having none of her fun. "Then why the face?" she asked.

"What?"

"If it's nothing, then why the face?"

"It is nothing. Just an android." He rubbed his chin. Something inside him was unsettled. He picked up his comm and said, "Wadi. Come back."

"Wadi here. What can I do for you, Yassin?"

"What's on the second docking bay ring?" he asked.

Wadi pressed some keys and pulled up the screen he needed. "Ten spaceliners, including Air Force One."

"Air Force One is on the docking ring where the droid entered?"

"Yes. But he's on a standard maintenance routine. I have it right here in front of me."

"Thanks, Wadi. That's all." He set the comm back down and glanced around the room. There was an assortment of small groups of terrorists gathered about in twos and threes throughout the spaceport. He counted twenty small groups in all.

He spotted Akim standing with a clique on the back wall near a kitchen. He said, "Akim, come here."

He then spied Vicki on the other side of the room. Ah, Vicki, with her dark hair hanging down around her shoulders. A natural beauty. If it weren't for Shakira . . . "Vicki!" he yelled.

She swung around toward him, and he waved her over.

She bid her companions goodbye and came over to Yassin.

Yassin waited until both Akim and Vicki had arrived. "I want you two to go to the second docking bay ring and check it out. Also check out Air Force One."

Akim and Vicki quickly glanced at each other. "What's up?"

"Nothing really. An android has entered the docking bay ring from space. It's probably nothing, but go check it out anyway." He made a shallow frown, and they stood still with empty stares. "Go, now," he said.

"We are on our way," they said. And they took off for a shuttle.

As he picked up his can of soda, he saw Shakira smiling at him.

"I thought you said it was nothing," said Shakira, teasing him a little. "And you said it several times. I heard it myself."

"It is, but they have nothing better to do. Better to send them on an errand and keep them busy."

CHAPTER 37

McKenna pulled himself beside Andy, who was standing at the exit doorway leading into the station proper. He watched as the blue progress bar quickly filled up to the hundred percent mark. In less than twenty seconds, the room had fully pressurized.

"Let's go," said Mat as he grabbed the door handle.

But before he could turn the handle, Andy placed his synthetic hand on top of McKenna's hand, halting his progress.

Startled and surprised, the sheriff said to the android, "We need to become familiar with all aspects of the station we might have to encounter. We need to be able to do little things like opening an exit hatch for ourselves."

"OK," said Andy in a voice that was little above a whisper. "However, we don't know what's on the other side of the door. You can open it, but you should let me go through the door first, and then I can let you know if it's clear."

Sam and Mat gave each other startled glances.

"Thanks," said Mat, releasing the handle and stepping back. "That's a good idea."

Andy opened the door and stepped out. The docking bay ring was empty. Sam and Mat came out of the room, and Mat closed the door behind him. The ring was essentially a large hollow tube, forming an *O*. Inside the tube were two rail tracks for shuttle lines, plus one maintenance walkway. Both shuttle tracks went clockwise. Connected to this docking ring were sixteen docking ports that the spaceliners attached to.

Other than the shuttles, only maintenance personnel actually used the docking rings. In an emergency, it would be possible for people to use the maintenance walkway to pull themselves along the ring and down the hub to the spaceport. It would, however, be a very long walk.

Mary Lu spoke. "Remember: Air Force One is to your left. There are two spaceliners docked between you and Air Force One."

"Roger that," said Sam.

They set off to the left, pulling themselves with the handrails just like they had in space. There was very little gravity. They passed the first spaceliner to their left. On their trip in, they had traveled in a shuttle, and neither Sam nor Mat had paid much attention to the details of what was going on; they just wanted to get to the spaceport. Now Sam and Mat fully recognized the benefits of the bay's design. Like how the shuttle pulled right up to the entrance of the spacecraft, relieving passengers of the need to travel manually in a near-zero-gravity environment. They appreciated the details that had gone into the designing and building of a major city in space.

Sam was looking out the large windows at the ships in

dock. They were all the same. Because there were only two competing aircraft manufacturers, there were only two basic designs for spaceliners. "Andy, what's that vehicle over there?"

"Those are other passenger spaceliners. Every docking bay ring can support six vehicles."

"No, not those—that small, stubby, boxy one over there. What is that vehicle?" said Sam.

"That's a tug."

"What's it for?" asked Mat.

"Every spaceliner has standardized attach points. The tugs can attach to them and fly them into the docking bays if needed. If a spaceliner or any large vehicle were damaged in flight and needed to go to the repair bay, it wouldn't be allowed to fly directly to the repair bay, so a tug would go intercept the liner and bring it safely into the docking bay. The tugs have the power to fly all the vehicles. They aren't fast, but they can smoothly and safely fly all the vehicles wherever they need to go."

Mary Lu joined the conversation. "The tugs are also used to fly space probes to a safe distance away from the city to launch. No one is allowed to launch a probe here at the city or anywhere near it. The repair shack, or the garage, also serves as an assembly plant for space probes. Actually, that's what the garage does ninety percent of the time. It's mostly used to assemble space probes. Remember, this is the home of NASA's space launch operations."

Mat asked, "Can you fly a tug, Andy?"

"Sure. They are easy to maneuver. I've done so many times. It's part of my training." Andy came to an abrupt stop. "We have company," he said simply.

"What's that, Andy?" asked Mary Lu.

"A shuttle is on its way here. It's moving toward us down the transportation tube along the docking bay shaft."

Damn, thought Mat. The tubes were clear in order to give the passengers the thrill of looking into space as the shuttle moved from the ring to the spaceport. "There is nowhere to go. We are completely exposed. Any suggestions, Mary Lu?"

"Go back. Go back to the spaceliner you just passed. Maybe you can hide in there," said Mary Lu.

Sam had swung around and was already heading back. "Mat, come on. We have no choice."

"All right, we'll try hiding," said Mat.

Andy arrived at the spaceliner entrance first.

"Now we're stuck in these suits. Remind me to take this off right away next time," said Mat.

"Next time? What next time? We shouldn't have to do this again," said Sam.

When Mat and Sam arrived next to Andy, he was already opening the first door. Two doors separated them from getting into the spaceliner: the first door was the station's docking bay door, the second was the door of the spaceliner.

Mat looked back at the shuttle. "It's almost here."

The shuttle stopped at the exit chamber not very far from them, and the terrorists emerged from the shuttle one at a time. Mat watched as they stood in front of the shuttle. "They don't seem to be in a hurry." He stayed as close to the door as possible, trying to remain hidden. "Two terrorists are headed toward us," said Mat. "I don't think they see us yet."

Andy opened the spaceliner door. Sam quickly entered the liner. But as Mat moved to follow her, the two terrorists started to run toward them.

"I think they just spotted us," Mat said as he followed Sam inside the spaceliner.

"Let me see what I can do," said Andy. He moved casually into the doorway, making himself visible. "Maybe they will think that they saw me and not you." He placed his finger into the maintenance slot and initiated a standard diagnostic check on the door.

The two terrorists were almost on him. Shortly, Akim and Vicki stood in front of Andy. Akim studied the open door of the spaceliner, then Andy. "You. What are you doing?" he demanded.

"I'm a maintenance android."

"Who came in here with you?" he asked. "I'm sure I saw someone else with you."

"Why would anyone else be with me?" asked Andy. "My job is routine and requires no special engineering skill that I do not possess. My neural network has been completely trained for the task that I have been assigned, and the entire purpose of my presence here is to eliminate the need of human intervention, and also—"

"Enough!" shouted Akim at the android standing in front of him.

Great answer, thought Mary Lu. She found herself almost laughing. Andy never ceased to surprise her.

"Stay here with this droid. I'm going inside," said Akim.

"I'll keep the droid company until you return." Vicki pointed her weapon at the droid.

Andy might have been the first android in history to yawn. "Sorry to interrupt, but are you threatening me?" he asked politely.

Andy was a military-grade android. His outer surface, his skin, was designed to absorb the impact of small particles of space debris. He did have a few spots that were vulnerable, but unless she knew exactly what spots to shoot at, she had little chance of harming him.

"Damn right."

"How interesting. I've never been threatened before."

Vicki stood silent for a second, gazing at this droid in front of her. "It won't be so interesting if I shoot you."

Andy decided it was best to just remain silent.

Mary Lu listened to the conversation through the comm connection with Andy. She was amazed. She could practically hear Andy thinking and feeling. Andy was *growing*. The engineer in Mary Lu was excited. This was why she'd accepted the job here. Then she felt ashamed that she was thinking about engineering at a time like this, when everyone's lives were at stake. If only it didn't involve these circumstances.

She thought of Mat. And that thought surprised her. The thought that she might hear him die wreaked havoc on her emotions. Her emotions toyed with her until she was almost crying, but she didn't. Now she was angry with herself. She needed to focus; they were going to need her.

* * *

Sam was racing, pulling herself as quickly as she could into the rear of the spaceliner. She was hoping to find a great place to hide. Mat scrambled down the alley far behind. The configuration of the docking ports was such that the liners rotated with the docking ring, creating a low level of artificial gravity. Just enough to help orient the passengers, making it easier for them to board and depart. To move fast, Sam had to pull herself along and forget any concept of walking. It was, for all intents and purposes, the same as being outside.

"Stop!" commanded Akim.

Mat stopped and slowly turned around. He was five rows of seats ahead of Akim. He hadn't made it very far. *Darn.* With the space suit on, he could not fire his weapon; the gloves were just too big to fit into the trigger. He hadn't thought this through enough. He should have gotten out of his space suit immediately after entering the station. If he had, he wouldn't be in this helpless situation.

He spoke to Sam calmly. "Stay hidden. No matter what happens, complete the mission. Take care of my niece."

"Shut up, I'm thinking," she replied.

He too was thinking. But all his thoughts led to the same result. He was captured, probably a dead man waiting to be tortured.

He decided at that moment, when his eyes met Akim's, that he would die fighting. There would be no capture. There would be no torture. The question now was when. He had to optimize whatever minuscule chance he had.

"Come here," said Akim.

The First Lady continued to move to the rear. She was hidden deep beyond the curtain that separated first class from everyone else. She was in the tail section when her feet bumped into each other and sent her tumbling in slow motion. She floated sideways, twisting slowly into a row of seats, making a soft thud.

"What was that? I think I heard something," said Vicki.

"Whoever is back there, come out now or I will kill this one in front of me," yelled Akim. Of course, Akim would not kill him now. Just shoot him in the leg. He'd kill him later.

Andy slowly slipped inside the spaceliner to see for himself what was happening. He stood in the front aisle near the exit. Akim was one aisle away. Mat was near the first-class curtain.

"Don't, Sam. I'm working on a plan," Mat lied, hoping it would stop her from coming out.

"You had your chance!" Akim yelled.

Andy eased forward toward Akim.

Vicki grabbed the docking bay's handrail just outside the cabin doorway. She leaned inward into the cabin so she could watch Akim and see what was going on.

Sam moved to the wall of the spaceliner. There was an empty spot along one of the rows where some of the seats were missing, and she used the space to hide. And to think. Her brain began to hurt. It felt like her head was at the bottom of the ocean. She felt pressure from every direction.

Mat said, "I'm coming." He moved forward toward the terrorist, hoping to reduce the distance between them.

Akim raised his weapon to fire, aiming at Mat's knees. This was going to hurt. The infidel was going to wish he were dead. Aiming the weapon, he pulled the trigger. Nothing.

The trigger had jammed. "What?" he said out loud.

Andy had, smoothly and gracefully, like an Olympic gymnast, slipped his right index finger between the trigger and the gun, preventing it from being pulled and fired.

Sam was out of ideas. Her mind was blank. Nothing. She pulled herself up. She would turn herself in.

Realizing what had happened, Akim shoved Andy away from him and pulled his weapon free. "You son of a bitch!"

Sam pressed the speaker button. "I'm coming!" screamed the First Lady. "Don't shoot!"

She stood facing the wall. She started to turn toward the aisle to leave but stopped suddenly, focused on the cabin wall next to her. Now she knew why the seats were missing.

She gathered herself up. "Mat and Andy, on the count of three, I need you to grab something solid."

"What?"

"Just do it," said Sam.

Sam grabbed the hook at the side of her suit and clipped it onto the metal frame of the chair in front of her. She pulled on it to make sure it was secure. She popped the panel next to the door, exposing the emergency release lever.

The terrorist shouted down the alley, "You have ten seconds to come out, or I will shoot." His voice sounded like sandpaper. His eyes became narrow and his face had become red.

"One." Sam reached for a lever under the window in the emergency panel and lifted up the second safety lock. The only thing holding the door in place was the pressure in the cabin. Designed into the door was a lever that would pry the door open.

She grabbed this lever. "Two."

Mat had no idea what was about to happen, but he grabbed the frame of the seat beside him. He watched as Andy did the same.

"Three!" said Sam. She pulled the lever. Not knowing exactly what to expect herself, she pulled it with all her might, and the emergency system shoved the door inward from the pressure inside the cabin.

In that instant, a decompressive explosion occurred in the spaceliner as air rushed out of the cabin. The emergency door was the first thing blown out of the cabin. Sam managed to grab the metal frame of the chair that she was clipped onto with her safety hook. She held fast with both hands.

Akim was blasted off his feet. He flew down the cabin aisle and out the emergency exit. Sam saw the shock on his face as he flew by her. She would never forget the horror expressed in his eyes.

Andy and Mat held firmly to the chair frames. They were lifted horizontally off the ground, their feet dangling toward the rear of the cabin. Vicki was lifted horizontally off the ground too, her head and chest in the docking bay, her lower torso and legs floating inside the spaceliner.

In less than a second, the sensors in the docking bay emergency door detected the emergency change in pressure. The docking bay AI unit acted to defend and protect the docking bay facilities from decompression. In another second, their AI units had amassed the required energy and sent an emergency command to their doors. With explosive power and force, the docking bay's door at the entrance of the spaceliner closed. Then it sealed.

The door sent an emergency status update to the maintenance center and the environmental control center simultaneously, informing them of the decompression event and the actions it had taken. Then the door sliced through Vicki just above her hips. Her chest and upper body floated inside the docking bay. The lower half of her body fell into the spaceliner.

* * *

In the environmental control center, emergency buzzers were going off and status lights on monitors were flashing crimson red. "We have an emergency hull breach at the transportation docking hub," said Omar.

"Where?" asked Wadi.

Omar studied his monitor. "Docking Ring Two, Docking Bay Door C."

"I'll be sure to notify Yassin," said Wadi. "No sense in both of us calling him."

"Agreed. Thanks."

CHAPTER 38

"Sam! Where are you? Are you OK?" asked Mat.

"I'm fine!" she yelled.

"What did you do?"

"I opened the emergency exit in the back."

"Well, it worked." Mat picked himself off the seats he was stretched across.

Mary Lu asked, "Sam, can you close the door?"

"No, the door is gone."

"You guys will have to reenter through the exit hatch again. Better get going."

"Why?"

"The station won't permit the door at the docking bay to open. The spaceliner is open to space. It won't hold air, so the door won't open. You have no choice; you will have to reenter. Now you'd better get going if you want to get to Air Force One."

Sam floated up toward first class. In a moment she had reached Mat and Andy. She stared at the lower half of Vicki. Undulating deep red spheres of Vicki's blood and bodily fluids, some large, some small like water droplets, floated about the cabin.

"Let's go," she said.

Sam, Mat, and Andy traveled to the back of the spaceliner, all the way to the blown exit hatch. Andy went out first, followed by Sam, then Mat.

Andy jumped the short distance to the docking ring with ease. He said to the two humans, "You will have to jump. There are no walkways to the ring from outside the spaceliner."

Megan and Mary Lu held each other's hands and watched through Andy's camera feed as Sam placed her feet carefully against the doorframe and pushed off gently for the docking ring. She was floating in space with no tether. Slowly she floated toward the docking ring. She arrived next to Andy. Andy reached out and grabbed her and pulled her onto the docking ring structure, holding her tightly until she was secured.

"One down, one to go," said Mary Lu.

Mat watched, and when it was his turn, he mimicked exactly what Sam had done. He carefully anchored his feet against the side of the emergency exit hatch, then gently pushed off toward Andy. Andy grabbed him and pulled him onto the docking ring.

"We made it," said Mat.

"Thank God. Now get going," said Mary Lu.

"Follow me," said Andy.

"Roger that," replied Sam.

They were off to the exit hatch as fast as they could go. They had to get back inside the docking ring and then down to Air Force One.

"Here we go again," said Sam.

"Back to the exit chamber and to Air Force One all over again," said Mat.

* * *

They reached the exit hatch, and Andy opened the door after the room was depressurized. Then Andy began to pressurize the room.

As soon as the room was pressurized, Mat stood up. "How do I get out of this suit?"

"It's easy," said Mary Lu.

She quickly walked Mat and Sam through the process of taking off the suits. The suits were designed so that workers could remove them quickly. Soon Sam and Mat stood side by side in only their jumpsuits.

"We'll leave these on," said Mat. They had no choice since underneath the jumpsuits they wore only their briefs.

Mat and Sam hung the suits up into the racks located along one wall of the exit chamber for that very purpose. The comm devices they kept on. They planned on wearing those until they got back home to Earth. Everyone would be able to communicate with each other no matter where they were. They would be talking in private.

CHAPTER 39

Shakira's eyes grew as large as a full moon in the desert. She stood up involuntarily, pointing at the monitor window showing a view of the docking bay, and said, "What in the world is that?"

Yassin looked to where she was pointing. In slow motion, he stood and leaned toward the monitor showing the docking bay. He then gazed up at the window overhead, his mouth open. "What in the hell?" he said slowly with a voice full of breath.

On the second docking bay ring, in the rear of a spaceliner, there was an explosion. The area was suddenly filled with debris. It was like a garbage truck had exploded out there.

Yassin picked up his comm. "Akim! Are you there?"

Static.

"Akim, come in. This is Yassin. Report in."

Static.

Yassin and Shakira looked at each other, their faces open and blank.

"Vicki! Are you there? Come in."

Nothing. He stared out the window.

"Yassin, come in," said Wadi.

Yassin spoke quickly. "Yes, Akim, what happened?"

"It's not Akim. It's me, Wadi. I'm in the control center."

"Wadi, we just saw some kind of explosion in the docking bay."

"I know. That's why I am calling you. There was a decompression event in one of the spaceliners at Docking Ring Two. Fortunately, the system worked perfectly and sealed the docking bay off."

"What caused it?" asked Yassin.

"We don't know. But the docking door has informed us that the event originated inside the spaceliner."

"I thought the doors were supposed to be closed."

"They are. Apparently, both the spaceliner door *and* the docking bay door were open. As it would be for boarding or departing a liner."

"So someone went inside the spaceliner? It's not Air Force One, right?"

"Correct, Yassin. This has nothing to do with Air Force One. I have no idea what to tell you, except that someone must have gone inside the spaceliner and caused the event accidentally. Whoever it was didn't know what they were doing."

"Why do you say that?" asked Yassin.

"Because whoever caused the decompression is no longer in the spaceliner. They are now in space."

"Right. Thanks, Wadi. Keep me posted. Bye."

Shakira sat quietly looking at Yassin. He set his comm down and returned her look. Their facial expressions mirrored each other's perfectly.

"It seems like a big coincidence that I send two people down to the docking bays and this happens. I bet Akim and Vicki went inside the spaceliner."

"You think they were playing around in there, don't you?"

"Yes." He stroked his chin. "OK, maybe . . ." He stopped rubbing his chin and took a drink of soda. "I don't know."

"I see," she said.

"I think it's possible. I think they might have gone inside the spaceliner to play around and caused this. Or . . ."

"Maybe they found someone in the spaceliner." She took a small drink from her soda.

"Yes, it's possible. But why would they find someone? This is just an ordinary spacecraft. It would be one thing if it were Air Force One. But just a regular liner?"

"I see your point."

He glanced around the room. "Anyway, there is only one way to know." He paused. "And I want to know."

He called out to Shali, who was sitting with a group at a corner table, and waved his arm for her to come over. Then he waved over Omar and Faheed from across the room.

When they'd all arrived at his table, he said, "Faheed, I want you to lead this team." He motioned to them. "I want the three of you to go down to the docking bay, Ring Two, and tell me what the hell is going on. Faheed, call me when you know something."

"Yes, sir," said Faheed. He turned and left with Omar and Shali.

CHAPTER 40

Andy arrived at Air Force One first, this time moving quickly enough to leave Mat and Sam far behind. He inserted his finger into the gate lock and opened the docking bay door. He then proceeded to the Air Force One door, which also needed to be opened. Mat and Sam arrived just as Andy had opened the door to Air Force One. Perfect timing.

"Do you know where the sat phone is?" asked Mat.

"Yes," said Sam. "I think so."

"Let's do it and get out of here," said Mat.

"Roger that." She moved past Andy and Mat and entered Air Force One.

Any aircraft or spacecraft with the president of the United States on board received the designation of Air Force One. This spaceliner was "borrowed" for this one trip, and a few slight, temporary modifications had been made to the spaceliner to accommodate the president and his staff. A small area in first class was designated the Presidential Suite, and the passenger area was assigned to the press corps. And, for visual impact, the spaceliner received the presidential coloring of Air Force One. It was only one flight, but the

White House chief of staff and the senior political advisor wanted Air Force One colors in the image of the ship since it would be filmed as it approached Liberty.

Sam moved as fast as she could. There were several places they could have placed the emergency sat phone. She arrived at the first place she thought it might be hidden: the presidential area. She turned to her side to say something to Mat, only he wasn't there. She scanned the cabin area behind her and didn't see him. She poked her head out through the curtain into the press section. He was nowhere to be found.

"Mat, where are you? What are you doing? I don't see you anywhere."

"I'm in the cockpit. I'm going to try to contact Washington and let them know we're still breathing."

Mat McKenna pulled himself into the pilot's seat in the cockpit and placed the pilot's headset over his head. He now wore two headsets: the small one from his space suit and the larger, padded one from the pilot.

"Hello, Air Force One," he said. He waited.

"Do you mean me? Are you talking to me, sir?" came a voice over his headset. The voice was female, professional, and somehow reassuring.

"I believe so. Are you Air Force One?" he asked.

"Yes, I am. I'm sorry, I don't recognize you. Are you authorized to be inside the flight deck, speaking to Air Force One?" she asked.

"We have an emergency. I need you to contact Washington on a military-secured line. Right now."

"May I ask who you are?" asked the AI of Air Force One.

"No you may not. Make the call now. National security

is at stake. You are not to record any of this conversation. Understood?"

"Yes."

"Then make the call," he repeated.

"Do you have the security code?"

"Grasshopper."

"Thank you."

The cockpit's AI had been programmed by the Secret Service with a few standard preset protocols. Soon the call was being sent to CIA headquarters, Washington, DC.

Thank you, Mary Lu, you nailed it, he thought. She had briefed him on what she thought he could expect, and she'd been absolutely right so far.

Sam worked her way into the spacecraft. She knew the equipment was here, she just didn't know for sure where. She had a list in her mind of all the storage areas; it had to be in one of them. The Secret Service had set several false panels into the spacecraft. One by one, she ran her checklist. On the fifth one, she hit pay dirt.

"I got it!" she said.

"Great," said Mary Lu. She flashed a smile at Megan and gave a thumbs-up sign. "Now get out of there."

Sam carefully went through the bag, confirming each item. Then she double-checked it. Then she triple-checked it all over again. Her adrenaline was running high. She felt a surge of energy and relief coursing through her. They had what they came for, and it was already packaged into a nice, neat little bundle inside a shoulder pack. They didn't even have to pack it.

She scrambled toward the cockpit to grab Mat and get the heck out of there.

CHAPTER 41

Washington, DC
White House
Situation Room

With the decapitation threat now dissipating, Acting President Sandy Ross wanted the meetings moved from the PEOC to the White House Situation Room, so they were. The room was gloomy, dark. They were diligently reviewing all that they knew.

Amy Henderson was displaying pictures from the failed X303 mission. "That's the debris field from the X303. The remains of the men cannot be recovered. NORAD tracks everything in orbit, every piece of space junk, and they have informed us that the three men have been identified and are free-falling back to Earth. They will burn up completely on reentry. Cremation, I suppose."

Acting President Ross examined the photos. "These photos are classified. Top secret. I don't want any of these pictures, especially of the men, making it into the press. Everyone clear about that?"

Everyone said yes. Acting President Ross continued to stare at the images of the men. "I feel like that's us."

"Pardon?" said Amy.

Acting President Ross looked up from the pictures displayed on the monitors around the room, then looked at the people around her at the conference table. Pointing to the pictures of the men falling back to Earth, she said, "I feel like that's us. It feels like the whole country is in a free fall."

Amy saw Deanna Hatch, one of her staffers who worked a comm center in the Situation Room, raise a finger to her. She walked over to see what was up. Deanna passed her the comm, and she put it on her head. After a second, she pulled it off and gave it back to Deanna.

"Listen up, everyone," Amy said in a strong voice for everyone in the room to hear. It was unusual for Amy to speak in such a loud, full voice. "We have Air Force One on the comm. Everyone now knows as much about this as I do."

Deanna moved the call to the comm device at the center of the table.

Amy sat down in her chair at the table. "This is Amy Henderson, NSA. Are you there?"

"Hi, Amy. This is Sheriff Mathew McKenna of Shady Oaks, Florida. I'm calling from Air Force One here at Liberty."

Everyone around the table looked at each other. *Air Force One?*

"What?" said the acting president.

* * *

Mary Lu broke in abruptly. "Bad news, you have company coming. I'm looking at a camera feed of the spaceport. A shuttle just departed and is headed your way."

Mat pulled off the pilot's headset. "How long do we have?"

"Hard to say. Not long. Longer if they depart the shuttle at the spaceliner that was decompressed, shorter if they come directly to Air Force One. Get out right now or you will be trapped."

"Understood." He was about to put the headset back on and stopped. *Time for plan B.* "Andy, go to the exit chamber now. Don't let anyone see you."

"OK," said Andy. He took off like a monkey, using his arms and legs in equal measure to pull himself down the hallway to the exit chamber.

* * *

"Hello, are you there?" asked Amy.

Silence, mixed with muffled voices.

"This is Amy Henderson, NSA. Are you there?"

Silence.

"Come again? Are you there?" asked Amy.

More silence.

* * *

Mat placed the pilot's headset back on. "Sorry for the interruption," said Mat.

"Who is this? Can you repeat that?" said Amy.

"This is Sheriff McKenna from Shady Oaks, Florida, calling from Air Force One. Sorry, I have to go. We have visitors coming. The First Lady is here with me. The president and his family survived the assault, as well as Agent Cass. As far as I know, he and Cass have not been captured.

The terrorists number about one hundred. They have semiautomatic weapons, and they are well trained."

Mary Lu's voice broke in. "Mat, you have to go. They are headed your way."

"Roger that," he said.

He continued with Washington. "They have the control center complex and the spaceport. The terrorists have implemented an emergency protocol that has divided the city into three sectors."

Sam leaned into the cockpit and yelled, "Mat. We have to go now. Now, Mat—*now*!"

Mat could feel the urgency of her voice. For a moment he thought that maybe she would grab him and drag him out of the chair.

Mat said, "We'll call later over the Secret Service emergency sat phone. Bye." He got up from the pilot's chair. "Cockpit, terminate call. I was never here."

"Understood," said the AI voice of Air Force One over the cockpit speakers. The call was terminated.

He ripped off the pilot's headset and moved as fast as he could with Sam.

* * *

The Situation Room suddenly had a pulse. A new energy rippled and permeated through it. The Situation Room had been a hopeless, dark place of ugly, forbidden, unspoken thoughts. Now suddenly everything seemed to have changed. Sure, not much had changed—just a phone call— but at least it was something. And something trumps nothing, no matter how small.

CHAPTER 42

"Andy, where are you?" asked Mat.

"I'm in the exit chamber."

"Andy, we're trapped in Air Force One. We can't escape the docking bay. The terrorists have us cornered in Docking Ring Two, they just don't know it yet. There is no way out for Sam and me. But I have a plan. We are going to need your help."

"I'll be glad to help if I can," answered Andy. "What do you want me to do?"

"You know that tug we asked you about?"

"Yes."

"I need you to get to that tug ASAP."

"I'm on my way," said Andy. He pressed a button on the control panel next to the exit hatch, and the room began to depressurize.

"Andy, report in to us when you get to the tug."

"OK."

"Andy?" said Mat.

"Yes?"

"Hurry."

"Understood."

Sam and Mat could hear voices approaching down the hallway of Docking Ring Two.

"Mat. They are almost here," said Sam.

"Follow me." Mat left the cockpit and headed to the curtain separating the presidential area from the press seats. He and Sam passed through the curtains and stepped into the press area. Mat reached back and grabbed the curtains to stop them from moving. He and Sam then went deep into the back seating, all the way to the last row of seats at the tail of Air Force One.

Mat reached down to the floor, flipped up a handle, and raised a panel in the floorboards. "This is a maintenance galley running along the belly of the spacecraft."

Sam examined the narrow crawl space below the floorboards. She leaned back up. "All right."

"There is also a panel door at the start of the galley just behind the cockpit, very close to the exit," said Mat.

From the front of Air Force One came rubbing sounds, like someone grappling with handrails. The curtains separating the presidential area from everyone else began to flutter as if from a breeze or someone softly bumping against them. Then came the sound of voices.

Mat held the floor panel door open as Sam quickly floated down into the crawl space headfirst like a ferret chasing a rabbit. Mat followed right on top of her and closed the floor door behind him. Her legs were underneath him.

"Sam, quietly move to the front. Go all the way forward, right up to the cockpit, and stop at the exit floor door."

"OK." Sam extracted herself from Mat, then pulled herself forward toward the front. With each pull, she was careful not to make any sounds. After a moment, she said, "I think they know we're here; they just don't know where. We will have to force our way out. We can't simply hide."

Sam and Mat propelled themselves forward one arm stroke at a time. They had to be quiet. They could hear the terrorists moving directly above them.

* * *

Over the comm, Megan listened carefully to the developing events. She felt like she was swimming underwater, holding her breath with the pressure of the water all around her, her lungs aching to breathe. This was one of the hardest things she had ever experienced. A torrent of memories and emotions flowed through her soul. It reminded her of when her parents . . .

She felt tears welling up inside her. She couldn't lose Uncle Mat.

* * *

"Yassin, this is Wadi in the control center."

"Yes, Wadi, what is it?"

"You know that android that entered the docking bay's second ring a while back?"

"Yes, I remember? What about it?"

"That same android just exited again a few moments ago."

"You sure?"

"Yes, Yassin, I'm sure. And he used the same exit."

"Thanks, Wadi. Over." He slowly set the comm down on the table in front of him with a blank stare.

What is going on? We can't stop one stupid maintenance droid?

"What's wrong?" asked Shakira. She watched Yassin carefully. She knew his every tic, every subtle move, and every nuance. Something was wrong. Whatever it was, it was really getting to him. She had never seen him like this. Uncertain, almost lost.

* * *

Faheed, Shali, and Omar all faced each other and shrugged. The intruders had to be here somewhere, but where? There was no way out.

Shali stood by the exit, and Faheed motioned for her to check the cockpit. Then he said to Omar, "I know someone is here. I can feel it." They scanned completely around, first left, then right. Nothing. "Omar, stay by the exit while we search."

"Yes, Faheed." He bowed his head once and went to the door where he took his position.

Mat heard Andy's voice break over their comm while Omar was talking. "I made it. I'm at the tug," said Andy.

Mat quietly whispered, his voice like a soft breeze. "Andy, I want you to attach the tug to Air Force One."

"OK." Andy inserted his finger into the android lock and initiated the engine start sequence.

Sam and Mat continued to swim forward. Stroke after stroke, they floated forward, careful not to allow their feet and legs to bump into anything. Everything depended on them getting into position without anyone knowing where they were. They continued pulling themselves along as the terrorists talked above them. The weightlessness helped them move quietly. They were getting quite good at this.

Shali removed her knife and stepped forward like a leopard. Her movements were fluid, sure, her muscles bristling with the anticipation of pouncing. Slowly she stalked toward the cockpit, expecting to strike out at her prey at any moment. She looked at the knife, the whiteness of her knuckles. She could feel the blood surge through her veins with each heartbeat. She concentrated on controlling her breathing. She opened the cockpit door and slipped inside.

Nothing. There was nothing there. Two empty seats, one for the pilot and another for the copilot. There was nothing else in the cockpit, no places to hide.

This was a spaceliner, not an airliner. Space and weight were at a premium, and the engineers who'd designed the spaceliners didn't waste either. There were no frivolous luxuries. Just enough room for a pilot and copilot. Only what they needed for the job, nothing more, nothing less.

Andy brought the engines online, disengaged from the dock, and throttled the engines up. The tug slowly pulled away from its docking berth. As the tug established a safe distance, Andy pivoted her around and headed into a standard coupling approach with Air Force One.

Sam and Mat arrived at the front of the spaceliner, and Sam stopped when the hatch was directly above her. She bent her knees and pulled her legs forward, making more room for Mat to get closer to the door.

Mat and Sam positioned themselves to bolt forward, their knees bent underneath them. Sam pulled her knife from her side. She showed the knife to Mat. He needed to do the same.

He got the message. He reached back and withdrew his knife from its sheath.

"You take the back. I'll take the front," whispered Mat.

"You got it," she said.

* * *

"Shali! This is Yassin. Report."

Shali clicked on her comm. "Somebody is here in Air Force One. We are looking for them. Let me call you back in a few minutes, OK?" she said.

"No. Not OK!" yelled Yassin.

Shali, Faheed, and Omar were all taken aback by the harsh tone in Yassin's voice.

Yassin said, "Look outside toward the spaceport. Someone is flying a small ship. Look!"

Shali darted to the side of the spaceliner opposite the exit door and leaned over a window seat to look out. She couldn't believe what she was seeing. "Look!" she yelled, pointing out the window toward the spaceport.

In the back, Faheed jumped to the side of the craft. With his hands on the tops of two seats, he leaned over and looked out like Shali. Omar joined Shali and leaned beside her to look out the window.

"What the hell?" said Faheed.

"What is he doing?" asked Omar.

They watched as the tug banked and moved toward them. "We were just over there. There was no one there," said Faheed.

"Go," said Mat.

Sam exploded through the floor hatch. The hatch door

flipped all the way over on its hinge and slammed to the carpeted floor. Sam was up and out. She drove toward Faheed like a linebacker charging a quarterback, and Faheed moved toward her.

Sheriff McKenna broke into the cabin and steadied himself quickly in the zero-g environment.

The First Lady opened the curtain and threw her knife at Faheed in a smooth motion. It flew cleanly through the cabin, rotating three hundred and sixty degrees. He tried to move, but in the zero-g environment moving from one place to another was slow, like he was moving underwater. The blade sank into the flesh of his left shoulder. Sam witnessed the grimace on his face from the pain.

Mat took a step forward as if charging at the two terrorists. "Get out, Sam."

Sam pulled herself around and moved to the exit door right behind him. At the door, she stopped and yelled, "I'm out."

She lied. It was a small lie. She wasn't about to just leave Mat alone.

Mat charged them with his knife raised in front of him.

Sam's mouth went dry, the corners of her mouth angled down in anger. "Mat, no!" she yelled. Mat would lose against the two terrorists in a knife fight. It was suicide.

The two terrorists braced for Mat; they too had knives, and their knives were ready. Only he wasn't bull-rushing them. Instead he raised both legs into the air in a crouching position, and when his feet made contact with the end of the seat row, he pushed off toward the exit door behind him. As he flew backward in the air, he threw his knife at the two terrorists. It hit the side wall, missing both of them. But it didn't matter. They flinched, shielding themselves.

That's all he needed.

At the exit door, he crashed into Sam. With his right hand, he managed to grab one of the passenger guide rails. His body swung around his handhold and slammed into the side of the docking bay ring wall just outside the exit door. Sam was knocked backward all the way out and into the hallway.

He regained his composure and reached inside Air Force One. He grabbed the door, yanking it closed as Shali and Omar arrived at the exit. But they were too slow, their movements sluggish and awkward in the zero-g environment. Advantage Mat and Sam. They were getting used to working in a no-gravity world.

Sam picked herself up and tried to close the docking bay's door. It wouldn't let her. Sam was not authorized to close the docking door.

"What was that?" screamed Omar. The spaceliner rocked, and Omar, Shali, and Faheed grabbed the nearest seats to keep their balance. The ship groaned.

Faheed glanced around the cabin.

Shali yelled, "It's that small ship! It rammed us!"

Faheed said, "No, I think it's docking with us."

There was the sound of metal on metal, and an electric humming could be heard echoing through the cabin. Faheed, Omar, and Shali huddled together, holding on to the back of the aisle seats at the exit door.

They glanced around nervously when they heard a loud *click*. Not only did they hear the click, they felt it.

It had come from below them.

CHAPTER 43

"Andy, we're out," said Mat. His voice was breathy with relief.

"OK." Andy sent a signal to Air Force One, and the ship responded by closing, locking, and sealing all hatches and entryways. Andy sent another command to the docking bay. The docking bay door started closing.

Yassin from the spaceport spoke into his comm. "Shali, Omar, and Faheed—get out now! You need to get out now!"

Shali yelled into her comm, "The door won't open. We can't open the door!" She heard a sound outside and looked out the window. The docking bay door was closing. "Omar! Quick, open the door!" she yelled.

He pulled the lever down, but nothing happened. Omar yelled back, "I'm trying! It won't obey my commands."

The lever that controlled the door wasn't mechanically in control of the door. When you pulled down on it, you were making a request to a computer to shut the door. Everything was by wire. Computers and AI systems controlled everything, and Air Force One's AI was ignoring the lever.

With the tug coupled to the spaceliner, it now had control of the spacecraft's systems. Air Force One's AI took

its orders from the tug, and the tug took its orders from
Andy. Air Force One had been ordered to close and seal.
Dutifully it had obeyed the order.

Yassin said, "Shali, you have to get out. Do whatever you
have to, but get out."

Shali said, "Step back." She raised her weapon to the
control panel as she and Omar backed away from the panel.
She raised her arm high, and with the butt of her weapon,
she smashed the control panel again and again until the silver
panel was completely obliterated, a jumble of shattered
nanochips hanging by the side of the door.

Still, the door remained shut and locked.

Air Force One sent the tug a status message, and in the
display panel that showed the status of the tug's coupled
partner, a status light went from red to green. The
spaceliner's door was closed and sealed.

Another light flipped colors from red to green. The
docking bay door was now closed, sealed, and locked as he
had requested.

Andy spoke to Sam and Mat. "I'll see you two in a few
minutes. Bye." He pulled back on the throttle, and the tug's
powerful thrusters kicked in. Slowly, with smooth, even
power, Air Force One and the tug pulled away from the
docking bay. The tug kept a steady, reliable, and dependable
thrust. After a moment, Andy piloted a slow pivot toward
Earth as Mat had requested.

* * *

Yassin could see what was happening. "Are there any space
suits on board?"

Shali and Omar exchanged glances, then quickly scanned the area around them. They scrambled around the ship as fast as they could in the zero-g environment.

"No, Yassin. There are no space suits on board."

Omar, Shali, and Faheed felt the ship lurch. They rushed to look out the windows. Then Air Force One was free and moving slowly away from the dock. They watched as the dock grew farther away.

"The cockpit!" exclaimed Omar as he swam toward the cockpit just a few feet away. Shali followed him, not knowing what else to do.

Andy maintained steady throttle on the large passenger liner. Having completed his turn, he increased the thrust and set the two vehicles into a rolling embrace as Mat had directed him.

"Andy, get out now. That's good," said Mary Lu.

The android popped the small hatch on the tug, then reached above him and pulled himself directly up and out. He faced toward the station, fired his small jet pack, and gently flew toward Liberty. Shortly he was at the Docking Ring Two exit hatch and on his way back inside.

CHAPTER 44

The First Lady, Sheriff Mat McKenna, and the android
Andy silently followed the structural beams from the
transportation docking hubs back to the city's rim. They had
to be careful; they didn't want to be caught on camera.
Occasionally they had to wait while Andy directed some of
the cameras to look in another direction, giving them time
to pass.

* * *

Yassin slammed his fist on the lunch table. The fries on his plate
and Shakira's plate jumped into the air and scattered across the
table as if trying to flee from Yassin. Anger burned through his
veins. "What in the hell just happened? Who were they? And
where did they go? Where *are* they? Search every ship in the
docking bays. They must be hiding in there somewhere."

"Yes, Yassin. We will find them. And they will pay for
this," exclaimed Hakim, pointing his finger in anger.

Yassin cautioned all the others there in the spaceport with
him. "Not a word to anyone about this. Let me talk to Aaziz
first." He glanced around the room, making eye contact with
each one there.

"Hakim," he said, placing a hand on one man's shoulder, "you're in charge here. I'm going to the control center to tell Aaziz."

"I am honored that you trust me," said Hakim.

"Hakim, I want twenty armed men searching every inch of the docking bay. When I get back from the control center complex, I will expect a full report."

"Yes, Commander Yassin. It will be done as you have ordered." Hakim bowed his head.

Shakira went to Yassin's side. "You know Aaziz dislikes you."

He smiled. "Dislikes is an amazing understatement."

"He thinks he should be in charge," she said quietly for his ears only.

"I know."

"He blames you anytime anything goes wrong."

Yassin agreed with her.

"Be very careful," she warned him.

"I plan to be." As he left, he picked up two loyal soldiers, and they headed for the exit.

CHAPTER 45

Washington, DC
White House
Situation Room

National Security Advisor Amy Henderson cleared her throat. "Let's get started. There is a lot for us to consider, so let's get everyone up to speed on what we know.

"We have some intel on the call from Air Force One that occurred several minutes ago. First, we have confirmed that the call came from Air Force One. That's why the call was brought in here. I assume everyone understands that. We have physical verification of that. Let me play this small clip from the call." Amy pressed a key on her laptop.

The recording sounded. "Mat, we have to go, now! Now!" played for everyone to hear.

Amy continued, "We have verified through voice analysis that this voice is in fact the First Lady of the United States, Samantha Devane." Everyone smiled. Amy went on to say, "The First Lady is alive. She has not been captured, and she is not being tortured. We will come back to the status of Air Force One later in this briefing. Let's continue.

"The call was originated by a man claiming to be a Sheriff

McKenna of Shady Oaks, Florida. We have verified that he is who he says he is. The sheriff of Shady Oaks is indeed a Mathew McKenna, and according to his office, he is currently visiting his niece on Liberty. Everyone on his staff has confirmed that the voice we heard was his. Therefore, we are satisfied that the call was made by Sheriff McKenna.

"So who is this Sheriff McKenna, and what is he doing on Liberty?" asked Amy. "I'll let the secretary of defense, Scott Chao, answer that." Amy sat down.

"Thanks," said Secretary Chao. "Here is what I have. His name is Mathew McKenna. Served twenty years in the United States Army, now retired. He volunteered for three tours of combat duty in the Iraqi intervention. Received two Purple Hearts and was awarded the Distinguished Service Cross for bravery in the Shiloh incident—I think you all remember the Shiloh incident. The disaster would have been a lot worse if McKenna had not acted. He held off an assault by himself, enabling the removal of his entire platoon. His bravery allowed half a dozen men to be evacuated from the battlefield, many of them severely wounded."

Secretary Chao went on. "I personally talked to Lieutenant Colonel Hastings just five minutes ago. Lieutenant Colonel Hastings was McKenna's commanding officer during his third and final tour of combat duty in the Iraqi intervention. He described McKenna as solid, brave, and 'a damn good man.' Wouldn't hesitate to take the initiative. He said that McKenna was soft-spoken and a little on the quiet side, but he warned not to let the quiet fool you. He described McKenna as 'a little bit cocky.' He said that there is a rebel in him, but he keeps him under control, at least usually. He also said that 'if you're in a fight, he's a good man to have at your side.' And that is a quote." The secretary concluded, "His record is excellent."

Sandy Ross said, "Thank you." Relief formed on the acting president's face. "So he has served in combat. That's good."

Jan McClusky, director of the FBI, said, "Here is what I have on Sheriff Mathew McKenna. His father was NYPD, precinct captain. McKenna's father retired thirty years ago and moved the family to Florida. Mathew's mother and father had two children later in life, both boys. Mathew had an older brother named Jeff.

"Jeff and his wife passed away in a car accident, leaving behind one teenage daughter, Megan. Sheriff McKenna is her legal guardian. She graduated from Central Florida with a degree in business and is currently employed on Liberty. Since taking the job, she has received two promotions. She is currently an assistant manager. It's her first job out of college. McKenna is single; he has never married, though he has had several serious relationships.

"We wondered how he ended up on Liberty. Here's what we found: he never purchased airline tickets to the city, but his niece did, and it was that ticket that he used to fly there."

The room filled with silence.

General Lee Solaski, chairman of the Joint Chiefs of Staff, said, "If you don't mind, let me remind everyone about my friend Samantha Devane, the First Lady of the United States." General Solaski paused for emphasis.

He continued, "Her maiden name was Samantha Johnson. Upon graduating college, she joined the military and served a tour of duty in the Iraqi intervention. She served her country as a Navy SEAL. She was deployed as a member of the Rapid Response Team. Her bravery in combat is unquestioned. She was highly trained in hand-to-hand combat.

"A tomboy as a kid, she has been athletic all her life. She went to college on an athletic scholarship. And of course, the Navy SEALs. Since leaving the military, she has remained very physically active. Currently she rides a bike for about an hour every other day. About once a week, she rides for three hours. She rides at a very fast pace. While riding, she enjoys listening to audiobooks, usually fiction, sometimes factual."

"Thank you for the information. We have additional news we need to share," said Amy. She grabbed her bottle of water and took a quick drink, then set the bottle down to her right. "There has been an event on Air Force One. The event occurred shortly after the call with Sheriff McKenna was terminated. It appears from these NSA photos that Air Force One is tumbling toward Earth." Amy displayed a series of images. "These images were taken by intelligence satellites." She pointed to a large shape attached underneath Air Force One. "This has been identified as a tug ship from Liberty. Why and how it became attached to Air Force One is a mystery."

"Is there anyone on board?" asked Acting President Ross.

"Yes," said Amy. "We have intercepted calls from the cockpit of Air Force One to the spaceport at Liberty asking for help. It appears, based on those intercepts, that there are three terrorists trapped on Air Force One. McKenna and the First Lady are not on board. Let me be clear: based on those intercepts, only the three terrorists are on board."

Acting President Ross asked, "Can we intercept Air Force One before she enters Earth's atmosphere?"

"No. There isn't enough time. In less than three hours, Air Force One will burn up as she enters Earth's atmosphere. Another thing. Air Force One is being forced to tumbling under control. The tug is locked onto her with a slow, steady rotational burn. Whoever attached the tug did that on purpose. The tug is forcing an uncontrolled entry. If it weren't for the tug, the ship could fly itself back to Earth and land safely."

Amy stopped and glanced around at the faces in the room. "That summarizes all we have at this moment." Amy took another drink of water.

Scott Chao said, "Let me state the obvious. We have two people on Liberty with combat experience. One is a sheriff, and the other is an ex-SEAL and the First Lady of the United States. At least that gives us something."

General Solaski spoke up. "Let's hope that he's able to call us back soon. Right now all we have is a clusterfuck wrapped in a disaster inside of a nightmare."

"Well, General Eloquence, I guess you won't get a disagreement about that," said Acting President Ross.

CHAPTER 46

Yassin walked into the control center and approached the first person available. "Where's Aaziz?" he asked.

Yassin had brought two loyal lieutenants with him, armed, as escorts. Aaziz was brave, an able fighter, tough, determined to win, loyal to the cause. And a hothead.

The soldier bowed his head and said, "He is in the middle conference room, Commander Yassin, the one you were using."

"Thank you." Yassin patted the soldier on the upper arm. Then he and the two escorts proceeded to the conference room. The door was open, and Yassin and the escorts walked in. He motioned to one of his escorts, who dutifully closed the door behind them.

Inside the room were three Aaziz confidants sitting at the table with him. Yassin mentally patted himself on the back for bringing his two escorts with him. His instincts had been impeccable.

"Aaziz, may I have a word with you?"

Aaziz and his three compatriots looked confused, as if they wondered what was going on. They all began to stand.

"No, please." Yassin motioned to them. "Please remain sitting."

"What's up, Yassin?" said Aaziz.

Yassin noticed that Aaziz didn't use the word "commander" like everyone else. "I bring glorious news, Aaziz."

"Yes, Yassin, and what is this glorious news?" He looked as if he doubted this claim.

"Faheed, Omar, and Shali will soon be martyrs for Islam," said Yassin with his arms open.

"Praise Allah," said Aaziz as he stood, and the others in the room joined in the praises. "Please tell us how they are going to do this."

"They went on a brave mission into the docking bays and were involved in an attack inside Air Force One. Air Force One is tumbling out of control toward the Earth and will burn up on reentry. Faheed, Omar, and Shali are inside Air Force One, and they will be cremated as the spaceliner burns up. Praise be to Allah for such brave soldiers."

He handed Aaziz a comm he had brought with him for this purpose. "Here, Aaziz. You may speak to Shali if you desire."

Aaziz exploded in anger. His blood was boiling; it burned the inside of his veins as it flowed through his body. He stepped toward Yassin to grab him. The two escorts with Yassin quietly lowered their weapons and pointed them at the people in the room. Aaziz bit his lower lip, tasting warm, salty blood. He stepped back. The two escorts had made their point.

Yassin said, "Praise to Allah."

They all repeated, "Praise to Allah."

Yassin said, "I came here, Aaziz, to honor your sacrifice

to our cause by personally coming to inform you of the bravery of our comrades. Especially Shali's bravery and sacrifice."

Yassin left the room and, after greeting everyone in the control center, slowly made his way back to the spaceport.

CHAPTER 47

When Sam and Andy walked into the office that was serving as their base, Megan and Mary Lu jumped up and hugged them. Andy froze while first Megan and then Mary Lu put their arms around him.

"I've never been hugged before," said Andy.

"How did you like it?" asked Mary Lu.

"I think I liked it."

"Where's Uncle Mat?" asked Megan.

Just then, he walked into the room.

"What took you so long?" asked Mary Lu.

"I wanted to make sure we weren't being followed."

Megan rushed up to him and gave him a bear hug. "Welcome back!" she cried. After a few moments, she released him.

But before she could get far, Mat reached out and hugged her again. "I told you I would be back," he said.

Mary Lu then hugged Mat. She seemed to be waiting her turn but trying hard not to show it. Sam and Megan exchanged glances as Mat and Mary Lu hugged. The hug seemed to last longer than the others had.

Then Mary Lu went back to Andy and gave him another

hug. "Welcome back, Andy, and thank you. That must have been hard for you, sending Air Force One tumbling out of control back to Earth with people on board."

"It was," he agreed.

"I am very proud of you."

Mat, Sam, and Megan gave Andy and Mary Lu some additional space. They all watched with keen interest and curiosity.

"You understand why you needed to do that?" she asked.

His eyes moved away from her for just a second, then his head and his eyes returned to Mary Lu. "Yes, I do."

"Everyone in Liberty is very grateful to you for helping us, even though they don't know it yet. You understand that the terrorists will kill everyone in the city. That's over a million lives at stake."

"Yes, about three million five hundred and sixty-four people. I know. They tried to kill the First Lady and Sheriff Mat McKenna and me too," said Andy.

They talked for several minutes about what Andy had experienced. Finally Mary Lu said, "If there is anything else that you would like to talk about, you know I'm here for you. OK, Andy?"

"OK." Andy sat down cross-legged on the floor next to Mary Lu. This experience was triggering a moment of inner perspective and self-evaluation inside him.

Mary Lu understood. His neural systems were experienced-based, just like biological entities. They'd been programmed from the factory with a skeletal base set of core rules and models that provided a foundation that helped his systems frame events and create new functional models of reality.

Everyone left Andy and Mary Lu alone, sensing that something personal was happening. It made them all feel uncomfortable to listen in, so they left the room to do other things.

"Mary Lu?" asked Andy in a soft voice.

"Yes, Andy? What is it?" she said.

He studied the floor for a moment.

Mary Lu thought about saying something, but she thought better of it and waited. Mary Lu had seen Andy grow since he was first assigned to her team. She wanted to hear what Andy was concerned about without interjecting any assumptions.

Andy raised his eyes up to Mary Lu. "Can I ask you a question?" Andy saw her tilt her head slightly. He had seen her do that with Sheriff McKenna but not with him. "A personal question?"

"Yes, of course you can, Andy. You can ask me anything."

"I mean . . ." He paused. "Are you my mother?" He studied her carefully, analyzing her facial expressions for interpretation. "It's OK if you're not." He found himself looking at the ground again, feeling lost inside.

Mary Lu put an arm around his shoulder and pulled him against her. "You can think of me as your mom if you like. I'm very flattered, incredibly flattered. You are a very dear friend, a very close friend, and as time goes by, we will grow even closer than we are now."

Andy nodded slowly. She was being honest, that he sensed.

"If you want to think of me as your mom, you can. We can think of each other as family. In time, you will know that we are really close friends. A kind of family not based on biology but based on caring."

"OK," he said. "I didn't know. I was just wondering."

Mat waited until they were done talking, then reentered the room. "Mary Lu, we need to set up the sat phone."

Mary Lu opened the sat phone bag and began removing its contents. There wasn't much there, just a transmitter-receiver and two phones. There was also a little pamphlet in the bag. She smiled at them. "This is pretty simple. What they are calling a sat phone is really just a NASA communications module. It utilizes the NASA global communications network. Makes sense. We point the transmitter-receiver toward Earth and NASA does the rest. The system just plugs into NASA's global network. We then just use the phones to talk. Simple."

"So where do we set up?" asked Mat.

"The transmitter-receiver should be outside. It needs a clear view of the Earth."

"So we need to go back out?" said Sam.

"No, we'll let Andy go back out and configure it. We'll just place it near the exit hatch."

"All right," said Mat and Sam.

"It's designed for easy use. They configured it for a Secret Service agent to plug and play in an emergency. It comes with the transmitter-receiver and two phones. The phones are, well, uh, phones. They have a huge range. The system was designed so that the Secret Service could follow POTUS around a city. It's completely self-contained.

"So we just set the dish up and walk away from it, and the phones should work fine anywhere in the city. The signal is scrambled." Mary Lu played with the phones for a moment. "These work like a regular phone. You can send pictures, video, whatever. Interesting."

"Let's do it," said Sam. "We need to talk to Washington, the sooner the better."

CHAPTER 48

Everyone gathered around in a semicircle on the floor, facing a cradle they'd made for the phone out of a folded shirt and a book. Mat picked up the sat phone. "Well, let's give this a try in conference mode. Let's see how well it works."

He picked up the phone and pressed the button to call Washington. The phone made three beeps in a tonal sequence, indicating that it was on. It reminded Mat of his Bluetooth headphones.

"Hello, is anyone there?" Mat waited the few seconds of silence as the call was passed to Delphi in the Situation Room of the White House.

Delphi, the comm cylinder sitting in the center of the White House Situation Room's conference table, lit up with a blue light and said, "Call from Liberty."

"This is Amy Henderson. Who am I speaking to?" said Amy.

"This is Sheriff McKenna from Liberty. Hold on one second, sorry." Mat pushed a button to place the phone in videoconference mode. He set the phone down into its T-shirt cradle on the floor so that the camera faced them.

Delphi directed the video to the screens that surrounded the room.

"Can you still hear me?" asked Mat.

"We hear you fine," said the acting president.

The video image of Mat, Sam, Mary Lu, and Megan popped up onto the walls around the Situation Room. People in the room gasped with excitement.

"We can hear you and see you too," said Acting President Ross.

Mat, Sam, Megan, and Mary Lu all waved to the camera.

Sam leaned forward and said, "Hi, Sandy. Hi, everyone."

Acting President Sandy Ross smiled. "Hi, Sam. Are you OK?"

"As well as you can be, hiding from terrorists, I guess."

Smiles of relief filled the Situation Room.

"I'm Sheriff McKenna. You can call me Mat. I have the First Lady here with me, as you already know. This is Mary Lu Hayashi, chief maintenance engineer at Liberty, and my niece Megan, and this is Andy. We are calling from our uh, little, uh, well . . . our base."

"Tell us what you know," said Amy.

"All right, let's start with the assault. Every Secret Service officer went down except for agents Laura Cass and Bill Dougan."

"Where were you when the assault took place? How did you get involved in this, Sheriff?" asked Glen Stevenson, CIA director.

"I was sitting with my niece, Megan, in Tier Two not far from the stage. As a police officer, I went to the stage to assist, and together with the First Family and Agents Cass and Dougan, we fled into the city. Agent Dougan died during that flight.

"We then went to the control center complex. The terrorists had taken the complex. As we escaped, we were split into two groups. Agent Cass, President Devane, Michael, and Sarah were in one group. Sam, Mary Lu, Megan, and I were in another. We haven't seen or heard anything from President Devane since that moment. We believe they are still at large and hiding somewhere."

"OK," said Amy Henderson. "You said something about the terrorists implementing a security procedure and dividing the city into emergency sectors. Did we hear that right?"

"Yes, you heard that correctly. The city has been sealed off into emergency sectors—some form of emergency protocol. The city is now divided into three sections or subcities. All transportation systems are down."

"Do you have any idea of the disposition of the terrorists in the city?"

"No, we don't. Frankly, we have only done two things to date: run like hell from them and then gather this comm equipment. Here's what we think. They occupy the spaceport and the control center complex. We think that all the terrorists are in the sector with the spaceport."

"We do have a little bit of data to send you. Hold on." Mary Lu transmitted the images of the two dead terrorists and the pictures of their photo IDs.

"Did you get the pictures?" asked Mat.

The images of the two dead terrorists popped up on the wall monitors around the Situation Room. "Yes, we're viewing them right now."

"Good."

"Mat, tell us about Air Force One," said Amy. "Why did you go there? If the terrorists control the spaceport, how did you get to Air Force One? Tell us about that."

"With the help of Mary Lu and Andy, Sam and I exited the city and went to the docking facilities, where we reentered the city at Docking Ring Two. We then went to Air Force One and got the comm equipment, which is when we called you that first time."

"Are you aware that Air Force One is tumbling to Earth?" asked Amy.

"Yes."

"Did you do that?"

"Yep, that was us. We were trapped inside it with no way out, so we had Andy attach a tug to her. And when we got out, the tug closed the doors. Then Andy flew her toward the Earth. We came back here to call you."

"Who is Andy?"

"He is an android. Works for Mary Lu."

Andy waved to them. Everyone in the Situation Room laughed. The image of Andy, sitting cross-legged on the floor next to Mary Lu, waving at them, was almost too much.

"Who is Mary Lu again?"

"She is the chief engineer here at Liberty. Any engineering issue. She keeps Liberty working."

Mary Lu smiled and waved.

"Where did you meet up with her?" said Amy.

"She was being held captive at the control center complex. She escaped with us when we got away. It's a long story. We will tell you when we get out of this. So far, we have killed two terrorists while escaping. The two that we sent the pictures of to you. Two more at a spaceliner as we went to Air Force One, and three more inside Air Force One. We've killed over nine terrorists so far."

"What are you planning to do?" asked the FBI director.

"Recon. Try to learn what they are up to. Thin their ranks whenever the opportunity is present."

"Well, it sounds like you guys have done one hell of a job," said Amy. She looked to the acting president and asked, "You exited the station? Could you do that again if needed?"

Everyone agreed. "I don't see why not. We will do whatever we can to assist you," said Mat.

"Stay safe and get some rest."

Sam had the last word. "Bye." She reached for the phone and took hold of it. Then she pressed a button and ended the call.

CHAPTER 49

Everyone grabbed a sandwich and something to drink from the food bag. Mat grabbed the weapons bag and emptied the contents onto the middle of the floor.

"What are you doing?" asked Megan.

"Taking inventory."

There were two semiautomatic weapons, two magazines of additional ammunition, and three extra magazines for their Secret Service handguns. He removed three knives and placed them next to the rifles.

"We lost two knives at Air Force One when we threw them," he said to Sam.

"And Mat and I each have one gun." Sam showed her weapon sitting in its cradle under her arm.

"Correct," said Mat. He pointed to his holstered weapon. Sam and Mat wore their weapons all the time.

"And everyone has a ballistic vest, right?" asked Sam.

Everyone nodded.

Mat handed a knife to Sam and one to Mary Lu, then took the last one for himself.

"Have you ever fired a gun before?" he asked Mary Lu as he took a bite from his sandwich.

"No."

Mat took a drink, then held the gun up in front of Mary Lu. He showed her the safety switch, making sure she understood which position was on and which was off. Then he handed her the weapon and showed her how to aim and how to shoot. It was a three-minute lesson.

"Never point a gun at anything you don't want to shoot."

"Do I really need this?"

"Yes, you do. If you stay hidden, hopefully you will never need to use it." He helped her put the holster on.

Mat handed a gun to Megan. "Put this on."

She took the weapon and opened her purse.

Mat grabbed her hand gently. "You should carry it on you."

They eyed each other for a moment, frozen. Then she said, "OK." She put the holster around her and secured the gun inside it.

Mat handed one of the assault rifles to Sam, along with the extra magazine. He took a gun and magazine for himself. Then he leaned back on the floor and took another large bite of his turkey sandwich.

"So, what are we thinking?" asked Sam.

He swallowed a gulp from his soda. "We? There's no 'we,'" he replied. "I'm going out to try to get some intel."

"I don't think that's a good idea," said Sam.

"I don't think so either," said Mary Lu. Her eyes were big.

"I don't think it's a good idea either," said Andy quietly.

"We have no choice. If we do nothing and stay here, my gut says we will all end up dead, along with lots of other people."

Sam touched his shoulder. "It's too risky."

"What's too risky? Staying here, doing nothing, and hoping they don't find us? Or going out and seeing if we can assist a rescue somehow?"

"OK, I get that. And I agree. But this has to be done together."

Megan broke in. "I'm not staying here alone. No. No. No." She leaned into him. "No, Uncle Mat. I'm going."

"Yeah, me too. I'm not staying here either." Mary Lu crossed her arms. Daggers flashed in her eyes. "I am *not* staying here. Besides, you might need me."

"I got my gun here, just like you asked." Megan patted the gun holstered under her arm. "We're going."

Sam got up off the floor and moved into her chair. She wolfed down the remnants of her sandwich in two bites, then gulped down a long pull from her soda and leaned back. "So what's the plan, Sheriff?"

Everyone got up off the floor and sat in their chairs, facing inward toward the middle of the room so they could all see each other easily.

"I think we should cruise the outer perimeter of the sector. If we can, then let's clear the perimeter. Learn what we can, if anything. If we come across stragglers, we should eliminate them. Every terrorist we can kill is one less that can kill us. Anything we can do to reduce their numbers would be helpful."

"OK, I'll buy that."

"They are up to something. They sealed the sectors for a reason. Maybe we can learn something about what they are up to. We need to do anything we can to throw a monkey wrench into their plans and their timetables."

Sam said, "Now that Washington knows we are here, they might come up with a plan. Anything we can do to help them helps us. Let me be clear about this: my family is out there. I can't just do nothing. Here's how I see it. We can't just sit here and wait for the terrorists to come get us."

"Sounds like we all agree," said Mat.

Sam rocked forward. "We just might find my family. It's a long shot, but who knows?"

They armored up.

The ballistic vests and the comm equipment they'd gotten from the space suits they now wore all the time. Next came the communications headset from the space suits. Mat picked up the two sat phones used to call Washington. He handed one to Mary Lu and pocketed the other. They shoved some soft drinks, fruit bars, and snacks into one bag. The other bag was empty. He handed both bags to Megan.

"What's this for?" she asked.

"In case we find something we need, like ammo. Anything. We have to be able to carry it," he answered.

"Got it." She folded the empty bag up neatly and placed it into the other bag.

"Good idea," said Mary Lu.

"Are we forgetting anything? Remember, we can't depend on coming back here. We may have to set up shop somewhere else, hence the food bag. Everything we need has to come with us," said Mat.

"And fit into one bag," added Sam.

Everyone scanned the office. After a moment, Sam said, "No, I think that's it."

CHAPTER 50

Mary Lu pulled up a map of the city on her tablet. "Let me orient you. This blue dot is where we are now. This is the exit chamber you took to Air Force One. This here is the control center complex, where you rescued me. And this is the spaceport."

"What's down here at the bottom?" asked Mat.

"That's the agricultural belt."

Sam pointed to the center of the sector. "That's the control center complex, and that's the spaceport?"

"Yes."

"We need to stay away from those areas," said Sam. "That means we need to screen this area around us now and then go down to the ag belt and go to the other side of the sector."

"Avoid the center of the sector," said Mat. "I like it. Avoid direct confrontation with the bulk of their force. Screen the perimeter."

Sam nodded. "Exactly. Let's test the waters first. Get a feel for this."

"We have another issue: guns. We have limited ammo. Better to conserve if possible. And if we shoot, we will likely pull them right down on us. We should use our knives if possible. Silent kills."

"Well, we both have extensive training in doing just that."

"Yep," said Mat.

"Mary Lu and Andy, do you know the general path we want to take?"

"Yes." Mary Lu smiled at Andy. "We do." She swung her tablet strap over her head and shoulder like a purse.

* * *

Mat stopped at the door. He glanced outside. Just hours ago, they were here on their way to Air Force One. It felt like a lifetime ago. He scanned the pedestrian walkways from the door window. The streets were still empty.

"Mary Lu, are there any hotels in this area?"

"I'm sure there are. Let me check." She searched on her tablet. In a minute, she'd found one. "There's the Sierra Hotel not far from here. It's that way." She pointed. "Just one block over crosswise."

Mary Lu showed Sam and Mat the location on her map. "Here."

"Why the hotel?" asked Sam.

"People should be there. I want to make sure that they're all right. Just a hunch. Mary Lu, you take the lead. You are the most familiar with the area."

Mary Lu crossed the street and moved one block tubular, going in the direction of the tubular center of the sector. She turned ninety degrees and headed into the center of the sector away from the city wall. Two buildings down, on the other side of the walkway, was the Sierra Hotel.

Sam was about to cross the street when Mat grabbed her arm and pulled her back. He pointed his finger.

A block farther down from the Sierra Hotel were six terrorists walking along the pedestrian path. The way they sauntered across the walkway reminded Mat of a street gang. They were fully armed and strutted like they were proud of it. They were headed this way and looking for someone to have their way with.

Sam glanced at the building behind them. It was a one-story building, like most buildings in Liberty. The front of the building was dark glass. There was a porch with an eave overhead and five small round tables with green tablecloths. Four stylish white-framed chairs were at each table. Above the door, a carved oval wooden plank hung from two chains located at the top left and right corners. The words *Alcove Restaurant* were carved into the wood and painted with bright colors.

Megan slid to the door on her belly, then reached up and grabbed the door handle and pulled on it. The door cracked open an inch; it was unlocked. She opened it a little more and slipped inside the Alcove Restaurant, followed closely by Andy and Mary Lu. Down the block, the terrorists had not spotted them, at least not yet.

Hunched low to the ground, Sam slipped in the door sideways, keeping it open only a crack.

The terrorists were joking with each other, occasionally pushing one another around and laughing. Sporadically they checked the buildings as they walked up the street toward them.

Like Sam, Mat slipped into the Alcove, hunched low to the ground. The terrorists were looking for trouble. And if there weren't so many of them, Mat would have given it to them.

The six terrorists stopped in front of the Alcove Restaurant.

"Everyone get in the back." Mat motioned to the back of the restaurant with a wave of his hand.

"You think they will come in here?" asked Sam.

Mat slipped off to the side. "Don't know." He watched from the corner of one of the dark windows. Sam did the same from the other corner of the window.

One of the men sauntered over toward the Alcove, and Mat and Sam slid over to hide behind the tables in the front corner, near the window.

He stepped up to the door and poked his head inside the Alcove. He glanced around the restaurant, and after a moment he pulled himself back and closed the door. Then he walked back to the center of the walkway and rejoined the others. Another man who was checking another building on the other side of the street joined back up as well, and they continued on their way down the street.

Mat peered out the window. "They're gone."

* * *

The team hid inside the building for a while. Mat and Sam carefully watched through a front window at the main entrance of the building across the street, the Sierra Hotel. No one came; no one left.

After ten minutes, Mat said, "Andy, go into the Sierra

and tell us if it's clear." *Andy is just an android. Nobody will pay attention to him.*

Andy walked across the street and into the hotel. The lobby and gift shop were empty. He walked the perimeter for a minute, then went into the gift shop, but he came out quickly. "It's clear. No one is here. But there is a dead woman in the gift shop behind the counter. Half her clothes are missing."

"That's what I figured," said Mat.

The team crossed the walkway and joined Andy. Mat quietly led the way down one of the hotel hallways. Mat and Sam had their knives out. They made a right corner and continued down, listening for anything unusual. In the third hallway, Sam heard something. Or thought she did. A muffled sound. "Mat, I'm checking here." She reached for the handle of the door.

"Let me unlock the door for you. The doors self-lock when closed," said Mary Lu. She withdrew her maintenance pass card.

Sam was waiting for Mary Lu to unlock the door when it suddenly opened. She found herself standing in front of a man with a bloodstained shirt and an assault rifle swung over his shoulder.

Sam was drawn to the scene on the hotel bed, where a girl was draped over the end, just into view. Her face was a battered pulp. One arm hung over the edge, dangling in the air. Her eyes were open and staring into space. In the corner of the room in a chair was an adult woman, a large red spot soaking her shirt in the chest. She was dead too.

The terrorist pushed Sam back with both hands. Sam

recovered and threw herself to the side, slicing the man's belly with her knife. As he reached down to his stomach, she slit his throat, and he collapsed to the ground.

Everyone entered the room. When Megan spotted the girl on the bed, she swung away and vomited.

Mary Lu looked away. "Can we go now? Please."

"Not yet." He closed the door, then grabbed the terrorist by the feet and dragged him into the shower.

"What should we do about them?" asked Sam as she grabbed a sheet to put over them.

"Stop. Leave them as they are."

"What?" Mary Lu was flushed with emotions. "Why?"

"They're dead; they won't care. We want to leave this room the way we found it. No clues to our presence."

Andy said nothing. He glanced around the room, then went over to Mary Lu and stood next to her quietly.

They left the room and continued down the hallway. After checking the first floor, they took the stairs to the second floor and began again.

They stopped at another door when they heard a woman scream, then what sounded like muffled voices pleading with someone. Mat and Sam gathered next to the door. Mat grabbed the door handle and Mary Lu unlocked the door. He gave one nod to Sam, then opened the door, and they went in.

There was a man kneeling at the side of the bed, his hands tied behind his back. A terrorist was holding him by the hair of his head, forcing him to look at the bed. On the bed was a woman, maybe in her twenties, guessed Mat. She was naked except for a pair of pink socks. On top of her was another terrorist with his pants down around his knees.

The terrorist at the side of the bed was facing them, smiling and saying something Mat didn't understand. Something foreign. Then the terrorist's eyes suddenly went wide.

Mat reached the terrorist in two strides. The man stood and tried to back away from Mat, but Mat grabbed the man by the back of his head and pulled as he plunged the knife up through the bottom of his chin and into the base of his brain. The man died instantly. Mat released him and he fell to the floor.

Sam charged the man on the bed before he had time to realize what was happening. She severed his spine at the back of his neck as he still lay on top of his victim. Sam pulled him off the bed and to the floor.

Megan, Mary Lu, and Andy walked into the room after it was all done. Mat leaned down to the man beside the bed. "It's over." He placed an arm around him and helped him to stand while Megan helped the girl on the bed find some clothes.

"We have to go," Mat said to the man and his young wife. "Don't dump the bodies into the hallway. It will just draw attention to you. I understand if you don't want to stay here."

The man and woman just looked at him.

"You can't wander around the streets. You need to find a place to hide until this blows over. All the hotels are booked. If you find an empty room, just take it."

"OK," said the man. The man and woman held on to each other, right where Mat had sat them down on the side of the bed.

Mat and Sam carried the two terrorists into the shower, and Mat grabbed the doorknob as he left the room. He paused and faced the couple still sitting on the bed. "Don't go wandering around. Stay hidden."

"OK," said the man. "Thank you."

"You're welcome." Mat closed the door.

Mary Lu said, "Isn't there anything else we can do for them?"

"Uncle Mat, we can't just leave them."

"No. There is nothing else we can do. And yes, we can just leave them. And we are." Mat walked down the hallway.

Mary Lu and Megan followed quietly. But every time Mat faced them, their eyes pushed him away.

They spent the next hour checking the hotel floor by floor. Whenever they heard something unusual, they checked it out. They didn't have the time or the manpower to do a room-to-room search. But the terrorists were loud, not expecting armed opposition. They tended to reveal themselves.

Over the next two hours, they cleared the two hotels in this part of the sector. When the team finally exited the hotel, Mat said, "Mary Lu, get us to the ag belt and across to the other side of the sector."

"You got it."

"This is why you wanted to go to the hotels in this area, isn't it?" asked Sam.

"Yep. I reasoned that if they were going to go out and have fun, it would have to be where the people were. In this sector, that means hotels."

"I can see that now."

"It also means that we have a chance to find them in ones and twos."

"Yeah, but we just left all those people. What are they going to do?" asked Megan.

"There is only so much we can do, Megan. We have to do what we can do and not dwell on what we cannot."

"I understand, Uncle Mat. But I don't like it. My God, those poor people."

"I don't like it either. If we survive this, counselors can be sent in for everyone. Right now, we have to focus on surviving. There are millions of people in the city, and they're all depending on us."

CHAPTER 51

The team was heading crosswise when Mary Lu stopped abruptly and fell in behind some trees. Everyone did the same. Four terrorists were walking along the street crosswise toward the wall.

These terrorists were different. Two of them had backpacks on. One was out in front, leading the way. He carried an assault rifle swung over his shoulder. The others carried their weapons in their hands and walked with purpose. They weren't out searching for adventure. These four were going somewhere. They were doing something. Something like work.

"What do you make of that?" asked Mat.

"I don't know," said Sam. "I have a bad feeling about it."

"Let's follow them and see what they are up to," said Mary Lu.

"Good idea."

The terrorists walked down the pathway in single file.

The team followed at a distance, cutting over one block and following on a parallel course. They followed for five minutes, staying one block behind the terrorists. Between buildings, they stopped to make sure the terrorists were still there. Mat removed the sat phone from his pocket and snapped a couple of pictures of the four terrorists. He pressed the Send button, then put the phone back in his pocket.

"They are headed for the wall," said Mary Lu. "Just one more block and we'll be at the wall."

The terrorists reached the wall at the corner of the sector and disappeared into a one-story gray cement structure.

"Interesting," said Mary Lu.

"What's in that building?" asked Sam.

"It's not what is in it, it's where it goes. It's a secured-access facility. Employees only. There are elevators inside."

"Elevators to where?" asked Mat. "The building only has one floor."

"The elevators go down to the agricultural belt."

They moved closer to the building. "The ag belt? Why would they be going there?" asked Sam.

"Andy, go inside and see if the way is clear. If anyone is there, act like you're doing maintenance," said Mary Lu.

"OK, Mary Lu. But what kind of maintenance?"

"Any kind. Make something up."

"Make something up?"

"Yes, ad lib. You will think of something. I trust you. You can do that."

"Make something up?" He walked away toward the building. Halfway there, he stopped and looked at Mary Lu. "Ad lib?" Then he continued on to the building.

Andy inserted his finger into the droid lock and disappeared into the gray building.

CHAPTER 52

Air Force One began to enter Earth's atmosphere. As it came in contact with the upper atmosphere, it began to tumble. Shali attempted to steer the ship, but the entry was too steep and every command she sent caused the ship to tumble more. The ionized heat enveloped the ship, and all communications stopped.

NORAD tracked the vehicle as it descended into Earth's atmosphere.

On Earth, people looked up into the night sky to see what appeared to be a bright meteor streaking across a dark sky. The meteor broke up and splintered into smaller chunks so that there was one large piece with three smaller ones near it. On the beaches near Orlando, Florida, tourists pointed into the sky as it passed overhead and flew into the distant horizon. Several miles out over the Atlantic Ocean, the chunks crashed into the sea.

NORAD notified the White House that the debris had fallen harmlessly into the Atlantic Ocean.

CHAPTER 53

"What do you see, Andy?" asked Mary Lu.

"No one is here. The room is empty. I think they left already."

The team got up from their hiding place and moved toward the building.

"Stay where you are, Andy, we're coming," said Mary Lu.

"OK. I'll be here."

"Andy, can you open the door for us?" said Mary Lu as they ran toward the building.

"Sure."

The door opened just as everyone arrived.

Mat was the second to arrive, behind Mary Lu. "Thanks, Andy," he said as he joined them inside.

Mary Lu pointed to the stairs next to the single elevator. "There is only one place they could have gone, and that's down to the ag belt."

The team headed down the stairs, Mat and Sam drawing their weapons on the way down. At the bottom of the stairs was just one door out of the room.

Through the door's window, Mat spied the four combatants heading out into the farmland, traveling along the circumference. They walked against the city wall.

"Do you see them?" asked Megan.

"Yep, they're out there. Let them get a little farther out before we open the door and follow."

Sam came up, and Mat moved away from the door window so she could look. "Thanks," she said. She moved forward and peeked out. "I see them." She watched for a moment and then stepped back. "Lots of places to hide. There's a whole field of corn out there."

"I wonder what they're up to," said Mat. "Any ideas?"

"I know. It doesn't make any sense. What would they want from the ag belt?" Sam shrugged.

"Don't look at me," said Mary Lu. "I have no idea what they could want."

Megan said, "Beats me."

Mat stepped up to the window again and peeked out. He placed a hand on the door and slowly opened it, watching to make sure they hadn't been spotted. He waved Sam through first, and then, one by one, they slipped out the cracked door and fled into the cornfield. The cornstalks were to the left and heading along the circumference. Grasses were along the wall. The cornstalks stood four feet tall. Tall enough to hide in, but not to stand upright.

"Don't bump the cornstalks, or they will see us moving in here," said Sam.

Hidden by the cornfield, the team moved left, farther away from the terrorists. They didn't want to get too close; no point in risking detection. With some distance between them and the terrorists along the wall to their right, the team headed along the circumference of the city into the cornfield. They ran low to the ground and parallel to the terrorists.

Mary Lu glanced over to Andy. "How are you doing, Andy?"

"This is fun. Very exciting," said Andy.

CHAPTER 54

"What are they going to do now? They are almost at the end of this sector. There's nowhere for them to go," said Sam.

Mary Lu was quiet. She watched them as they reached the corner of the sector where there was a small building.

"What's in that building?" asked Mat.

Mary Lu answered, "Nothing is in it. It's the emergency sector pass. It's just like an exit chamber, but instead of leading into space, it leads into the adjacent sector. Normally they aren't used because the sectors are never sealed. The emergency sector pass is exactly like an airlock, only it allows emergency teams to pass from one sealed sector to another safely."

"First they seal off the city into three sectors. Now they are going into one of the sectors they sealed off," said Sam.

"Whatever they are up to, it can't be good," said Megan.

Mat said to Mary Lu, "I assume you can get us through there?"

"Yes, I can get you through. So can Andy. The passes require a security code or an override from the control center." Mary Lu smiled at Mat and leaned toward him just a little. "It's a good thing I came along."

The four men reached the emergency pass and disappeared into the chamber. Mat and Sam ran up to a window in the wall that divided the two sectors.

"There they are," said Sam.

"Yep. Marching along the wall into the sector," said Mat.

"Well, we will have more crops to hide in. What are those anyway?"

"Beans, I think." The plants stood about two feet tall, maybe three, but were in fairly dense rows.

"What kind of beans?"

"I have no idea. I'm a sheriff, not a farmer." Then Mat said to Megan, "You doing all right?"

"I'm fine."

"Arms getting tired?" asked Mat. Megan was carrying the satchel, the emergency office in a bag.

She smiled. "A little, but I will be all right."

Andy asked Megan, "Want me to carry those for a while?"

Mat and Mary Lu both nodded that it would be all right, so Megan said, "If you don't mind."

"It would be my pleasure," said Andy.

Megan slipped the satchel strap over her head and off her shoulder and handed it to Andy. "Thanks, Andy."

"You're welcome." He took it and held it by the handle.

Sam said, "I think we can go now. They are far enough into the sector that we should be able to slip inside."

Mat glanced out the window; she was right. It was time to move.

Mary Lu arrived at the emergency sector pass first. She

slipped off her passkey from around her neck and inserted it into the lock. She opened the door, and everyone stepped inside the chamber. Once everyone was in, she closed the door. "The system won't allow both doors to be open at the same time. Just like an exit chamber." Mary Lu walked across the room to the other side.

Mat peered out the small window in the door. The terrorists were still marching away. "I think we're clear to go."

Mary Lu opened the door just enough for them to slip out. Sam left first and went straight for the bean field, and everyone followed, hiding among the leafy green rows.

They trailed the terrorists, hunched down low to the ground. The cornfield had been easier. The beans were lower to the ground. A lot lower.

After two minutes, Mat stopped and took a knee. His back was killing him. He placed a hand on his back and tried to stretch a little, careful not to expose himself above the beans. Everyone joined him in taking a rest and stretching. Everyone except Andy, who moved monkey-style on his front knuckles. Then they set off following the terrorists again, running hunched over and aching.

Over an hour had passed when the four terrorists came to a halt in the tubular middle of the sector. The one in front made a motion with his arm and pointed to the ground, and the two men with the backpacks laid them on the ground where he had pointed.

"What the hell?" said Mat. "I wish I had binoculars."

"Well, I don't think they are setting up to have a picnic," said Sam.

"I guess that's what this mission was all about," said Mary Lu. "Gathering intel."

Sam nodded. "True."

The man who was the leader sat down in the grass and watched. One of the men who had carried a backpack also sat down but not next to the leader.

Everyone noticed that and quietly laughed. "He doesn't want to get too close to him," said Sam.

Megan scrunched her face. "I wonder if it's BO."

"Or his amazing personality," said Mary Lu.

Sam nudged Mat. "It reminds me of the way we treat Sheriff McKenna."

Mat said, "Yep." He placed his index finger against his lips. *Don't get too loud.* Everyone got the message.

The other two men walked over to where the backpacks lay, then bent down and unzipped them. They removed items from the bags and placed them carefully on the ground. It appeared that they were being placed in some sort of order.

The team was too far away to see what was being removed. They dared not move closer. They would just have to wait. Mat picked up the sat phone and snapped a couple more pictures. He then pressed the Send button and sent the pictures to Washington.

Two of the men . . . Wait. It was now obvious to Mat that the smaller man was actually a woman. She had short, dark hair and wore a bright red T-shirt and blue jeans. There was no doubt of it; her profile was definitely female, and her movements were fluid, agile, and feminine.

They watched as the woman wearing the red T-shirt

grabbed one of the packets about the size of a traditional red brick. She walked over to the wall and began to unthread the brick and place it against the wall. It looked like putty on a roll of tape, or maybe sculpting clay. She spread it in a line, forming a large circle about three feet in diameter. The man working with the woman also wore a T-shirt, but his was black with lettering on the front. It was some sort of sports logo and lettering, but he was too far away to tell what it was. He had a small rectangular black object in his hand, which he set on the ground next to the wall. He ran two wires up from the object to the bottom circle of the clay and inserted the wire ends into the clay. He then handed another small rectangular black object to the man sitting in the grass, the one who had led them out.

"That has to be plastic explosives. What else could it be?" asked Sam.

"They're going to blow a hole in this sector? I can't believe this—that will kill everyone inside. There are hotels in this sector. There have to be at least a million people in this sector," said Mary Lu.

"Now we know why they sealed the sectors. They plan to kill everyone sector by sector," said Mat.

"Oh my God," said Megan.

"This could be just a threat. 'Do what we say or we'll kill everyone here,'" said Sam, looking first at Mary Lu, then turning to Mat. "Right?"

Mary Lu shook her head. "No, I really think they're going to blow this sector and kill everyone. These people are killers. I've experienced it."

"They aren't going to blow this sector," said Mat. His

voice was even. Confident. Calm.

"They aren't? How do you know?" said Mary Lu.

The corners of Sam's lips tightened, and she crossed her arms disapprovingly like a mom. "Mat, how could you possibly know what they are or aren't going to do?"

"They aren't going to blow anything up because as soon as they leave, we are going to remove whatever it is that they have planted."

"Oh yeah. That's right." Sam smiled and tried to control an embarrassed laugh.

"Good point," said Mary Lu with a laugh.

They watched the terrorists for a few more minutes. Then Sam asked Mat, "Do you want to take them out?"

Sheriff McKenna answered, "No, we want them alive so they can report in to their superiors. We want them to believe that their mission was accomplished. Otherwise, they will just do it all over again."

The five of them stayed low in the bean field for what seemed like an eternity, watching and waiting for the terrorists to leave. The man with the black T-shirt walked to the wall and examined everything again, as did the woman.

A little over half an hour after they'd begun, the woman and the man backed away from the wall and began to put everything still on the ground back into the two backpacks. The woman and the man walked over to the leader, who was still sitting on the grass. They appeared to talk for a while. Occasionally the woman would nod or shake her head no.

The leader stood up. The other two men grabbed the backpacks, and Mat watched as the four terrorists then began walking away from the wall.

Wait.

"Mat, what are they doing?" asked Sam.

He watched as the leader set off into the bean field. He was walking crosswise. "I don't know."

Megan's voice rose. "Guys, they're headed right for us! Uncle Mat!"

"Oh no—they are!" said Mary Lu. "They are headed right for us."

"Let's get out of here. Stay low, everyone. Follow me." Mat headed back down the bean row as fast as he could crawl. "Stay low."

The team scrambled between the bean rows. They had to stay very low to the ground or else they would be spotted. They had to get away fast.

"They're getting closer," said Sam.

"Keep moving." Mat felt his knees and thighs burning, but he continued to crawl and run.

They fled for another twenty seconds, seconds that seemed like hours. They moved away from the terrorists as far as they could. The problem was, the terrorists had an excellent view down between the bean rows. They had to be very careful to not be visible between the rows as the terrorists passed by. If they looked down the row, they might spot them.

"Stop, everyone," said Mat.

Everyone stopped and watched the terrorists.

Mat continued, "Slowly move into the next bean row. Try not to disturb the plants. If you shake the plants, they'll see you."

Mat slowly bent one plant down and occupied its space.

Everyone watched and copied him, slowly bending one plant down and moving on top of it. "Good job, everyone," said Mat.

Mat held his gun. He now wished he had taken one of the assault rifles. Too late now; the handgun would just have to do. Mat flexed his fingers that were wrapped around the gun grip. He felt the circulation return to his hand. The lead terrorist stepped into their row of beans.

Everyone froze as the terrorists approached. *Please, don't let them see us,* thought Megan.

Mat regripped the weapon. He watched. He waited.

They all waited, but Megan and Mary Lu both stared down at the dirt; they didn't want to see. Megan could feel her heart beating. It felt like her chest was exploding with each beat.

Mary Lu closed her eyes. *Mat will protect us,* she thought.

The leader passed into the next row. Two more terrorists stepped into their row. Mat looked away for just a second. *Don't stop. Keep walking.* He glanced up, and they were walking into the next row of beans. Mat watched the woman in the red T-shirt; she was the last one. She took another step and passed beyond their row of beans.

"Don't move, anyone," said Mat. "They passed us by, but they're real close. Don't move. Stay frozen."

Ten seconds passed. "Stay frozen," said Mat.

Another ten seconds passed. "Don't move."

Another ten seconds. "There's a small storage shed, a mini barn, located on the other side. I think that's where they are headed," said Mary Lu.

More seconds passed by. "OK, you can move between

the bean rows. Stay down," said Mat.

Everyone could hear everyone else sigh and breathe with relief over the comm.

Mat and Sam holstered their weapons and came to rest next to each other. They watched as the terrorists disappeared into the shed.

"Just what I thought," said Mary Lu.

CHAPTER 55

Now they waited.

Megan shifted on her knees. "So what the heck are they doing in there?"

"No idea," replied Mary Lu. "Nothing would surprise me."

"Maybe they are going to blow up the tractors because they hate farmers," said Megan.

"Very funny, Megan," said Sam.

They all smiled.

Then the door to the shed slipped open and the leader emerged, followed by the two men. The woman wearing red was last. She closed the door to the shed before hurrying to catch up with the others.

"Well, there they go. Back the way they came," said Sam.

"So now we know why they went to the shed," said Mat.

"We do?" asked Sam.

"Look at them. None of them are wearing a backpack. They left the backpacks in the shed."

Everyone examined the terrorists as they walked back to the emergency sector pass. Mat was right: the backpacks were gone.

After the terrorists disappeared into the emergency sector pass, they all got up and went to the shed. Mat grabbed the door handle and slid the door open. The shed was twenty by thirty feet in size, not very big. Inside the shed was a small AI tractor and trailer. The tractor was the size of two TOD cars, also not very big.

There was some harvesting equipment that the tractor could pull. On the other side of the shed were miscellaneous farm tools, simple tools that the ag droids might need. Shovels, pliers, hammers, a pallet of seed bags, and a couple of pallets of fertilizer bags.

"Anyone find the backpacks?" asked Mat.

The team fanned out into the shed to search for them.

Mary Lu opened a large foot locker. "Here they are, I think."

Sam and Mat walked over to her, and they each reached in and grabbed a backpack. "Yep, that's them," said Mat.

Everyone walked out of the shed. Mat and Sam set the bags on the ground and opened them up. Mat reached in and withdrew a brick of putty stuff. There were also two small black boxes. One had wires coming out of it.

"This bag is empty," said Sam.

They all passed around the brick of the putty stuff and examined it. It eventually came back to Mat. It looked like plastic explosives to him, but what did he know? He wasn't an explosives expert. Hell, he wasn't even an explosives amateur.

Mat reached into his bag and pulled out a small rectangular black box with wires coming from it. He handed it to Sam.

"Detonator," said Sam as she handed it back to Mat.

He handed her another small, flat rectangle not much bigger than a credit card. It had two buttons on it and a small light.

"Controls the detonator," she said. "Press this and *boom*." She handed it back.

Mat put the detonator and the putty, or whatever it was, back into the backpack and zipped it up. He swung the pack over his shoulder.

Sam placed her hands on her hips casually. "Interesting. It's not like any of the plastic explosives that I've seen or worked with, but it is similar. The detonators are familiar." She bit her bottom lip gently. "Hmm." She bent down and picked up the empty backpack.

Mat, Mary Lu, Megan, and Andy watched the First Lady carefully. After a moment, Mat asked her, "You worked with plastic explosives before?"

"Yes. Not a lot." She shrugged. "I helped out, a little, on two separate occasions that involved plastic explosives." She paused. "While I was in the SEALs."

Sam folded her backpack up neatly into something resembling a square and handed it to Andy. "Put this in the bag, please."

Andy took it and placed it into the bag he was carrying for Megan.

"OK, let's go back to the wall and undo what the terrorists just did." Mat began walking across the bean field toward the wall.

When they arrived, Mat and Sam carefully examined the putty that had been placed on the wall. The terrorists had cleared away some dirt so the putty could be placed lower to the ground and out of sight.

Mat took more pictures and transmitted them to Washington. He took several close-up pictures of the putty. "Maybe they can figure out what it is," said Sam.

Mary Lu said, "I'll take some microscopic photos of the stuff that we can send to Washington too."

"Good idea," said Mat.

Sam pulled the two wires out of the putty and carefully stuck the leads down into the ground. Then she pulled out her knife and began to remove the putty from the base of the wall.

Mat removed his backpack with the putty and set it on the ground. He watched Sam for a while, then he removed his knife and began to help her scrape the putty from the wall.

Megan and Mary Lu found two plastic bags lying on the ground where the terrorists had thrown them. As Sam and Mat removed the putty, they handed it to Megan and Mary Lu, who wrapped it up in the clear wrapping as best they could.

After a few minutes, they were done. Mary Lu and Megan placed the plastic-wrapped putty into the backpack with the other putty. Sam knelt down next to the detonator. Mat knelt next to her with the device between them.

"We don't want them to know that we have removed their handiwork," said Mat.

"Are we ready to go?" asked Sam.

"No, not yet. We have a problem," said Mat.

"Like what? What's on your mind?" said Sam.

"Remember, their plan was to blow the sectors one at a time, killing everyone in the sector."

"Agreed," said Sam. Everyone nodded.

"It doesn't make sense that they put these leftovers in the shed unless they were done with them. That means that another sector is probably set to blow, just like this sector was."

"That means that we have to check the other two sectors. Is that what you're saying?" said Sam.

"Yep. That's what I'm saying."

Mary Lu said, "Do you have any idea how far that is? It took us forever to walk here. It would take at least one whole day to walk all the way around the next sector. Maybe two days."

"Yeah. I was afraid of that. It is what it is. The sectors have to be searched and disarmed. We have no choice," said Mat.

"Actually, we do have a choice," said Mary Lu.

Mat studied her for a moment. "How's that? If you have an idea, let's hear it."

"Andy is more than capable of doing this. And he'll do it a lot faster than any of us," said Mary Lu.

Mat didn't say anything. Trusting something this important to an android caused him to pause.

Mary Lu added, "Andy can do this. Really. Andy was not designed to work fast food."

Mat said, "Andy, do you know what we are looking for?"

"Yes." He faced Mary Lu. "I can find it for you. And I'll be a lot faster than any of you."

Mat smiled at Mary Lu, unconvinced. "Really?"

Mary Lu ignored him and walked toward Andy. "Andy, check the ag belt of the other two sectors. Walk down both walls, and stay hidden from the terrorists. Can you do that?"

"Yes, I won't let the bad people see me or get me."

"If you find anything, call us. We want the putty carefully placed inside the bag. Leave the detonator alone. Remove the wires from the putty and place the ends into the dirt on the ground, just like we did here. Can you do that?"

"Yes."

Megan took the bag back from Andy, then reached in and handed him the empty backpack.

"Good luck, Andy," said Mat. "See you when you get back."

"Bye," he said, and he was off. He ran like a cheetah, using all four limbs.

Mat's mouth fell open. *What the hell?*

Mary Lu laughed out loud. "You didn't realize how fast he could move, did you?"

"Wow."

"You do know that he is designed to function in an extreme environment—space. His purpose is to save lives. He is designed for a crisis where time is everything and where millions of lives may depend on him acting accurately and quickly. Yes, he certainly is a gifted athlete."

As Mary Lu spoke, Mat, Megan, and Sam watched him run like an animal. It was mesmerizing.

Mat took another look at the wall where the putty had been. "Well, we definitely have something to tell Washington."

CHAPTER 56

The team arrived back at their base, exhausted. It had been a long day. Mat's back was still sore from running through the bean field, hunched over to the ground. Megan grabbed her bag with the two toothbrushes, hair shampoo, and soap.

Mat and Sam each grabbed a pitcher for water from the coffee center in their office. Together, they went to the restrooms, where they spent the next thirty minutes washing. They used the pitchers to pour water over their heads to rinse out the shampoo, and they dried their bodies with paper towels.

When everyone was done, they took the elevator to the fifth-floor cafeteria and grabbed some food for dinner. Then they headed back down to their office to eat and call Washington.

Soon Andy reported in. He had found the putty set up in the ag belt, just like the one they had found. He had removed the putty and placed it into the bag, but he left the detonator where it was. He was now done checking the other two sectors and on his way back.

As they settled into the office, they gathered themselves on the floor in a semicircle as they had before, facing the phone. Everyone had their dinner in front of them.

"Are you guys ready?" asked Mat. "We are going to do this as a conference call again."

The First Lady cleared her throat. "Do it."

Mary Lu smiled at Megan. "We're ready."

* * *

Delphi interrupted everyone in the Situation Room. "Incoming call from Liberty," she said.

All conversations were suddenly terminated or suspended as Delphi put the image of the conference call on the monitors located around the room. An image popped up of Mat, Sam, Megan, and Mary Lu huddled around in a semicircle in the office.

"Hi, everyone. We got those pictures you sent us," said Amy Henderson.

Mary Lu spoke. "I'm going to try to get some microscopic pictures of the putty stuff for you later."

"That would be great. Send them to us as soon as you can."

"We had a long day today. We need to get you guys up to speed. First we scouted the perimeter, staying as far away as we could from the terrorists. When we came across small units of two to three terrorists, we eliminated them. We eliminated a total of four terrorists today. Those were the photo IDs we sent you," said Mat. He took a drink.

"We figured that's what those were," said Amy.

"While scouting the perimeter, we came across four more terrorists. It seemed that they were on a mission. All the other pictures we sent you were from them. We followed the four guys down to the ag belt. They then went to an exit pass and left the sector. They walked to the tubular middle of the sector, planted the putty on the base of the wall, and wired it with a remote detonator. You should have all those pictures. Then they left and went back where they came from. We removed the plastic explosives, but we left the detonator. We also retrieved additional putty and detonators that they had placed in a small shed.

"We sent Andy to inspect the walls in the second and third sectors, and he found that they had wired it with plastic explosives just as they had in the other one. We had the android remove the explosives, but we kept the detonator as they had it set.

"I guess we now know why they implemented the emergency protocol and divided the city into three sectors. They intend to blow the other two sectors one at a time."

"Did they wire the sector that they are in with the explosives?" asked Amy.

"No, they did not."

"If I heard you correctly, they wired the other two sectors but *not* their own sector."

"Correct."

"Interesting.. Is there anything else?" said Amy. It was almost midnight on Liberty.

"No. I think that covers it," said Mat.

The acting president gave a single nod, and Amy said, "Thank you, Sheriff McKenna, and thank you to everyone there with you. You did a hell of a job. Get some rest. We will talk later. Goodbye."

Everyone waved goodbye, and Mat picked up the sat phone and ended the call.

Day Three

CHAPTER 57

Mat fixed a fresh mug of coffee and watched Mary Lu. She had been busy at the desk with her tablet since early this morning, over two hours ago, and she was still at it.

He slid his chair next to hers at the desk and sat down. "Mind if I ask what you are doing?"

"I was looking some things up. I'm just about done." She lifted her face away from her tablet and toward Mat. Her brown eyes shone. There was an energy there.

Mat felt himself drawn to Mary Lu in ways he couldn't explain, but this was not the time for those thoughts. But still, her eyes were beautiful. They stared at each other for several moments, not saying anything.

Then Mary Lu smiled, the corner of her lips moving upward, and she shied away from him gently. She picked up her tablet again. "I have found some things I need to share with everyone."

"About what?"

"I know what that putty is." Her eyes were narrow, focused, all business.

"You mean now?"

"Yes, now would be good."

Mat pulled a couple of the empty chairs around to the front of the desk. Soon the team came back from the hallway and the bathrooms as everyone completed their morning rituals, and they sat down in front of Mary Lu. The meeting was ready to begin.

"What's up?" asked Sam.

Mary Lu said, "The putty that we found yesterday is not ordinary plastic explosives."

"What is it?" asked Megan. She sat next to her uncle.

"Andy ran it through the substance analyzer over at NASA last night. The analyzer broke it down chemically and took microscopic photos of it. This morning I transmitted the results to Washington. I have been looking at the results of the test with my tablet. I called Washington back with what I found, and they have confirmed it."

"So what is it?" asked Sam.

"Well, I've never heard of it before. It's called dermite."

"What's dermite?" asked Sam.

"It's a material used in the building demolition industry. You've seen videos of buildings being brought down by demolitionists, where the buildings fall straight down, right?"

Everybody nodded, and Sam said, "Sure."

"Many companies use dermite to do that. It's not just an explosive. It burns at a very high temperature; it will burn right through just about anything. It can be used almost anywhere. It contains its own oxygen supply in the compound itself. You can use it for underwater demolition.

"However, this is not ordinary dermite; it's molecular

dermite. Very pure. It requires a very high level of manufacturing technology. It's a nanotechnology product. This dermite is military grade. I just wanted everyone to know what we learned about it."

Megan, Sam, and Mary Lu all stood up to leave, but Mat remained sitting. He said, "I have an idea that we need to discuss. Now would be a good time."

They all glanced at each other and sat back down. "OK, what's your idea?" asked Sam.

"We cannot allow the terrorists to destroy the city sector by sector. Millions of people would be killed. If we can stop that, then we have to."

"Of course. I agree with that." Sam glanced around to everyone in the circle. "I think all of us agree with that. So what's your idea?"

"I think we should plant the dermite to blow the spaceport sector. Almost all the terrorists are in this one sector. With the sectors sealed, no one else in the other sectors would be hurt."

"We can take what the terrorists have planned and use it against them," said Mary Lu.

"Yes, something like that."

Sam shuffled in her chair and said, "But that means that my husband and my family will be killed."

Mat said, "It's possible. We will try to find them first. But—"

Sam interrupted him and said loudly, "Wait a minute. I am not going to rush off and kill my family! There must be other options. No."

"Yes. If it is our only option," said Mat.

Sam stood up. "*No!*" She looked at everyone in the circle

and came to a stop at Mat, staring at him in disbelief.

Mat had expected this reaction. That's why he wanted to mention it now so that it could germinate and grow, so they might still have a chance when no other credible options emerged. "We can't do nothing and let them kill millions of innocent people."

"I know! But . . . but . . . there must be another way!" demanded Sam.

"We don't have to do this now. But it's an option that must be on the table." Mat stood up. "The clock is running. We don't have forever. I am not saying we should decide this today. But if no other option becomes available, then we have to consider it. That's all I'm saying."

"*No!* I will *not* kill my family!" The blood vessels on Sam's neck were bulging.

Mary Lu cleared her throat, and everyone faced her. "Everyone, sit back down. I think there just might be another way."

Everyone sat down except Sam. She crossed her arms and stared at Mat, her eyes filled with pain and betrayal. She stared at him like that for several seconds. Then, finally, she faced Mary Lu and sat back down.

Mary Lu pulled up an image of the city and moved her tablet so everyone could view it. "These are the three sectors that have been sealed. This here is the spaceport, the sector that we are in. Now, let's go back in time. Back to when they built Liberty. The first thing they built was the repair shop, the garage. It's here at the very center of the city, at the hub." She pointed to it.

"They built it first because they needed it to build the

other sections and modules that make up the city: the exit chambers, emergency pass chambers, the docks in the docking bay, things like that. Things they had to have but were too big to ship up from Earth. All the large components that make up Liberty were manufactured there.

"The next thing they built were the docking rings and the docking bays. They needed them to assist in bringing in supplies and construction workers to and from Liberty. They then built outward to the city's tube structure, the city proper. The spaceport and housing for the workers who would live at Liberty while it was under construction were next. Today, what was the worker housing area is now called the control center complex.

"They needed to build housing for the workers, and they needed to be able to control the environment of the city to support life as it was constructed. They needed fresh air, water, sanitation, waste removal, stuff like that. So the housing, the control complex, the spaceport, and the docking bays were all built first, out of necessity. The rest of the city was built from there. That's why the control center complex and the spaceport are all together at the same location in the city."

Mary Lu zoomed in on the spaceport and the control complexes. "So this was built first. The construction workers lived here. It was pressurized, sealed off from the rest of the facility as they built. So in this sector is a small subsector. This small pressurized area housed all the workers. Does everyone see that?"

Everyone studied the map. "Yes, I see," said Megan.

Sam said carefully, "I know what you're saying. This

small area that today is the spaceport and control complex used to be housing for the workers when they were building Liberty."

"Exactly," said Mary Lu. She continued, "The structures used to seal off this core are still there. We don't have to blow the entire sector. Just the subsector, the core. The core is where most of the terrorists are anyway. As you can see from the map, there are a couple of hotels, some shopping plazas, and a few parks in the core today. But if we blow only this core, it would save a lot of lives."

"That's it!" said Mat.

Sam was more cautious. "Say that again from the beginning."

Mat went on. "It also means that Sam and I can check those two hotels and get at least some of the people out. It reduces the area we have to search to a reasonable size. We can search those two hotels and see if the president and First Family are there. That might be doable." He waited for Sam's reaction.

Sam said, "Can you say all that again? I'm sorry, I wasn't listening as well as I should have been."

"Sure," said Mary Lu. She walked back through it all. She explained how the city was built and how they only had to blow the core and not the entire sector.

When Mary Lu was done, everyone was quiet. They all watched the First Lady to see what her reaction would be.

Silence.

Then Sam spoke. "I see. Well, I think that is as good a solution to this mess as we will ever have. Blowing the core should be our plan," she said to Mat. "We need to let

Washington know. If they have a better plan, then great. Otherwise, they can coordinate an assault with us."

Everyone agreed.

Mary Lu said, "There are three areas and five walls that need to be sealed to make the core airtight. Everything hinges on that. When the city was completed, they opened up these two passages to the right and to the left of the core. They converted the structure in the ag belt into what is now the primary storage facility for agriculture.

"I believe that those large vault sections are still there. These wall-like doors are like hangar bay doors for aircraft, only they are huge. They are still there, just permanently open. They are on wheels, and they slide open and closed like sliding glass doors—but they have never been closed since they were opened when the structure was completed."

"Why are they still there?" asked Megan.

"They just left them there. They are too big to be hauled away; they would have to be cut into pieces to be removed. Besides, you never know when you might need them. Why bother? Frankly, it was cheaper and easier to just leave them. People walk by them every day and have no idea that those walls are actually sliding doors."

Megan said, "And now those doors are the key to saving the whole city."

CHAPTER 58

Mary Lu, Mat, and Sam gathered around Mary Lu's tablet.

"When are we going to plant the dermite?" asked Mat. He leaned toward Mary Lu. "Look, there's no point in putting this off. Let's get it done."

"I agree. So where do we place the dermite?" asked Sam. Now both she and Mat questioned Mary Lu with their eyebrows raised.

"Wait a minute. I don't know. I've never done anything like this before! Don't just look at me. Don't you dare dump this on me." She crossed her arms and made a point of looking back at both of them, one at a time. "Besides, Mrs. First Lady of the United States, weren't you the big-shot Navy SEAL? Isn't this up your alley? Hmm?"

Mat laughed out loud. This was so unreal.

Megan was quietly drinking a soda in the corner of the office, trying to stay out of the discussion. She raised her left eyebrow; she knew that Uncle Mat had just made a mistake. She had seen it before, and she figured that she would probably see it again.

Mary Lu pivoted and aimed her eyes at Mat. "Aren't you

Sheriff McKenna? Aren't law enforcement people supposed to know about things like this?"

"We didn't mean to dump this on you. Sorry, Mary Lu. But Mat and I need your help," said Sam.

"How about if we just do this together," said Mat.

"Thanks." Mary Lu smiled.

Mat spoke mechanically, just the facts. "It needs to be someplace we can get to without being noticed. Someplace they wouldn't look or stumble upon. And it needs to be someplace where it will work and get the job done."

"Exactly," said Sam. "What are the options, Mary Lu? Any suggestions?"

"Can it be inside or outside? Does it matter? Do we know?" asked Mat.

Mary Lu said, "I would say we should plant it inside. We know what it does underwater, but we have no idea what it would do in the vacuum of space. Fluids boil in space. I don't know what this stuff would do. Why risk it? Put it inside."

Mat rubbed his chin. "OK, inside it is. Where inside? Let's start by elimination. Forget the spaceport, forget the control complex. That leaves the docking bays—"

Mary Lu interrupted. "No, forget the docking bays. They will seal and protect the rest of the sector. The dermite has to be on the tube structure of the city. The docking bays are designed to shut down."

"So that narrows that down," said Sam. "What a shame. It would have been easy to get to since we can get there from space." Then she pointed to the map. "Why can't we just go to the ag belt and plant it like they did?"

Mary Lu enlarged the map and examined it. "That's a great idea. We need to seal the door to the agricultural storage building anyway. Why not plant the putty there and seal the door at the same time? Two birds with one stone."

"I like it. Why would the terrorists be in the storage building? We can get there from the ag belt," said Sam.

"It's perfect," agreed Mat.

"Time to call Washington?" asked Sam.

Mat nodded. "Yep."

CHAPTER 59

Delphi spoke in a clear, commanding voice. "Incoming call from Liberty." Images began to pop up on the monitors of everyone gathered around the phone, sitting cross-legged on the floor.

National Security Advisor Amy Henderson glanced at her watch. "Hi, everyone. Is everything all right? Has anything changed?"

Mat got right to the point. "We have a plan that we are going to implement, unless you have a better one, but we are hoping that you will coordinate with us."

Everyone in the room was taken aback by the aggressive nature of the comment. "Let's not be too quick about this just yet," said Amy.

"What's your plan?" asked Scott Chao, the secretary of defense.

"It's obvious that the terrorists plan to kill everyone in the city one sector at a time. I guess you could say that we plan to do to them what they were going to do to us." Mat took a drink from his soda. "We plan on planting the dermite in their sector and blowing it."

Secretary Chao leaned back. This was something. Tangible. Real.

Amy spoke to the comm cylinder at the center of the table. "Delphi, show us a map of the orbital city of Liberty."

An image popped up on the screens around the conference table. "Is this one all right?" Delphi asked.

"Show a map containing the emergency sectors," said Amy.

Another map came up, clearly showing the city divided into three sectors. "Better?" she asked.

"Yes. Thanks," said Amy. "Now highlight the sector with the spaceport. Show the spaceport and control center complex."

The image outlined the spaceport and the control center complex. "OK?"

"OK," said Amy.

Mat jumped back in. "There's more. Let me give you the short version; you can look it up easier than we can later on. When the city was built, first came the repair shack. It was needed to build the major structural components, like exit hatches and gates. Next they added the docking bay and the docking rings. They needed them to fly supplies from the Earth and the moon, and they needed the docking facilities to fly workers and supplies to and from the construction site.

"They then built the tube frame of the city. Inside that frame, they built the core first. What is today used for the spaceport and the control complex was initially used to house the workers who built the city. This core was airtight;

the workers lived there for many years while they built the city. This core is a subset of the sector. We plan to seal the core from the rest of the sector, then blow the core."

"Hold on just a minute," said Amy quickly. "Delphi, do you know what he is talking about?"

"Yes."

"Show me."

Delphi displayed the outline of the core within the sector.

Amy commanded, "Delphi, analysis. Can they seal the sector?"

"Yes, if they have the proper tools. And assuming no one stops them, of course."

Scott Chao leaned forward on his elbow and examined the map. He then abruptly said to the acting president, "Sounds like we just might have a plan."

Mat interrupted. "There is still more."

The acting president grabbed her mug of coffee that had been sitting idle on the table for over an hour. She sat back in her chair with her cold coffee. "Well, by all means, continue."

"The docking bay structure is part of the core. It has been designed to seal and close in an emergency. We plan on closing the docking bay off. The docking bay and its docking rings will remain pressurized. We hope that you will coordinate an attack with us and dock at the ring when we blow the core. We will open the boarding gate." Mat breathed in and exhaled. "Copy?"

Everyone in the Situation Room began talking to one another.

Mat repeated, "Copy?"

Amy replied, "Copy. Can you give us a few minutes while we look at this?"

"Can you keep the comm open so we can listen?" asked Mat.

The acting president answered, "You got it, Mat."

* * *

Mat, Sam, Mary Lu, Megan, and Andy listened in. It was odd. It was also a chance for them to relax, to become detached and to let someone else deal with this nightmare. In a bizarre way, they were free of the problem. They were spectators in their own show.

As they relaxed, they listened to the discussions in the White House Situation Room. They learned that the White House had been training Marines and a variety of specialists for potential operations. Educating troops about the city environment. Interesting.

* * *

Amy asked, "When do you plan on setting the dermite?"

"Today," said Mat.

"Today? Why so soon?" she asked.

"No point in putting it off."

"When do you plan on blowing it?"

"Tonight, when most of the terrorists are asleep. We can't seal the core until the moment we want to blow it. We need to seal it when no one is around. Night is our best chance."

"All right. We will have our demolition experts talk with

Mary Lu later. Call us when you are done," said Amy.

"We gotta go."

"Good luck to you. Sounds like you have a real job ahead of you tonight. Let us know when you get the dermite planted," said Amy.

"Roger that." Mat reached up and took hold of the phone and terminated the call.

Mat stared out the window for several minutes, thinking. It was only nine o'clock in the morning. *Today is the day.*

Andy unplugged himself from the wall. "I have an idea."

Everyone was startled. They all wanted to hear what he was going to say.

Mary Lu asked him, "What's your idea, Andy?"

"I should ask the service droids that work in the restaurants and hotels if any of them have seen the president or the First Family."

"That's an excellent idea," said Sam.

"I will ask them to keep an eye out for them and to let me know if they hear anything." He added, "I will let them know it is top secret."

"Even better," said Mary Lu.

Andy smiled. "I'm not a microwave oven or a refrigerator, you know. I can think."

Mary Lu explained to the group, "Andy will be able to question them in digi talk, so humans won't even know they are talking. No one will know anyone is even asking."

"Digi talk?" asked Sam.

"Yes, that's a digital language that robots and androids use for direct communications. The service droids use digi talk to talk to devices, like phones, blenders, thermostats, or whatever. It's a wireless world. The terrorists won't even know they're talking. If it is possible for us to find them, this is the only practical way for us to do it. A droid might overhear a conversation. Who knows?"

"It's settled then," said Mat. "We go to the ag belt to plant the dermite and seal the storage bay door. Then Andy talks to the droids to see what he can learn."

CHAPTER 61

Mary Lu and Andy had a short conversation, and then Andy left. Mat and Sam checked their weapons, making sure they were fully loaded. They each carried an extra magazine and a knife. Mat picked up one of the sat phones and pocketed it. He handed the other sat phone to Sam, then grabbed the backpack containing the dermite and handed it to Megan. And they were off.

Mat, Sam, Mary Lu, and Megan traveled down to the ag belt. Even though no one was in sight, they proceeded with caution, using the bean field as cover, walking hunched over along the city wall.

When they were moving parallel to the storage facility, located in the tubular center of the sector, they stopped and waited. They all looked carefully out over the leafy green fields. After a moment, Mat gave the go-ahead, and they crossed the bean field to the large central ag storage bin. Nobody was there to spot them.

They opened the large garage door to the storage bin and walked inside. They were now in the core. When the city was completed, the builders had converted this large room into the main storage facility for the ag belt.

"Follow me to the cellar," said Mary Lu.

"Cellar?" asked Sam.

"This huge storage bin doesn't have any dirt. Understand, the ground we just walked on is six feet of dirt. There is no dirt in here." They walked into the storage bin, came to the cellar steps, and went down to the very bottom. "All right, we made it. On the other side of this floor is outer space."

They scanned the room. Where to plant the dermite? They walked over toward the center of the floor between two aisles of fertilizer. Megan lowered the knapsack from her shoulder. They removed the dermite and laid it out just as the demolition expert from the White House Situation Room had advised.

Mat removed the sat phone and took a picture of the dermite. He zoomed in and showed the wiring, then took another snapshot of the detonator.

They moved some bags around and spent the next thirty minutes reorganizing part of the room to hide the putty, then Mat pushed a button on the sat phone and called in to the Situation Room. "Did you get the photos?"

"Yes. The demolition team and I are looking at the pictures now," said Amy.

A few moments passed.

"They look good," said Amy. "You did it. Get out of there."

"Amy, we are thinking of blowing this between three and five this morning Liberty time."

"Based on our last conversation, we figured as much. The team is moving toward launch standby. Should be ready in about five to six hours. We have six spaceliners being prepared on the ground to be ready to lift off. On your word, we will launch two of them. Understand, they will have to dock two hours after taking off, or they will have to come back to Earth."

"Understood."

"On your orders, they will launch." Amy wanted to make sure.

"Roger that. When I give the order, they launch. They will arrive two hours later."

"Correct."

"They won't be ready for another five hours at the earliest," said Mat.

The secretary of defense silently nodded.

"Roger that," said Amy to Mat.

"Bye." Mat hung up the sat phone and slipped it into his pocket.

They walked back up the cellar stairs and out of the storage facility, but Mary Lu just stood at the door.

No one said anything for a few moments. Then Mat asked, "What are we waiting for?"

"We are waiting for Andy. He's bringing some things we need to seal the doors—this one and the others too. I also want Andy here so he can see it done."

They waited a few more minutes, and Mary Lu said into her comm, "Andy, are you OK?"

"I'm coming, Mary Lu. I'm in the ag belt now. I have the supplies you requested."

They all looked around the ag belt for him.

"There he is!" said Megan. She pointed.

Andy was coming at them fast. He had a bag in his hand. Presently he arrived.

Mat realized that there was one annoying thing about androids: no matter how hard and fast they worked, they were never out of breath. It was like they were always fresh and never tired. An obvious design flaw.

"Let's close it and seal it," said Mary Lu. Andy dropped the bag that Mary Lu had requested. She removed the contents.

"Andy, we are going to close and seal this door. If you have any questions, let me know."

"OK. It's pretty simple. The doors are already designed to be sealed. Nobody does it, but they could," said Andy.

"True. But in life, things are often not as easy as they should be."

Mary Lu swept the edges of the door with a handheld broom and then rolled the giant door into place like a large sliding glass door. She inserted a key into the door and locked it into place and then pulled a lever down, which wedged the door into the wall. Then Mary Lu removed something from the bag that looked like a tube of caulking material. She applied it all around the edge of the door, leaving an inch-thick gray material.

"What's that?"

"Insurance. It's emergency sealant for small gashes. It's stronger than steel, designed for emergency repairs to the structures. It's already dried. It dries and sets almost instantly. It has to."

Mat touched it. She was right; it was dry. "Let's go."

"One down, four to go," said Mary Lu.

CHAPTER 62

They arrived back at their base at midafternoon. The plan was to go into action at two o'clock in the morning. They would seal the core and blow it.

Hopefully, Andy would return with some information. They would evaluate what he said. If they did not know where the president was, they would move forward anyway; too many lives depended on them. Odds were that the president would not be in the core. It was a gamble they had to take. Sam hated it, but she understood.

Mat's watch read 6:05. He stood up. "I'm going to the cafeteria. Anyone want anything?" He had to do something. He could not just sit and wait.

"I'm coming too," said Sam.

"I'm not hungry or thirsty. Surprise us, Uncle Mat." Megan smiled at him. "You can bring me something if you want."

Mary Lu jumped all over that. She walked up to Mat. "Yeah! Pick something out for us." She spun around like a ballerina and walked away.

Mat watched the soft, round curve of Mary Lu's jeans as she left. A pair of blue jeans had never looked better. Then he glanced over to find the First Lady watching him. *Great. The First Lady of the United States is watching me admire Mary Lu's ass. Well, the female form is beautiful.*

The First Lady forced a smile at Mat. *Here we are, my children's lives are at stake, and Sheriff McKenna is looking at a woman's ass. Men. No wonder the world is so messed up.*

Mat grabbed their food bag. He and Sam waved goodbye and left for the elevator.

* * *

They didn't come up to the cafeteria often. It was on the top floor of the office complex, so coming there to replenish the small supply of food and drinks in their office cooler was like a mini trip. Mat grabbed a diet soft drink for Megan.

"What are you going to get for Mary Lu?" asked Sam.

"I don't know. She likes green tea."

"She does." Sam paused.

He grabbed a chicken salad sandwich for Mary Lu and an Italian sandwich for Megan. He grabbed chips and a healthy snack bar for each as well, along with a handful of other snacks. What the heck?

Sam laughed. *Smart move; he's got every base covered.* Their little satchel was getting full. He then put some ice into plastic freezer bags and threw them into their food bag, along with a couple more sandwiches and drinks.

"Sam? What are you getting?"

"I don't know. I'm not really hungry."

"Mat! Sam! Where are you?" yelled Mary Lu into the comm.

"What is it?" asked Mat.

Sam and Mat came running down the hallway toward the stairs.

Megan called out. "Uncle Mat! You better come here fast."

Mat and Sam dropped everything and sprinted down the stairs as quietly as they could. They pulled their weapons when they reached their floor and ran past the elevator.

"Coming," said Mat. "We'll be there in a minute. Hold on."

They quietly snuck into the office complex.

"Hurry!" cried Megan.

As they approached the hallway leading to their office, Mat and Sam slowed down. They quietly came toward their office and stopped just outside the door. It was closed.

Using hand gestures to each other, they positioned themselves by the door. They might have only one crack at this. Failure could easily mean death. Sam would open the door and Mat would go in first, followed by Sam.

Sam lipped, *One.*

Mat nodded. He understood.

Two.

Sam gripped the doorknob and turned it slowly so that no one would notice.

Three.

She threw open the door, and Mat exploded into the room, weapon raised.

Megan opened her mouth to scream but nothing came out, as Mat's gun was pointed at her head, and Mary Lu made an unintelligible guttural sound when Sam swung into the room with her weapon pointed at her.

Mat and Sam scanned the room. It was empty. There was no one else in the room, just Megan and Mary Lu. Slowly Sam and Mat lowered their guns.

"What is it? What's wrong?" asked Mat.

"You guys scared me to death!" said Megan.

"Well, what do you think you just did to us?" said Sam.

Sam and Mat were still panting from all the energy from charging down.

"So what's up?" asked Mat between breaths.

They pointed to Mary Lu's tablet. It was showing the news broadcast.

Mary Lu stood up and motioned for Sam to sit down in her chair. Quickly Sam sat down while Mary Lu and Mat grabbed chairs for themselves. They all gathered around, watching the local news broadcast.

President Devane had been captured, along with his two children and Agent Cass. The news broadcast replayed them being walked out of an apartment building with their hands tied behind their backs.

When the broadcast was over, they gathered around Sam, who remained sitting, staring at the monitor. Tears streamed down her face; she was terrified of what they would do to her family. And Sarah. Especially Sarah.

She slowly faced Mat. "You promised me we would get them. You promised! And what have you done? Nothing!" Her hands were shaking.

"I'm sorry," said Mat.

Sam slapped him as hard as her body would permit. The sound was loud like a gunshot. The movement was crisp, clean, athletic, the blow delivered with precision. "You bastard. Now those barbaric two-legged animals have my babies and my husband." Her lips quivered, her eyes sharp as needles.

"I'm sorry," repeated Mat. He absorbed the full impact of the blow. The side of his face became white, and then his face became bloodred. He felt numb. He slowly withdrew from Sam, leaving her alone in the room with the rest of them.

Fear gripped the First Lady for several minutes as she wept, occasionally bordering on sobbing. Slowly she came back to them as she regained control of her emotions.

Mary Lu walked over to Mat. "What do we do now?" she asked in a quiet voice so no one else could hear.

Mat replied, "We wait for Andy. Let's see what he finds out. It's still early evening; it's only six thirty-five. There is still time."

From across the room, Sam could see the swelling of Mat's face where she had struck him. She was sorry for striking him. But she wasn't in the mood to apologize.

CHAPTER 63

It was seven in the evening when Andy showed up. "Did you learn anything, Andy?" asked Mat.

Andy slowly looked at Mary Lu and then Mat. "About the terrorists?"

"Yes."

"Yes, I think so. A little."

They all pulled up their chairs and gathered around in a loose circle. This was going to require them, all of them, to glean as much information from what he had heard from the other droids as they could.

"What did you learn?" asked Mat.

"Yassin is the leader. His favorite dinner is sirloin with baked potato. He won't eat the green beans or the salad. Hates the salads. Loves fried shrimp. His girlfriend is named Shakira."

Sam's mouth was open slightly, her eyes narrowed a bit as she leaned back in her chair. She brought her soda closer to her chest.

"Go on," said Mat.

"He likes to eat dinner at six, usually in one of the restaurants in or near the spaceport complex. He sleeps in the hotels in the spaceport. The command center for the terrorists was supposed to be the control center complex, but Yassin doesn't like being in there. He thinks it's boring and prefers to be where the food, wine, and women are. He thinks that's the spaceport.

"There is no second-in-command. He has an array of commanders that he sometimes delegates various tasks to. Aaziz is one of these men. Aaziz is angry at Yassin, hates him in fact. The others fear Aaziz. Aaziz has a small but loyal following. You know the woman who was trapped on Air Force One?"

"Yes."

"That was Aaziz's woman. Her name was Shali. He hates Yassin for letting her get trapped on Air Force One. Blames him for it. Blames him for not doing anything about it."

"Do you have more on him?"

"Yes."

"Go on," said Mat. He could not believe the level of detail that he was hearing.

"He and some of his troops blame Yassin for allowing you and the president to escape. In their opinion, he let the president escape not once but twice. The first time was at the celebration. The second time was when you showed up at the control center complex."

"Anything else?" asked Sam.

"Yes. Many of the terrorists believe that he has shamed Islam with the many failures in this operation."

Now it was time for the big question. He dreaded what the answer was likely to be. He had to ask. "Do you know where the president is?"

"Yes."

Mat stood up. *Oh my God.*

Andy continued, "The president is being kept at the Palms Hotel along with his two children, Sarah and Michael. The children are in the room adjacent to the president. Agent Cass is being kept in a separate location. She has been tortured. The damage is not permanent, not yet. They know about you, Sheriff McKenna."

"I'm flattered," he said.

"Was that information obtained from Agent Cass?" asked Sam.

"Yes, I think so," answered Andy.

"Anything else?" asked Mat.

"Everyone has left the hotels in the spaceport. The terrorists have taken them over. The hotel and restaurant chefs are forced to cook. Everyone else is gone."

"Andy, you learned all this from the service droids?" asked Mat.

"Yes."

"Thanks, Andy," said Mat. "Great job. Unbelievable."

Sam stood up next to Mat, and they embraced for several minutes.

* * *

At seven fifteen came another breaking news story about a major new development. In response to the United States' refusal to meet their demands, the terrorists announced that the president would be executed at nine o'clock. The execution would be streamed live.

CHAPTER 64

"Listen up, everyone," said Mat. "Here's the plan. Sam, Andy, and I will get the First Family. As soon as we are out of the core, we will let Mary Lu know. Andy will then go and help Mary Lu. Mary Lu and her team of droids will seal the core off, then Megan will blow the core. After the core is blown, we will regroup and get down to the docking bay and then let the combat troops in.

"The detonator is yours, Megan. If we can't rescue the president or if anything happens to us, blow the core."

"No."

"Yes. I'm depending on you."

"Uncle Mat—"

"Megan, there is no one else. Everyone else is going to be exposed. If we were captured with the detonator, it would be game over for everyone in the city. Millions of lives would be doomed."

"OK, Uncle Mat, but you'd better not die on me."

"Mary Lu, when we take the president, maybe the terrorists will be too busy trying to kill us to notice you and your droids. Hopefully, you will be free to close the doors."

"We only need a moment. They won't be expecting this."

"Mary Lu and Megan, both the sat phones are yours. Mary Lu, I will let you know when to tell Washington that they need to launch."

CHAPTER 65

Washington DC
White House
Situation Room

The president was led down a hallway with his hands tied behind his back. His two children followed. Cass was last. She had been struck in the face repeatedly. Her left eye was swollen shut.

Two terrorists escorted them and two followed behind. Another was filming them as they were led down the hallway of the apartment complex.

The images were from the apprehension earlier in the day. Everyone in the Situation Room knew that these images would be replayed all day long on every broadcast news agency in the world.

Amy Henderson sat with her head in her hands.

"Amy, can I get someone to bring you some aspirin?" said Delphi.

"No, thanks."

She was remembering when President-Elect Devane had first approached her for the job. It was over a dinner. She had just delivered her first baby, Faith. The president-elect had promised her that she would be able to work at home, at least some of the time. She could have several special assistants to facilitate her ability to take the job. He really needed her. The country needed her. The job was everything she wanted professionally. At least that's what she thought before she had her baby.

What she'd wanted was to be with Faith and her husband. Even more than that, she wanted a world where Faith would be safe and could live a life filled with joy.

She watched the monitor. Her president and his two children were marched out of the apartment complex for the world to see. Her eyes narrowed. *OK, you bastards.*

The terrorist announced an execution time. At nine o'clock tonight, the president would be executed. *Prime time.*

Amy turned to General Lee Solaski. He shook his head no. He bit his bottom lip in a grimace. He knew what she was asking, pleading. There was nothing they could do.

It was clear the terrorists wanted to build tension for their barbaric act. The moderator also suggested that they had been told the children would be given a chance to convert to Islam and would not be executed if they did. Publicly, however, the terrorists had said nothing about the children.

* * *

"We have a call from Liberty. This is not a conference call," said Delphi.

"This is Amy Henderson. Are you there?"

"Yes, I'm here. The plan is a go," said the female voice.

"And who are we speaking to?" asked Amy.

"This is the chief engineer of Liberty, Mary Lu Hayashi. We are proceeding with the plan. You should launch immediately."

"Is Sheriff McKenna available?"

"No, and I won't be either in another minute."

"And why is that?"

"Because Mat and Sam are on their way to extract the president."

"How're they going to do that?" asked Amy.

"I have no idea, but I know he will get it done. We know where the president and First Family are being held. We know where the agent is being held too, but she isn't in the core."

Megan spoke up. "Uncle Mat said that they would rescue the president, so the president will be rescued."

"And who is this?" asked Amy.

"I'm Megan. I'm the one with the detonator, so you'd better be ready. Bye."

Mary Lu said, "I have to say goodbye too."

"Wait one moment." Amy made a silent motion to Delphi.

"Comm silence."

Megan and Mary Lu could no longer hear the conversation.

"Delphi, voice analysis."

"Voices are under duress. Tired, stressed out. Voice stress analysis indicates a ninety-two percent probability that they are telling the truth when identifying the location of the president."

Amy said to the acting president, "Only on your command."

The acting president slowly stood up. "Command given." She walked over to the coffee station and fixed another mug.

"Delphi, connect to Liberty," said Amy.

"Done," said Delphi.

"Mary Lu?"

"Yes?"

"It's a go. They are on their way. Call us back when the core is blown."

"You got it." Mary Lu hung up and put the phone in the back pocket of her jeans.

CHAPTER 66

A ndy entered the service entrance of the hotel. "It's clear."

Sam and Mat moved up to the service entrance with Andy. They went down the hallway and took the stairs to the second floor. Mat carefully cracked the stairway door open and peeked out into the hallway. It was empty.

"We need an empty room near where they will be headed. Let's get between the room they are being held in and the elevators."

It was clear that the hotel staff was gone. Too many of the rooms were open, the doors left ajar. "Are you sure they're down there?"

"Yes. They made no attempt to hide anything from the droids."

Mat stepped into the hallway and quietly raced toward one of the rooms where the door was partially open. The lights were off in the room; it was dark inside. He slipped into the room. It took a moment for his eyes to adjust. Mat glanced around the room. It was empty. Mat went back to the door and waved to Sam and Andy, who joined him in the room.

The terrorists had left the hotel almost barren. They were arrogant; they clearly assumed that they had total control of the area. They felt no threat.

"Now we wait and let them bring the First Family to us. If they are headed to the main entrance of the hotel, they will pass right by us."

"Agreed," said Sam. "One thing is for sure: we will never be able to rescue them once they are surrounded by their troops. We take them now or never."

"Yep," said Mat. "As soon as they pass by, we will emerge and take them down."

Mat cracked the door open just a hair so he could look. They all waited quietly by the door, watching.

"I want you to go to the back stairs. It's the only other way they could go. They should not be going that way, but if they do, I want you to tell us. Then I'm going to have a job for you."

"What?" asked Andy.

"Plan B," responded Mat.

Andy left the room and went to the back stairs. If the terrorists went the back way, at least they would know.

Soon they heard the ding of the elevator. Voices were suddenly heard from that direction. They heard people walking toward them, several people. Presently two camera crews of two people each walked by as they headed down the hallway. They reached the end of the hallway, where it made an L-turn, and disappeared.

"See anything, Andy?" asked Mat.

"No, but some people just came up to the room and are standing outside. I can't see them, but I can hear them. I don't have a line of sight."

"Where are you?"

"I'm in a utility closet. If they come this way, I will know."

Mat placed a hand on Sam's shoulder and squeezed it gently but firmly, and her eyes fell on him. He didn't say anything. He didn't have to. He pulled his weapon from its sheath and rechecked his knife. She did the same. It was ten till nine. The terrorists meant to make a show of this. And it was close to showtime.

Andy heard a door open down the hallway, and then he heard someone talking about the live pictures of the president and his children. The sounds became fainter. "I believe they are out of the room and headed your way."

"Thanks, Andy. Now go get us five jumpsuits and five helmets. Bring them back into the core and back to us."

"Five jumpsuits from the space suits and five space suit helmets. Roger that," said Andy.

Mary Lu's voice broke in. "Hey, that's a good plan B."

"You don't think we will make it out of the core, do you?" said Sam.

"Nope. I don't."

CHAPTER 67

Mat glanced out from the side of the cracked door. There were six terrorists: two in the front escorting and two in the rear. One terrorist was at the side of the president, another was with the two children. Four people were reporters, one camera team in the front and the other in the back. Mat had the distinct impression that the camera crews were with the terrorists.

The president and the children had their hands tied behind their back and were blindfolded with black scarves. Cass was not there. The president and his two children were being led down the hallway, toward the hotel room where Mat and Sam waited. National journalists were covering the event. The terrorists wanted everyone to witness their triumph.

Beyond the door, the sounds in the hallway became louder. The terrorists were getting closer. Mat stepped away from the door. Why take the chance of being spotted through the crack? The voices were louder now, more distinctive. Mat could make out the voices from different individuals. Mostly it was the reporters who were talking. They were getting very close.

Mat and Sam waited for them to pass the door; then they would strike. Mat wanted the terrorists to walk past them.

That way, the terrorists would have to turn around to see them. Advantage Mat and Sam.

Mat watched the light under the door dim, and he heard the voices of the journalists pass by.

* * *

Amy Henderson watched the president of the United States and his two children being walked out of the hotel room on live television. *So much for the rescue,* she thought. *This is going to be the worst day of my life.*

Everyone in the Situation Room watched. No one wanted to, but they needed to know everything they could, so they watched. The terrorists were almost to the elevator. The Situation Room was quiet. Dead quiet.

* * *

Mat nodded once and slipped out the door, Sam right behind him. Mat raised his weapon and fired two shots at the two terrorists escorting the group. They fell where they stood. Sam fired two rounds, striking the two terrorists in the back of the group. Two shots, two kills.

That left two terrorists, one next to the president and one with the children. The journalists backed up and got out of the way, but they kept filming this unfolding historic event.

Sam held her gun with both hands in a crouched firing position, aiming at the man holding her children. He was hiding behind the kids, trying to use their bodies as a shield.

The man next to the president grabbed him around the neck and spun him around in front of him. Mat raised his gun and leveled it at him.

Sam fired three shots just over her daughter's shoulder at the man hiding behind her kids. The first shot hit the man in the base of the neck and struck his spinal cord. The second shot struck him in the face; the third grazed the top of his skull. He collapsed to the ground.

The terrorist held the president from behind. "Lay down your guns or I will shoot!" He had his right arm wrapped around the president's throat, his gun pointed at his head.

Really? Is that right?

Mat squeezed the trigger. A split second passed and he squeezed again.

The man's pupils went wide, and two red dots formed on his forehead. The arm around the president dropped down. His hand holding the gun fell to the side, and the man staggered backward one step. He wavered a moment as the two red dots grew redder. The man then collapsed to the floor, dead.

Mat pulled his knife and cut the president's hands loose. He ripped off the blindfold. Sam had already cut her kids free and had removed their blindfolds.

Sarah and Michael exploded in happiness. "Mom!" they cried and jumped into her arms. Sam was on one knee, large round tears raining from her eyes. She held both of them in one giant hug.

They could hear yelling in the distance. Stunned, angry yells. And the yells were getting louder.

"Let's go," said Sheriff McKenna. He grabbed Sam by the shoulder and pulled her to her feet.

* * *

Amy Henderson found herself watching the others in the room as much as the monitors. No one said anything as the president of the United States was escorted as a prisoner with his two children. The acting president watched the monitors with her left arm draped on the top of a table, her right hand open across her mouth and chin.

There was a blur of motion to the side of the hallway. *Pop, pop . . . pop-pop.* The images showed men falling, then the views became blurry as the camera moved around quickly from place to place, not knowing what to show. The blurring stopped. Sheriff McKenna was pointing his weapon at the man holding the president. The terrorist yelled, "Lay down your guns or I will shoot!"

A wide shot revealed four men on the ground, dead.

Amy stopped breathing as everyone stood frozen in time. Mat pointed his gun at the terrorist while the terrorist had his gun pointed at the president's head.

Pop, she heard. *Pop.* She watched; she could see nothing. Mat was still pointing his gun— No, he was reaching for his knife. She saw the two dots on the terrorist's forehead, and he dropped his gun as he stepped backward one step. Mat was at the president's side, cutting him loose. The terrorist Mat had shot collapsed to the ground.

The next image on the screen showed Sam holding her children. They were crying. Sam was on one knee, giving her kids the biggest hug Amy had ever seen. Amy reached up to her cheek and wiped away a tear.

Everyone in the White House Situation Room was on their feet with their mouths open. The room was silent. The rescue had just been broadcast live everywhere.

"Damn!" exclaimed General Lee Solaski happily.

* * *

Andy watched the television monitors and saw the rescue. He had anticipated this. The terrorists were dazed and in shock. The terrorists could not believe that this was happening again. The commanders shouted orders to their troops. The troops were everywhere! Yassin ordered thirty of his men to go after them. The troops began yelling, shouting, cursing. Then they ran toward the hotel in pursuit.

Andy began to speak in digi talk. Suddenly, androids and servant droids from fast-food restaurants, along with hotel and office droids of all kinds, emerged into the hallways. The entrances to the hotel were blocked by a wall of androids. They poured out from the rooms, clerks' offices, and the hotel's front offices. The androids were everywhere!

The soldiers ran up to the front of the hotel, but there was nowhere for them to go. The passageways were blocked by the androids. The soldiers tried to push the androids out of the way, but there were too many of them.

"Arrrggh!" screamed Aaziz. "Go another way! Go around to the rear of the hotel! *To the rear!*"

Andy walked past the hotel and went to a path back behind the hotel. "Thank you," he said in digi talk. "You did an excellent job. You stopped the bad people."

Andy darted out of the spaceport, then broke into a full sprint like a cheetah using all four of his limbs, running at full speed. It was a moment like this that he had been designed for. He had to get those space suits.

* * *

Mary Lu was watching everything from Andy's comm feed. "Oh my God! I can't believe it," she said, laughing out loud.

"What?" said Megan.

Mary Lu continued to laugh. "Andy just had all the service androids block the terrorists from chasing Mat."

"You're kidding me."

"He did that on his own. That many droids had to be prearranged, prepositioned," she said, thinking out loud. "Andy did that all by himself." Mary Lu smiled at Megan.

CHAPTER 68

Aaziz rushed up to Yassin. "Blow the sector!" he commanded.

"What?" Shakira, who was standing next to Yassin, gave Aaziz a dirty look.

"Blow the sector, now. Make them pay for this humiliation!" he screamed. Aaziz was getting angrier with every second. His blood vessels were about to pop.

Shakira looked at Aaziz with eyes brimming with hatred. *How dare he speak to Yassin that way,* she thought.

"You don't give me orders," answered Yassin. He reached for his gun, but before he could pull it out, a man grabbed his hand from behind him.

"Wha—" Yassin yanked his arm away and said to the man who had held his wrist, "How dare you!"

Aaziz reached to his side and pulled his sidearm. He leveled the gun at Shakira and fired once. The bullet plowed through Shakira's chest, deforming and tumbling into her heart before punching its way out of her back.

Shakira fell dead to the ground.

"How does it feel to have your woman killed?" he asked Yassin.

Before Yassin could answer, Aaziz shot Yassin in the forehead, and he fell dead.

Aaziz reached down and grabbed Yassin's comm from his dead hand. "This is Aaziz. I am now in charge. We will make the infidels pay for this, I promise you. They will pay dearly."

Aaziz called Wadi in the control center complex. "Wadi, this is Aaziz. I'm in charge now. Understand?"

"Yes, Aaziz, I understand. What can I do for you?"

"Do you have the detonator for the first sector?"

He spotted the device sitting on the right side of his desk. "Yes, Aaziz. It's right here."

"Keep it with you. Don't let anyone else have it."

"Yes, sir."

"On my command, I want you to detonate it." A smile touched the corners of his lips. He would blame POTUS for this. "Have the cameras showing the outside and the inside of the sector turned on. Then I want you to send the feeds to the broadcast unit. I want the world to see this."

"Yes, sir." Wadi flipped some switches, and the cameras came on: two external shots showing where the dermite would burn a hole and two distant internal shots showing people moving about in public in the sector about to be destroyed.

The monitors inside the spaceport flipped, and the images of the sector popped up.

Aaziz stood in front of the camera. "Because of the temporary escape of the president, this is what happens when you resist."

He picked up his comm. "Wadi, blow the sector."

"Yes, sir." Wadi pressed the button.

Everyone was staring at the images of the sector, including Aaziz. Nothing happened.

"Wadi, did you hear me? Detonate the sector. Now."

"I did." He pressed the button again. Then again, and again. "Nothing is happening." He motioned to the cameraman. "Turn off the camera!"

The image of people inside the sector vanished.

"Aaziz, I've pressed it over and over. What's wrong? Didn't it blow?"

"No, it did not. Nothing has happened!"

Aaziz ordered the men who had set up the dermite to go see what they had done wrong. He ordered two of his own men to go with them.

Before the men left, Aaziz pulled his two men aside. "Tell me when they fix what they did wrong."

"OK," they said.

After they fixed what they did wrong, he would have them executed for incompetence. Unlike Yassin, Aaziz believed there had to be consequences for failure. He would see to it.

"And do it as fast as you can."

CHAPTER 69

Mat led the group down the hallway to the back stairway. He pushed the metal door to the stairway open, and they headed downward toward the floor. Behind Mat came Sarah and Michael, then the president, with Sam covering the rear. Mat reached the bottom and exited the stairs.

He moved for the side exit of the hotel. Then they saw it—androids everywhere, blocking the terrorists from chasing them. *What the hell?*

The terrorists saw them as they broke out of the side exit and onto the street. They were pointing at them, screaming, jumping.

"Mary Lu, are you in position?"

"Yes, Mat, I'm ready."

"We're not ready. Don't seal the core yet," he said.

"I won't, but hurry."

"Megan, I need you to give us directions. Can you do that?"

"Yes, I'll try," she said. Megan pulled out her phone. "Just a minute, Uncle Mat." She opened up a map of the city and zoomed in to his location at the hotel.

"First, where the hell are we?"

"Uncle Mat, go across the street to the other hotel, the Shanton Hotel. Do you see it?"

"Yes."

Mary Lu broke in, "Go inside and up to the third level; there is a platform you can take. The platform runs crosswise."

"Will this get us out of the core?"

"No, but it might get you away from the terrorists," said Mary Lu. "Mat, the inbound Marines and the Navy SEAL assault teams are twenty minutes away."

* * *

Mat led the First Family across the street and into the Shanton Hotel. They ran past the gift shop. When he stopped to get his bearings, he spotted a stairway at the corner of the building, and they ran for it.

"Andy, do you have the suits?" Mat pushed the door open, and they all entered the stairwell.

"Yes, I have five jumpsuits, one for everyone. I'm on my way to the Carlson Steak House."

"Is that where you are going to place the suits?"

"Yes. I should have the suits there in ten minutes."

Ten minutes? thought Mat. "Megan, I need you to direct us to the Carlson Steak House."

"OK, hold on. Let me punch it up."

Mary Lu placed a dot on her tablet where the Carlson Steak House was. "What?" She gasped.

"What is it?" asked Sam.

"It's across the street from the control center complex."

Mat took the stairs two steps at a time. The others were falling behind.

"C'mon. Keep up, people!" said Mat. "Do like me. Two at a time. Go."

The others copied him and began to charge up the stairs.

"Andy, what are you doing? The Carlson Steak House is smack in the middle of the core," said Mary Lu. "Andy?"

"I know, but the terrorists have the core sealed off. They are trying to trap you; they have shut down all avenues of escape. The restaurant is empty."

"Andy, how do you know that?" asked Mat.

"The service droids told me. Everyone is chasing you. The droids who work in the steak house say it's empty. First time in days that no one is there."

"How's it looking where you are, Mary Lu?" said Mat.

"Everyone is here. Terrorists are everywhere. I don't think we can seal it."

"OK, this will work out fine. The steak house it is!" said Mat.

Mary Lu was beside herself. "Fine? Fine? *Fine?* What do you mean fine? Mat, you're going in the wrong direction! You'll be smack in the middle of the core. It's *not* fine!" Her voice quivered around the edges in a mixture of anger and despair.

"Andy, are you almost there at the steak house?" said Mat.

"Yes, almost. Another few minutes," said Andy.

"Mary Lu, seal the core as soon as you can. Andy, as soon as you drop off the suits, help Mary Lu seal off the core. Andy, don't put the suits where anyone can find them," said Mat.

"OK. I'll hide them and then go help Mary Lu," said Andy.

"I got it, Uncle Mat. Mary Lu's right. Go to the third floor and you will see an elevated crosswalk. Take it. Let me know when you get there."

"Roger that."

Mat and the First Family sprinted up past the second floor. Mat could see terrorists coming at them. Mat stopped at the door as Sam led her family past him. He grabbed his rifle and jammed it into the door handle. Then he bounded after the First Family.

Mat was darting up the stairs two at a time when he heard a loud *bam!* behind him. The terrorists had reached the door. He hoped the rifle would hold. He sprinted up the stairs; behind him he heard the door *bam!* against the rifle repeatedly.

At the third floor, the First Family stopped and waited for Mat. Sam angled her head to see where he was. He had just reached her side.

"C'mon!" he said as he slammed through the door and into the third floor of the hotel. "We are at the third floor," said Mat.

"Good. Take the crosswalk. All the way to the end."

* * *

Andy carefully placed the suits down in the back room; next to the suits, he set down the two boxes of helmets. "The suits are at the steak house. They're in the back room."

"Thanks, Andy. Now go help Mary Lu."

"On my way," he said.

Mat and the First Family raced across the elevated

walkway all the way to the end. There they took the steps down to ground level. The terrorists were coming toward them from two blocks farther down on the circumference.

* * *

Mary Lu rose from where she was crouched. They were gone. She waited another moment and looked around again. The pathways were open, clear. The terrorists had all left.

* * *

The two spaceliners had obtained low Earth orbit and were steadily rising to match the orbital height of Liberty. Each spaceliner carried two hundred Marines.

The seat light clicked off, and Commander Pash unbuckled his seat belt and stood up. He stood in the aisle next to his seat and said, "Suit up." His voice boomed throughout the spaceliner.

The two hundred combat Marines went through their weapons checklist.

In the zero-g environment, Commander Pash floated down the middle of the aisle the full length of the spaceliner. He wanted his presence felt. He wanted every soldier to know that he would be there with them.

In another spacecraft flying a parallel course, a similar scene was underway. The Marine assault teams were ready and eager.

* * *

"Andy, how's it looking where you are at? Any terrorists?" Mary Lu asked.

"No, Mary Lu. They all left to kill Mat and the First Family," he answered.

Mary Lu had seven maintenance droids at her command. All seven were present: four with her and three now with Andy.

She had already told all of them what their tasks were. She had directed them to act with emergency status protocol three. For these droids, this was an emergency protocol event. They would not stop until their task was completed. All life depended on it.

"Go," ordered Mary Lu to the worker androids.

The four droids with her went to work. The large sliding hangar bay doors were dislodged from their moorings, and the powerful droids drove the doors across the walkway. The large metal structures rolled across the floor and slammed into the old moorings and grooves on the other side. Mary Lu unlocked a panel on the wall next to the door and pulled a large handle down until it clicked and locked into place. The doors were closed and locked.

Mary Lu then grabbed another handle and pulled it down until it clicked into place. The huge door was now pressed against the wall and sealed, and a droid began to spray the edge of the door with emergency sealant.

Mary Lu ran to the door on the other side, two blocks over. She locked and then sealed that door in place as well. The two droids with her began to apply the emergency sealant around the outside seams of the door.

"Mat, one side is sealed," said Mary Lu. "Status report, Andy."

"Sealed," he said.

"Both doors?"

"Yes."

"Have you applied the emergency sealant?"

"Doing it now."

"Tell me when you are done."

Mary Lu ordered the droids back to standard maintenance; quickly they were gone.

"Mat, there are two terrorists taking notice of these new walls," said Mary Lu.

"Are you hiding?"

"Yes. Mat, this won't hold them. It won't take much for them to open these doors."

"OK."

"Mat, I'm moving to a new location. I don't feel safe here," said Mary Lu.

"OK."

"Mary Lu, we're done," said Andy.

"Mat, I have bad news," said Mary Lu. "There are three men in the spaceport heading toward the docking bay shuttles. They must have detected the inbound assault force. Each one of them has what looks like a shoulder missile, like those other guys had before. If they make it into the airlock, we won't be able to stop them and they'll be able to shoot down the inbound Marines."

"Uncle Mat, when you exit from the stairs, keep going in that direction. You're going along the circumference two blocks and then you will be there. The Carlson Steak House will be on your right," said Megan.

"Mat, hurry!" said Mary Lu. "The men have boarded the shuttle and are on their way to the docking bay rings."

Mat was exhausted and completely empty. *Almost there,* he told himself. Michael and Sarah were beat. It was obvious that they had not slept in a while. They ran like they were about to topple over, their movements sluggish, their eyes sunken deep into their faces. Then Mat saw the sign for Carlson Steak House and felt a surge of energy. "There it is." He pointed. "Run!"

Mat swung around and fired three shots down the street where the terrorists were coming toward them. One of the bullets struck a man in his upper thigh. The rest of them dove to the ground for cover.

Mat ran into the restaurant and was greeted by two droids. "Sheriff McKenna?" asked one of the two droids.

"Yes?" he said.

"We have been expecting you. Follow us," said the service droid. The two droids headed toward the back.

The restaurant had a three-foot dividing wall separating the back of the restaurant from the front. Against the wall were two boxes of space suit helmets and a stack of folded jumpsuits.

"Thank you," said Mat. "I advise you two to hold on to this wall and don't let go until I say so."

The droids briefly conversed together in digi, then did as he said. They leaned up against the wall and held on to the top.

"Tell all the droids you can to grab something solid."

The restaurant droid said to Mat, "That's what Andy said too. I think all the droids know, but we will pass it on."

Three terrorists dove into the restaurant and leaped behind the small desk at the entrance. Mat fired two shots at the door to the restaurant as more tried to come inside.

Sam said to her family as she helped them get into the jumpsuits, "As soon as you are suited up, hold on to this wall and hold on."

"Sam, are you done?" asked Mat.

"Almost." She picked up a helmet and helped Michael put it on. Then she locked it into place.

"Mat! The three terrorists have just disembarked from the shuttle. They will be at the docking bay exit any moment!" said Mary Lu.

Mat grabbed a helmet and handed it to the president. The president slipped it over his head, and Mat locked it into the dog collar while Sam helped Sarah do the same.

Done! They were all suited up!

Terrorists began storming into the restaurant. They all moved aside as one terrorist entered the restaurant and walked toward the First Family.

Sam took a helmet and slipped it on, then locked it into the dog collar. She reached down and grabbed the last helmet and pitched it to Mat, and he slipped it on and locked it in place.

Aaziz walked up toward them, four others at his side. They pointed their weapons at them. Aaziz spotted Sheriff McKenna, even wearing the jumpsuit. "If it isn't the mighty Sheriff McKenna." Aaziz and four others surrounded them. Aaziz approached Sheriff McKenna. "Drop your weapons. Now!" said Aaziz.

Mat nodded to Sam. "Do as he says." He dropped the service weapon to the ground. Sam followed in kind.

Taking a chance, Mat grabbed Sarah's hands and moved

them to the top of the wall. Mat looked to Sam. She got the message, and quickly she had all members of her family holding on to the top of the dividing wall.

"Megan? Could you do your favorite uncle one small favor?" asked Mat.

"And who are you talking to?" demanded Aaziz. "Are you praying? It will do you no good. You will wish, infidel, that I had killed you here and now. But I won't. I will make sure that you pay for the blood of the men you killed. I will make it my personal responsibility that you suffer."

Mary Lu said in a voice pregnant with exhaustion, "Mat, the three terrorists have reached the airlock. As soon as it pressurizes, they will go inside. When they exit the airlock, they will destroy the inbound Marines. If they get inside the airlock, it will be too late; we won't be able to stop them." The emotional frustration in her voice cut him deeply.

"Megan?"

"What?" said Megan. Her voice wavering. She was trying hard not to let Uncle Mat hear her cry. "What is it uncle Mat?"

"Blow the core."

CHAPTER 70

The pilot pressed a button on his comm to speak to everyone in the vehicle. "We'll be docking at Liberty in three minutes."

He made a small adjustment to the flight path, as the ship's nav computer recommended. They needed to time the approach with the rotation of the docking bay ring. Given the ring's rotational speed and his own speed and distance, he was now on target to mate up with the docking bay.

"Sparrow Two, this is Sparrow One. Docking calibration complete."

"Copy that, Sparrow Two, over."

"What the hell! Do you see that?" said the pilot.

"Holy crap!" said the copilot.

"Sparrow Two, this is Sparrow One. Do you see what I see?"

"Sparrow One, this is Sparrow Two. Unbelievable! Look at all that crap Liberty ejected!"

"Sparrow Two, recalibrate approach. Cut speed in half. We don't need to fly into the debris field at this speed."

"Copy that, Sparrow One. Reduce approach speed by half. Recalibrating approach to docking bay."

CHAPTER 71

The explosion ripped throughout the core. Mat, Sam, Michael, Sarah, and the president were huddled along the three-foot-high dividing wall, hanging on to the edge, when the air blew out of the core. Adjacent to them were two service droids who were also hanging on to the wall.

The core held.

Mat and Sam both had an idea of what it would be like from their previous experience, but this was unreal. They held tight and made sure the others were secure. Everyone crouched behind the low wall, pressing themselves against it. They held on to each other with one arm and grabbed the top of the divider wall with the other. The first three seconds were the worst. Then the pressure dropped and the force exerted on them by the escaping air diminished rapidly.

Mat stood up and surveyed the area, not sure what he would find. The First Family had survived. He waved to them, and they carefully waved back at him. The eyes of Michael and Sarah were wide, Their hands still clinging to the top of the wall. Over toward the far end of the small divider wall were the two droids. They too had survived.

One second Aaziz was in front of him, and then he

wasn't. Mat never actually saw anyone go. They were just gone. The air was filled with debris. Everything loose became airborne. Many died from collision with flying debris. Mat lived in Florida; it reminded him of a hurricane, but it resembled more of a tornado.

It was brief, and then it was over.

CHAPTER 72

Mat, Megan, and Mary Lu watched the news as it showed reports of the mop-up operations of the Marines and Navy SEALs. Sam was with her family now, flying home to the White House.

After the core had been blown, Mary Lu had Andy seal off the docking bay and pressurize it. Andy opened the docking bay so the Marines could enter. The moment the docking bay had been pressurized, the assault team docked and stormed the facility.

Mary Lu and her team of androids immediately began to implement repairs on the structural hole in the ag belt. They worked on the inside and the outside simultaneously, thereby creating two seals very quickly.

The core was then repressurized. More passenger liners quickly followed, transporting additional combat troops. The fighting was intense, but the outcome was never in doubt. Eventually the last terrorist was killed.

None surrendered. These were true believers.

The Marines found Secret Service Agent Cass, alive. She had not been in the core when it was blown. She had a broken arm and a fractured left leg. The physical injuries

would heal after several surgeries and therapy. Cass was a
survivor.

EPILOGUE

Lori got up from her desk and walked up to Sheriff Mathew McKenna's office. She knocked on the door twice, even though the door was open, and took two steps inside. "Mat, don't forget you have that celebration to go to tonight."

Mat raised his eyes up from his monitor. "OK, I won't forget." Then his eyes fell back to the screen.

She stared at him. "You have to go to this," she said firmly but respectfully.

He looked up from his desk again and gazed at his secretary.

"You have to go," said Lori. "The First Lady of the United States of America personally has invited you. You told her that you would be there, on time . . ." Her hands moved to her hips while her gaze remained fixed. A moment passed. She continued, "You gave her your word as a man, and you represent the people here in Shady Oaks, Florida. It is your duty. You have to go. Period."

He knew she was right. The time for him to wiggle out of this thing had passed when Sam Devane called him personally to invite him. He had been invited earlier by a

White House administrative assistant. He had committed himself to go, but he had left a door to back out of wide enough to drive a pickup truck through.

OK, so he had to go—but he didn't have to look forward to it. He tried to imagine himself at a dinner with a bunch of politicians.

Lori knew the fight was over. She dropped her arms from her hips and took a step back out of his office. "You do know that you are technically a politician yourself. As a matter of fact, your reelection is a little more than a year away."

"I know." Lori always amazed him that way. She always knew what he was thinking, sometimes even before he himself knew.

The celebration dinner was in Orlando. About an hour away. Not bad. At least it wasn't in Washington. Sam Devane was sending a presidential limo to pick him up. He figured she didn't trust him to show up, at least not completely.

Lori said in a gentler voice, "Do you know what you are wearing?"

"Lori, I'm forty-five years old. I believe I can dress myself."

"Well, of course you can. But the First Lady—she seems very sweet, by the way—had some recommendations."

"Yes, she is. And what did she recommend?"

"You can wear your dress boots and casual dress slacks with a nice shirt. Like maybe that blue one with that subtle tone-on-tone pattern. Very sweet. Wear a nice belt. Not that brown one. Forget the tie. Don't need a tie. Do you even have a tie? Never mind." She smiled and left to go back to her desk chair. When she pulled up to her desk to do some paperwork, Mat was standing at his door. He knocked twice and Lori turned her head to him.

"Thanks, Lori." He smiled. "And yes, of course I have a tie. I think I have two, actually." He went back to his desk.

* * *

The limo arrived right on time. He locked the front door to his house. The chauffeur was holding the passenger-side door open. Mat was about to get in when he saw that there was no one else inside. He stood back up and asked the driver, "Am I your only passenger on this trip?"

"Yes," he said politely.

"In that case, mind if I sit up front?"

"Be my guest." He laughed. "We aim to please."

Before the driver could open the door for him, the sheriff opened it himself and sat down in the seat. "Thanks."

* * *

An hour later, the limo was pulling up to the entrance of the restaurant La Salle. It was early, thank goodness. Maybe he could get out of there after a couple of hours. With all the White House people, who would notice if one small-town sheriff had left? Who would care? That is, besides Sam anyway.

He thanked the driver and closed the door to the limo, then walked up to the entrance of La Salle Restaurant. Very high-end. Maybe he could get a good steak anyway. He could always hope.

Once inside the door, he was greeted by an attractive

young woman he guessed was in her early twenties, standing behind a small desk.

"Good evening," she said with a smile as he walked up.

"Good evening," he replied as he handed her a card provided by the White House. He had been instructed to show it.

The woman took the card and examined it briefly, then handed it back. "Welcome to La Salle, Sheriff McKenna. If you will, please follow me."

Mat was impressed. He couldn't remember when he had last been in a restaurant where he was greeted by a real human. Androids worked all the fast-food franchises now. Cooking and cleaning was done by androids. Heck, even the drive-through windows were manned by androids. Only the managers, owners, and customers were people.

And it wasn't just fast food either. Most, if not all, national restaurant chains used androids. The greeters, waitresses, and cooks were all androids. Only the nice restaurants that the wealthy attended were still manned by humans. It was the dividing line. The one good thing about the androids was that if you ordered anything from a national chain, it tasted exactly the same everywhere. It was claimed to be a good thing. The restaurants were all clean. Very clean. Thanks to the penetration of androids into the marketplace, bathrooms everywhere sparkled. Now that was very definitely a good thing.

The woman escorted Mat past several tables. All were empty. He glanced around; the whole restaurant was almost empty. It was, after all, just six fifteen in the evening on a Wednesday night.

She walked up to a small table in a corner of the room. "And here you are," she said as she motioned at the table. "A server will be with you shortly."

McKenna laughed. "Thank you," he said to the woman.

But his laugh and smile were not for her. They were for the woman sitting at the small table. It was Mary Lu.

Mary Lu stood up. "Hi, Sheriff McKenna!" She presented a hand for him to shake.

He took her hand and held it firmly for a moment. He hated to let her have her hand back. He could have held it all night. "Hi, Mary Lu. Just call me Mat." He walked to her side of the table and held her chair for her as she sat back down.

"OK, Mat."

"So where is everyone? Are we the first ones here?" asked Mat.

"I just got here myself, but it sure looks that way," she answered.

As Mat sat back down, a waitress was already approaching their table. "Sheriff McKenna?" she asked, looking to him for confirmation.

"Yes, I'm Sheriff McKenna. How can I help you?"

"I was asked to give you this." And she handed him a small envelope with a card inside.

"Thank you." He opened the card and began to read the note.

Hi Mat!

The three of us were to be the only ones attending this special night, and regretfully, I won't be able to make it, so it will be just you and Mary Lu. The bill is all taken care of. Also, here are two tickets for a rock concert tonight. It starts at 9:00. The limo is yours for the whole evening (or as long as you need it). By the way, Mat, the band is Alt Control—one of Mary Lu's favorites.

Thanks again for everything you two did.

Love,
Sam Devane

P.S. The limo driver will be expecting you to leave the La Salle by 7:40 to make it to the concert in time. He knows where it is.

Mat held the two tickets in his hand and examined them for a second.

Another waitress walked up to the table. She said, "Can I get you two anything? Maybe a drink?"

"I'll take a glass of merlot, thanks," said Mary Lu.

"I'll have the same. Thanks," said Mat.

Mat cleared his throat. "Would you like to go to a rock concert tonight? I just happen to have two tickets for the Alt Control concert."

"What? Really? They're one of my favorites!" Mary Lu angled her head sideways a little, and the corner of her lips turned up slightly, hinting at a smile. "So . . . are you asking me out on a date, Sheriff McKenna?"

"Yes, I am."

"I'd love to."

Her brown eyes sparkled, and her smile made his soul want to dance.

Mat decided that if Sam Devane ever ran for president, he would be her campaign manager.

Thank you

Thank you for purchasing Free Fall.

If you enjoyed this book, I hope that you will consider leaving a review.

About the Author

Visit John Parrish's website at AuthorJP.com

Sign up for John's mailing list so you'll be updated when a new book or event is coming up.

Thank you!

Made in the USA
Coppell, TX
10 May 2022

77621761R00224